BY KURT VONNEGUT

A Man Without a Country

Armageddon in Retrospect

Bagombo Snuff Box

Between Time and Timbuktu

Bluebeard

Breakfast of Champions

Canary in a Cat House

Cat's Cradle

Deadeye Dick

Fates Worse Than Death

Galápagos

God Bless You, Dr. Kevorkian

God Bless You, Mr. Rosewater

Happy Birthday, Wanda June

Hocus Pocus

Jailbird

Like Shaking Hands with God (*with* Lee Stringer)

Look at the Birdie

Mother Night

Palm Sunday

Player Piano

The Sirens of Titan

Slapstick

Slaughterhouse-Five

Timequake

Wampeters, Foma & Granfalloons

Welcome to the Monkey House

SOME OF THESE ARE GALAXIES.

WHILE
MORTALS
SLEEP

KURT

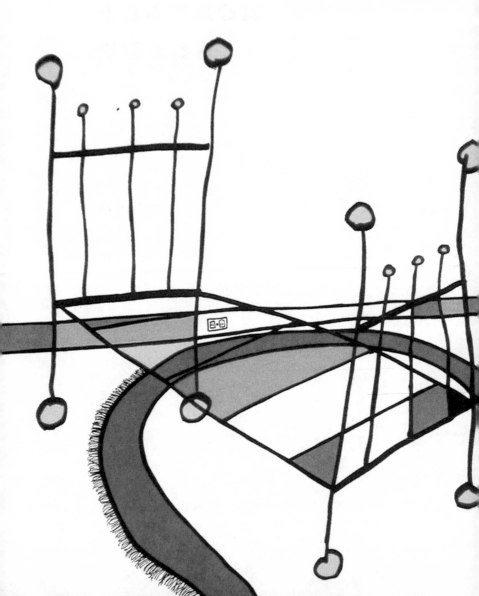

VONNEGUT

WHILE MORTALS SLEEP

UNPUBLISHED SHORT FICTION

Delacorte Press ▰ New York

Copyright © 2011 by The Kurt Vonnegut, Jr., Trust
Foreword © 2011 by Dave Eggers

All rights reserved.

Published in the United States by Delacorte Press, an imprint of The Random House Publishing Group, a division of Random House, Inc., New York.

DELACORTE PRESS is a registered trademark of Random House, Inc., and the colophon is a trademark of Random House, Inc.

Cover illustration by Kurt Vonnegut. Copyright © 1973 Kurt Vonnegut / Origami Express, LLC. www.vonnegut.com
For complete credits for the original illustrations by Kurt Vonnegut contained in this work, see page 255.

ISBN: 978-0-385-34373-2
eBook ISBN: 978-0-440-33987-8

Printed in the United States of America on acid-free paper

www.bantamdell.com

9 8 7 6 5 4 3 2 1

First Edition

Book design by Liz Cosgrove

FOREWORD

by Dave Eggers

I've been thinking a lot about what we lost when we lost Kurt Vonnegut, and the main thing that keeps coming to mind is that we lost a moral voice. We lost a very reasonable and credible—though not to say staid or toothless—voice who helped us know how to live.

With the internet, god bless it, we are absolutely overrun with commentary and opinions. Can't tell just yet, but so far, this seems fine. The access for everyone—commentators and their audiences—is more democratically available, and this is surely good. We have a million or so people offering daily advice, insight, perspective, and the occasional attempt to help us live in better harmony with our planet and our fellow humans. On the other hand, to get attention on the internet (and on television, for that matter), a commentator, more often than not, has to be loud, radical, or insane. And so the vast majority of such commentary is all three.

Then we have our novelists and short-story writers. By comparison, these people seem sane and well mannered. The catch is, they are, by and large, very quiet. They toil in the woods or on campuses or in Brooklyn, and they are so polite that they would never tell anyone, let alone their readers, how to live. And so the majority of contemporary literature, though it truly is brilliant and wonderful in myriad ways, is also free of moral instruction.

Now, I'm not saying that literature must tell us how to live, or must offer clear moral directives. No. No. I'm not saying that, internet commentators. But I am saying that it's okay for *some* contemporary literature to do so. In a pluralistic literary environment—and we need such a thing, we need to maintain it, to nourish it so that dozens of styles and genres can coexist free of the misguided notion that there is one miraculous form that obviates all others—in such an environment, couldn't there be a few writers who come out and say, "This is bad, that is good?"

But precious few writers do so. We have collectively shrunk from any clear instructive *point* in our work. As a result, our short stories—let's talk, here, about short stories primarily, given our present context—are full of lovely sentences and nuance, but they are also lacking, too often, in *punch*.

I will be the first to admit that I, too, have been trained to shy away from offering a tidy end, or moral point, to a story. Come to think of it, I'm not sure I've ever sent a simple declarative message in any short story. I came of age as a writer when to do so would have been out of the question. I was at least two generations removed from the days when a popular and literary short story would attempt to deliver a neat ending to a story, a conclusion that would cause the reader surprise and also recognition of a point made clearly and well.

But Vonnegut has always done so. And increasingly, what he did seems rare and necessary. Most of his short stories have resolutions that make abundantly clear that a lesson has been learned, by the characters (usually) and the reader (always).

I've been an avid reader of Vonnegut since I was a teenager, but it wasn't until I read these last two posthumous collections of stories, *While Mortals Sleep* and *Look at the Birdie,* that I've realized just how strong a moralist Vonnegut was. I knew that as a man and as an essayist, he was not shy about making his opinions known. He spoke highly of Jesus Christ, and he made clear and simple pronouncements such as, "Goddamn it, you've got to be kind." And because he looked a bit like a hippie Mark Twain and appeared older than he was, he could carry it off. He seemed, even in early middle age, to be one of those elder statesmen who could declare his opinions, grumpily, about anything, and people would attach to these statements a certain gravitas—well earned through his exemplary work and life. When you have fought in WWII, when you have survived Dresden, when you have supported your own family and also taken in the four orphaned children of your sister (after she and her husband died only days apart), then you've got some credit in the moral-authority bank.

And so we have these stories, which were written early in his career, when Vonnegut was trying to make a living as a writer. He was writing a great deal of short fiction at the time, and he was trying—often successfully—to sell these stories to magazines like *Collier's* and *The Saturday Evening Post,* which were then publishing a good deal of short fiction. Clearly, the way he wrote at the time was influenced a certain amount by what he knew these publications wanted. They wanted stories of relatively unadorned prose, tight plotting, simple conflict, and ideally an unexpected twist at the end.

These are what might be called mousetrap stories. This

was once a popular, if not dominant, form. But you don't see it much anymore. We're now in the age of what might be called photorealistic stories. What we have with most contemporary short stories is a realism, a naturalism, that gives us roughly what photography gives us. A gifted photographer will frame reality in a way that seems both real and novel. His or her work will "hold a mirror" to our lives, but in such a way that we see ourselves anew. All art forms attempt this mirror-holding, but photography, and the contemporary short story, are particularly well-designed delivery devices for this aim. And thus the contemporary short story gives us characters who breathe, who seem three-dimensional, who live in real places, who have real jobs and struggles and pain. The stories are to a great extent in service to these characters. The characters make realistic moves in their lives, realistic choices, and the outcomes are plausible and perhaps even pedestrian.

Not as much so in a mousetrap story. A mousetrap story exists to trick or trap the reader. It moves the reader along, through the complex (but not *too* complex) machinery of the story, until the end, when the cage is sprung and the reader is trapped. And so in this kind of story, the characters, the setting, the plot—they're all more or less means to an end.

This isn't to say the characters aren't real-seeming, aren't believable or sympathetic or any of the other things we might want characters to be. On the contrary, Vonnegut is masterful at quickly sketching a character who you instantly recognize and immediately are willing to follow. But in the end, their routes are determined by the master mousetrap maker, their fates in service to the larger point.

And so, when you start a story in this collection, you

know you are being set up. And you know what? It's fun to be set up. This collection is full of relatively simple stories, about relatively simple problems. In one story, a husband plays with his model trains too much, neglecting his wife in the process. (A far cry from *Cat's Cradle.*) In another, a newspaper editor who derides Christmas learns something about its true meaning when forced to judge a holiday lighting competition. A young woman inherits a fortune and finds the burden crushing and her new suitors untrustworthy. (Note just how many of these stories involve the pursuit of mid-century ideas of success—a quick fortune, a stretch limo, nice dividends on a stock portfolio; Vonnegut, working as a PR man, was no doubt struggling to get over a financial hump himself.)

In any case, no matter what the plot, you as the reader know that by the end of the story, you will get somewhere. That Vonnegut will tell you something with candor and clarity. That being a decent person is an achievable and desirable thing. That faith has value. That wealth solves few problems. Simple enough messages, sure, but there's a reason to be reminded of such things, and relief in having them expressed artfully but with a certain lack of obfuscation.

These early-career stories are different from Vonnegut's later novels, where the tone is darker, grimmer, more exasperated, where the nuances are many and the lessons more complex. Though while writing these stories, Vonnegut had already seen the decimation of Dresden, had tramped amid the charred bodies of thousands of civilians, had spent time in a German POW camp, the stories in *While Mortals Sleep* have the bright-eyed clarity of a young man just beginning to understand the workings of the world. You can almost imagine a kindly looking guy in a cardigan and penny loafers writing the stories in a malt shop, filling the juke box with quarters, typing happily away.

But of course he wasn't that. He was a man with kids trying to support his family while edifying the readers of *Ladies' Home Journal*. Later, of course, he'd be writing, repeatedly, about the end of the world. And sometimes incest, and often enough about the folly of war, and the greed and depravity of our industries and government. But for now, we have the eager young mousetrap maker, and we are his willing prey.

CONTENTS

WHILE
MORTALS
SLEEP

JENNY

George Castrow used to come back to the home works of the General Household Appliances Company just once a year—to install his equipment in the shell of the new model GHA refrigerator. And every time he got there he dropped a suggestion in the suggestion box. It was always the same suggestion: "Why not make next year's refrigerator in the shape of a woman?" Then there would be a sketch of a refrigerator shaped like a woman, with arrows showing where the vegetable crisper and the butter conditioner and the ice cubes and all would go.

George called it the Food-O-Mama. Everybody thought the Food-O-Mama was an extra-good joke because George was out on the road all year long, dancing and talking and singing with a refrigerator shaped like a refrigerator. Its name was Jenny. George had designed and built Jenny back when he'd been a real comer in the GHA Research Laboratory.

George might as well have been married to Jenny. He lived with her in the back of a moving van that was mostly filled with her electronic brains. He had a cot and a hot plate and a three-legged stool and a table and a locker in the back of the van. And he had a doormat he put on the bare ground outside when he parked the van somewhere for the night. "Jenny and George," it said. It glowed in the dark.

Jenny and George went from appliance dealer to appliance dealer all over the United States and Canada. They would dance and sing and crack jokes until they'd collected a good crowd in a store. Then they would make a strong sales pitch for all the GHA appliances standing around doing nothing.

Jenny and George had been at it since 1934. George was sixty-four years old when I got out of college and joined the company. When I heard about George's big paycheck and his free way of life and the way he made people laugh and buy appliances, why I guessed he was the happiest man in the company.

But I never got to see Jenny and George until I got transferred out to the Indianapolis offices. One morning out there we got a telegram saying Jenny and George were in our neck of the woods somewhere—and would we please find them and tell George his ex-wife was very sick? She wasn't expected to live. She wanted to see him.

I was very surprised to hear he'd had a wife. But some of the older people in the office knew about her. George had only lived with her for six months—and then he'd hit the road with Jenny. His ex-wife's name was Nancy. Nancy had turned right around and married his best friend.

I got the job of tracking Jenny and George down. The company never knew exactly where they were. George made his own schedule. The company gave him his head. They just kept rough track of him by his expense accounts and by rave letters they'd get from distributors and dealers.

And almost every rave letter told about some new stunt

that Jenny'd done, that Jenny'd never been able to do before. George couldn't leave her alone. He tinkered with her every spare minute, as though his life depended on making Jenny as human as possible.

I called our distributor for central Indiana, Hal Flourish. I asked him if he knew where Jenny and George were. He laughed to beat the band and said he sure did. Jenny and George were right in Indianapolis, he said. They were out at the Hoosier Appliance Mart. He told me Jenny and George had stopped early morning traffic by taking a walk down North Meridian Street.

"She had on a new hat and a corsage and a yellow dress," he said. "And George was all dolled up in his soup and fish and yellow spats and a cane. You would of died. And you know how he's got her fixed up now, so's he knows when her battery's running down?"

"Nossir," I said.

"She yawns," he said, "and her eyelids get all droopy."

Jenny and George were starting their first show of the day when I got out to the Hoosier Appliance Mart. It was a swell morning. George was on the sidewalk in the sunshine, leaning on the fender of the moving van that had Jenny's brains in it. He and Jenny were singing a duet. They were singing the "Indian Love Call." They were pretty good. George would sing, "I'll be calling you-hoo," in a gravel baritone. Then Jenny would answer back from the doorway of the Mart in a thin, girlish soprano.

Sully Harris, who owned the Mart, was standing by Jenny

with one arm draped over her. He was smoking a cigar and counting the house.

George had on the dress suit and yellow spats Hal Flourish had laughed so hard about. George's coattails dragged on the ground. His white vest was buttoned down around his knees. His shirt bosom was rolled up under his chin like a window blind. And he had on trick shoes that looked like bare feet the size of canoe paddles. The toenails were painted fire-engine red.

But Hal Flourish is the kind of man who thinks anything that's supposed to be funny *is* funny. George wasn't funny if you looked at him closely. And I *had* to look at him closely because I wasn't there for a good time. I was bringing him sad news. I looked at him closely, and I saw a small man getting on in years and all alone in this vale of tears. I saw a small man with a big nose and brown eyes that were just sick about something.

But most people in the crowd thought he was a howl. Just here and there you'd see a few people who saw what I saw. Their smiles weren't making fun of George. Their smiles were kind of queer and sweet. Their smiles mostly seemed to ask how Jenny worked.

Jenny was radio-controlled, and the controls were in those trick shoes of George's—under his toes. He would punch buttons with his toes, and the shoes would send out signals to Jenny's brains in the moving van. Then the brains would signal Jenny what to do. There weren't any wires between Jenny and George and the van.

It was hard to believe George had anything to do with what Jenny was up to. He had a little pink earphone in his ear, so he could hear everything anybody said to Jenny, even when she was a hundred feet away. And he had little rearview mirrors on the frames of his glasses, so he could turn his back to her and still see everything she did.

When they stopped singing, Jenny picked me out to kid around with. "Hello, tall, dark, and handsome," she said to me. "Did the old icebox drive you out of the house?" She had a sponge rubber face at the top of the door, with springs embedded in it and a loudspeaker behind it. Her face was so real, I almost had to believe there was a beautiful woman inside the refrigerator—with her face stuck through a hole in the door.

I kidded her back. "Look, Mrs. Frankenstein," I said to her, "why don't you go off in a corner somewhere and make some ice cubes? I want to have a private talk with your boss."

Her face turned from pink to white. Her lips trembled. Then her lips pulled down and dragged her whole face out of shape. She shut her eyes so she wouldn't have to look at such a terrible person. And then, as God is my judge, she squeezed out two fat tears. They ran down her cheeks, then down her white enamelled front to the floor.

I smiled and winked at George to let him know how slick I thought his act was, and that I really did want to see him.

He didn't smile back. He didn't like me for talking to Jenny that way. You would have thought I'd spit in the eye of his mother or sister or something.

A kid about ten years old came up to George and said, "Hey, Mister, I bet I know how she works. You got a midget in there."

"You're the first one who ever guessed," George said.

"Now that everybody knows, I might as well let the midget out." He motioned for Jenny to come out on the sidewalk with him.

I expected her to waddle and clank like a tractor, because she weighed seven hundred pounds. But she had a light step to go with that beautiful face of hers. I never saw such a case of mind over matter. I forgot all about the refrigerator. All I saw was her.

She sidled up to George. "What is it, Sweetheart?" she said.

"The jig is up," George said. "This bright boy knows you're a midget inside. Might as well come on out and get some fresh air and meet the nice people." He hesitated just long enough and looked just glum enough to make the people think maybe they were really going to see a midget.

And then there was a whirr and a click, and Jenny's door swung open. There wasn't anything inside but cold air, stainless steel, porcelain, and a glass of orange juice. It was a shock to everybody—all that beauty and personality on the outside, and all that cold nothing on the inside.

George took a sip from the glass of orange juice, put it back in Jenny and closed her door.

"I'm certainly glad to see you taking care of yourself for a change," Jenny said. You could tell she was crazy about him, and that he broke her heart about half the time. "Honestly," she said to the crowd, "the poor man should be dead of scurvy and rickets by now, the way he eats."

An audience is the nuttiest thing there is, if you ever stop to think about it. Here George had proved there wasn't anything inside Jenny, and here the crowd was, twenty seconds later, treating her like a real human being again. The women were shaking their heads to let Jenny know they knew what a trial it was to get a man to take care of himself. And the men were giving George secret looks to let him know they knew what a good pain it was to have a woman always treating you like a baby.

The only person who wasn't going along with the act, who wasn't being a boob for the pleasure of it, was the kid who'd guessed there was a midget inside. He was sore about being wrong, and his big ambition was to bust up the act with truth—Truth with a capital T. He'll grow up to be a scientist someday. "All right," the kid said, "if there isn't a midget in there, then I know exactly how it works."

"How, honey?" said Jenny. She was all ears for whatever bright little thing this kid was going to say. She really burned him up.

"Radio controls!" the kid said.

"Oooooo!" said Jenny. She was thrilled. "That would be a *grand* way to do it!"

The kid turned purple. "You can joke around all you want," he said, "but that's the answer and you know it." He challenged George. "What's *your* explanation?" he said.

"Three thousand years ago," said George, "the sultan of Alla-Bakar fell in love with the wisest, most affectionate, most beautiful woman who ever lived. She was Jenny, a slave girl.

"The old sultan knew there would be constant bloodshed in his kingdom," said George, "because men who saw Jenny always went mad for her love. So the old sultan had his court magician take Jenny's spirit out of her body and put it in a bottle. This he locked up in his treasury.

"In 1933," said George, "Lionel O. Heartline, president of the General Household Appliances Company, bought a curious bottle while on a business trip to fabled Baghdad. He brought it home, opened it, and out came the spirit of Jenny—three thousand years old. I was working in the Research Laboratory of GH at the time, and Mr. Heartline asked me what I could provide in the way of a new body for Jenny. So I rigged the shell of a refrigerator with a face, a voice, and feet—and with spirit controls, which work on Jenny's willpower alone."

It was such a silly story, I forgot it as soon as I'd chuckled at it. It took me weeks to realize that George wasn't just hamming it up when he told the story from his heart. He was getting as close to the truth about Jenny as he ever dared get. He was getting close to it with poetry.

"And, hey presto!—here she is," said George.

"Baloney!" the scientific kid yelled. But the audience wasn't with him, never would be.

Jenny let out a big sigh, thinking about those three thousand years in a bottle. "Well," she said, "that part of my life's all over now. No use crying over spilt milk. On with the show."

She slunk into the Mart, and everybody but George and I toddled right in behind her.

George, still controlling her with his toes, ducked into the cab of the moving van. I followed him and stuck my head in the window. There he was, the top of his trick shoes rippling while his toes made Jenny talk a blue streak in the Mart. At nine o'clock on a sunshiny morning he was taking a big drink from a bottle of booze.

When his eyes stopped watering and his throat stopped stinging he said to me, "What you looking at me that way for,

Sonny Jim? Didn't you see me drink my orange juice first like a good boy? It isn't as though I was drinking before breakfast."

"Excuse me," I said. I got away from the truck to give him time to pull himself together, and to give me time, too.

"When I saw that beautiful GHA refrigerator in the Research Laboratory," Jenny was saying in the Mart, "I said to George, 'That's the flawless white body for me.'" She glanced at me and then at George, and she shut up and her party smile went away for a couple of seconds. Then she cleared her throat and went on. "Where was I?" she said.

George wasn't about to get out of the cab. He was staring through the windshield now at something very depressing five thousand miles away. He was ready to spend the whole day like that.

Jenny finally ran out of small talk, and she came to the door and called him. "Honey," she called, "are you coming in pretty soon?"

"Keep your shirt on," George said. He didn't look at her.

"Is—is everything all right?" she said.

"Grand," George said, still staring through the windshield. "Just grand."

I did my best to think this was part of a standard routine, to find something clever and funny in it. But Jenny wasn't playing to the crowd. They couldn't even see her face. And she wasn't playing to me, either. She was playing to George and George was playing to her, and they would have played it the same way if they'd been alone in the middle of the Sahara Desert.

"Honey," Jenny said, "there are a lot of nice people waiting inside." She was embarrassed, and she knew darn good and well I'd caught him boozing it up.

"Hooray," said George.

"Sweetheart," she said, "the show *must* go on."

"Why?" said George.

Up to then, I'd never known how joyless what they call a joyless laugh could be. Jenny gave a joyless laugh to get the crowd to thinking that what was going on was simply hysterical. The laugh sounded like somebody breaking champagne glasses with a ball-peen hammer. It didn't just give me the willies. It gave everybody the willies.

"Did—did you want something, young man?" she said to me.

What the hell—there was no talking to George, so I talked to her. "I'm from the Indianapolis office. I—I have a message about his wife," I said.

George turned his head. "About my what?" he said.

"Your—your *ex*-wife," I said.

The crowd was out on the sidewalk again, confused and shuffling around and wondering when the funny part was going to come. It sure was a screwy way to sell refrigerators. Sully Harris was starting to get sore.

"Haven't heard from her for twenty years," George said. "I can go another twenty without hearing from her, and feel no pain. Thanks just the same." He stared through the windshield again.

That got a nervous laugh out of the crowd, and Sully Harris looked relieved.

Jenny came up to me, bumped up against me, and whispered out of the corner of her mouth, "What about Nancy?"

"She's very sick," I whispered. "I guess she's dying. She wants to see him one last time."

Somewhere in the back of the van a deep humming sound

quit. It was the sound of Jenny's brains. Jenny's face turned into dead sponge rubber—turned into something as stupid as anything you'll ever see on a department store clothes dummy. The yellow-green lights in her blue glass eyes winked out.

"Dying?" said George. He opened the door of the cab to get some air. The big Adam's apple in his scrawny throat went up and down, up and down. He flapped his arms feebly. "Show's over, folks," he said.

Nobody moved right away. Everybody was stunned by all this unfunny real life in the middle of make-believe.

George kicked off his trick shoes to show how really over the show was. He couldn't make himself speak again. He sat there, turned sideways in the cab, staring at his bare feet on the running board. The feet were narrow and bony and blue.

The crowd shuffled away, their day off to a very depressing start. Sully Harris and I hung around the van, waiting for George to take his head out of his hands. Sully was heartbroken about what had happened to the crowd.

George mumbled something in his hands that we didn't catch.

"How's that?" Sully asked him.

"When somebody tells you you've got to come like that," George said, "you've got to come?"

"If—if she's your ex-wife, if you walked out on her twenty years ago," Sully said, "then how come you gotta fall apart now on account of her—in front of my customers, in front of my store?"

George didn't answer him.

"If you want a train or an airplane reservation or a company car," I said to George, "I'll get it for you."

"And leave the van?" George said. He said it as though I'd

made a very fatheaded suggestion. "There's a quarter of a million dollars' worth of equipment in there, Sonny Jim," he said. He shook his head. "Leave all that valuable equipment around for somebody to—" His sentence petered out. And I saw there wasn't any sense to arguing with what he was saying, because he was really getting at something else. The van was his home, and Jenny and her brains were his reason for being—and the thought of going somewhere without them after all these years scared him stiff.

"I'll go in the van," he said. "I can make better time that way." He got out of the cab and got some excitement going— so no one would point out that moving vans weren't famous as fast transportation. "You come with me," he said, "and we can drive straight through."

I called the office, and they told me that not only could I go with Jenny and George—I *had* to go. They said that George was the most dedicated employee the company had, next to Jenny, and that I was to do anything I could to help him in this time of need.

When I got back from telephoning, George was off telephoning somewhere else himself. He'd put on a pair of sneakers and left the magic shoes behind. Sully Harris had picked up the magic shoes, and was looking inside.

"My God," Sully said to me, "it's like these little buttons all over an accordion in there." He slipped his hand into a shoe. He left it in there for about a minute before he got nerve enough to push a button.

"Fuh," Jenny said. She was perfectly deadpan.

Sully pushed another button.

"Fuh," Jenny said.

He pushed another button.

Jenny smiled like Mona Lisa.

Sully pushed several buttons.

"Burplappleneo," said Jenny. "Bama-uzztrassit. Shuh," she said. She did a right face and stuck out her tongue.

Sully lost his nerve. He put the magic shoes down by the van the way you'd put bedroom slippers by a bed. "Boy—" he said, "those people aren't gonna come back here. They're gonna think it's a morgue or something after that show he put on. I just thank God for one thing."

"What's that?" I said.

"At least they didn't find out whose voice and face the re-frigerator's got."

"Whose?" I said.

"You didn't know?" said Sully. "Hell—he made a mold of her face and put it on Jenny. Then he had her record every sound in the English language. Every sound Jenny makes, *she* made first."

"Who?" I said.

"Nancy, or whatever her name is," Sully said. "Right after the honeymoon he did all that. The dame that's dying now."

We made seven hundred miles in sixteen hours, and I don't believe George said ten words to me the whole time. He did do some talking, but not to me. It was in his sleep, and I guess he was talking to Jenny. He would say something like "Uffa-mf-uffa" while he was snoozing next to me. Then his toes would wiggle in his sneakers, signalling for Jenny to give him whatever answer he wanted to hear.

He didn't have the magic shoes on, so Jenny didn't do anything. She was strapped up against a wall in the dark in the back of the van. George didn't worry much about her until we got within about an hour of where we were going. Then he got as fidgety as a beagle. Every ten minutes or so he'd think Jenny had busted loose and was crashing around in her brains. We would have to pull over and stop, and go around in back and make sure she was fine.

You talk about plain living: the inside of the van looked like a monk's cell in a television station's control room. I'd seen floorboards that were wider and springier than George's cot. Everything that was for George in the van was cheap and uncomfortable. I wondered at first where the quarter of a million dollars he'd talked about was. But every time he passed his flashlight beam over Jenny's brains I got more excited. Those brains were the most ingenious, most complicated, most beautiful electronic system I'll ever see. Money was no object where Jenny was concerned.

As the sun came up we turned off the highway and banged over chuckholes into the hometown of the General Household Appliances Company. Here was the town where I'd started my career, where he'd started his career, where he'd brought his bride so long ago.

George was driving. The banging woke me up, and it shook something loose in George. All of a sudden he had to talk. He went off like an alarm clock.

"Don't know her!" he said. "Don't know her at all, Sonny Jim!" He bit the back of his hand, trying to drown out the pain in his heart. "I'm coming to see a perfect stranger, Sonny Jim," he said. "All I know is she was very beautiful once. I loved her more than anything on earth once, and she broke everything I had into little pieces. Career, friendships, home—*kaput.*" George hit the horn button, blasted the be-jeepers out of the dawn with the van's big bullhorn. "Don't ever idolize a woman, Sonny Jim!" he yelled.

We banged over another chuckhole. George had to grab the wheel with both hands. Steadying down the truck stead-ied him down, too. He didn't talk anymore till we got where we were going.

Where we were going was a white mansion with pillars across the front. It was Norbert Hoenikker's house. He was doing very well. He was assistant director of GHA research. He'd been George's best friend years before—before he'd taken George's wife Nancy away from him.

Lights were on all over the house. We parked the van be-hind a doctor's car out front. We knew it was a doctor's car be-cause it had a tag with those twined snakes on it up above the back license plate. The minute we parked, the front door of the house opened, and Norbert Hoenikker came out. He was wearing a bathrobe and slippers, and he hadn't slept all night.

He didn't shake hands with George. He didn't even say hello. He started right out with a rehearsed speech. "George," he said. "I'm going to stay out here while you go in. I want you to consider it your house while you're in there—with com-plete freedom for you and Nancy to say absolutely anything you have to say to each other."

The last thing George wanted to do was to go in there and face Nancy alone. "I—I haven't got anything to say to her," he said. He actually put his hand on the ignition key, got ready to start up the van and roar away.

"She has things to say to you," Mr. Hoenikker said. "She's been asking for you all night. She knows you're out here now. Lean close when she talks. She isn't very strong."

George got out, shambled up the walk to the house. He walked like a diver on the bottom of the sea. A nurse helped him into the house and closed the door.

"Is there a cot in back?" Mr. Hoenikker asked me.

"Yessir," I said.

"I'd better lie down," he said.

Mr. Hoenikker lay down on the cot, but he couldn't get any rest. He was a tall, heavy man, and the cot was too little for him. He sat up again. "Got a cigarette?" he said.

"Yessir," I said. I gave him one and lit it. "How is she, sir?" I said.

"She'll live," he said, "but it's made an old lady out of her like that." He snapped his fingers. It was a weak snap. It didn't make any noise. He looked at the face of Jenny, and it hurt him. "He's got a shock coming in there," he said. "Nancy doesn't look like that anymore." He shrugged. "Maybe that's good. Maybe he'll have to look at her as a fellow human being now."

He got up. He went to Jenny's brains and shook a steel rack that carried part of them. The rack didn't give at all. Hoenikker wound up shaking himself. "Oh, God," he said, "what a waste, what a waste, what a waste. One of the great technical minds of our time," he said, "living in a moving van, married to a machine, selling appliances somewhere between Moose Jaw, Saskatchewan, and Flamingo, Florida."

"I guess he is pretty bright," I said.

"Bright?" Hoenikker said. "He isn't just George Castrow.

He's *Dr.* George Castrow. He spoke five languages when he was eight, mastered calculus when he was ten, and got his Ph.D. from M.I.T. when he was eighteen!"

I whistled.

"He never had any time for love," Hoenikker said. "Didn't believe in it, was sure he could get along without it—whatever it was. There was too much else to do for George to bother with love. When he came down with pneumonia at the age of thirty-three, he had never so much as held the hand of a woman."

Hoenikker saw the magic shoes where George had put them, under the cot. He slipped off his bedroom slippers and slipped on the magic shoes. He was pretty familiar with them. "When pneumonia hit George," he said, "he was suddenly in terror of death and in desperate need of a nurse's touch many times a day. The nurse was Nancy."

Hoenikker turned on Jenny's master control switch. Her brains hummed. "A man who hasn't built up a certain immunity to love through constant exposure to it," he said, "is in danger of being all but killed by love when the first exposure comes." He shuddered. "Love scrambled poor George's brains. Suddenly love was *all* that mattered. Working with him in the laboratory, I was forced to listen eight hours a day to tripe about love. Love made the world go round! It was love and love alone the world was seeking! Love conquered all!"

Hoenikker tugged at his nose and closed his eyes, trying to remember a skill he'd had a long time ago. "Hello, Baby," he said to Jenny. His toes wiggled in the magic shoes.

"Heh-le, Hah-uh-u-duh-suh-um," Jenny said. There wasn't any expression in her face. She spoke again, put the sounds together better. "Hello, Handsome," she said to Hoenikker.

Hoenikker shook his head. "Nancy's voice doesn't sound like that anymore," he said. "Lower, a little rougher now—not so liquid."

"Huh-ear, huh-ut fuh-uh thu-uh suh-a-fuh uf-fuh Guh-od guh-o-yuh-oooo," Jenny said to him. She smoothed that out, too, "Here, but for the Grace of God, go you," she said.

"Say," I said, "you're good. I didn't think anybody but George could make her talk."

"Can't make her seem alive—not the way George can," Hoenikker said. "Never could—not even after I'd had a thousand hours of practice."

"You put that many hours in on her?" I said.

"Sure," said Hoenikker. "I was the one who was going to take her out on the road. I was the footloose bachelor who didn't have much of a future in research anyway. George was the married man who was to stay home with his laboratory and his wife, and go on to bigger things."

Life's surprises made Hoenikker sniffle. "Designing Jenny—" he said, "that was supposed to be a little joke in the middle of George's career—an electronic joke off the top of his head. Jenny was a little something he was to tinker with while he came drifting back to earth after his honeymoon with Nancy."

Hoenikker rambled on about those olden days when Jenny was born. And sometimes he would make Jenny chime in, as though she remembered those days, too. Those were bad days for Hoenikker, because he fell in love with George's wife. He'd been scared to death he would do something about it.

"I loved her for what she was," he said. "Maybe it was all the pap George was spouting about love that made me fall in love with her. George would say something ridiculous about love or about her, and I'd think up real reasons for loving her. I wound up loving her as a human being, as a miraculous, one-of-a-kind, moody muddle of faults and virtues—part child, part woman, part goddess, and no more consistent than a putty slide-rule."

"And then George began spending more and more time with me," said Jenny. "He took to going home from the laboratory at the last possible moment, wolfing down his supper, and hurrying back to work on me till well past midnight. He would have the control shoes on all day long and half the night—and we would talk, and talk, and talk."

Hoenikker tried to give her face some expression for what she was going to say next. He punched the Mona-Lisa-smile button Sully Harris had punched the day before. "I was excellent company," she said. "I never once said anything he didn't want to hear—and I always said what he wanted to hear exactly when he wanted to hear it."

"Here," said Hoenikker, undoing Jenny's straps so she could step forward, "is the most calculating woman, the greatest student of the naïve male heart that ever walked the face of the earth. Nancy never had a chance."

"Ordinarily," said Hoenikker, "a man's first wild dreams about his wife peter out after the honeymoon. The man then has to settle down to the difficult but rewarding business of finding out to whom he is really married. But George had an alternative. He could keep his wild dreams of a wife alive in Jenny. His neglect of the imperfect Nancy became a scandal."

"George suddenly announced that I was too precious a mechanism to be entrusted in anyone's care but his own," said Jenny. "He was going to take his Jenny out on the road, or he would leave the company entirely."

"His new hunger for love," said Hoenikker, "was matched only by his ignorance of the pitfalls of love. He only knew that love made him feel wonderful, no matter where it came from."

Hoenikker turned off Jenny, took off the shoes, lay down on the cot again. "George chose the perfect love of a robot," he said, "leaving me to do what I could to earn the love of an imperfect, deserted girl."

"I—I'm certainly glad she's well enough to say whatever she's got to say to him," I said.

"He would have gotten the message in any event," said Hoenikker. He handed up a slip of paper. "She dictated this, in case she wasn't up to saying it to him personally."

I didn't get to read the message right away, because George showed up at the back door of the van. He looked more like a robot than he'd ever made Jenny seem. "Your house again—your wife again," he said.

George and I had breakfast in a diner. Then we drove over to the GHA works and parked in front of the Research Laboratory.

"Sonny Jim," George said to me, "you can run along now, and start leading a life of your own again. And much obliged."

When I got off by myself, I read what Nancy had dictated to her second husband, what she'd said in person to George.

"Please look at the imperfect human being God gave you to love once," she'd said to George, *"and try to like me a little for what I really was, or, God willing, am. Then please, Darling, become an imperfect human being among imperfect human beings again."*

I'd been in such a hurry to get off by myself that I hadn't shaken George's hand or asked him what he was going to do next. I went back to the van to do both those things.

The back door of the van was open. Jenny and George were talking inside, very soft and low.

"I'm going to try to pick up the pieces of my life, Jenny—what's left of it," George said. "Maybe they'll take me back in the Research Laboratory. I'll ask anyway—hat in hand."

"They'll be thrilled to have you back!" said Jenny. She was thrilled herself. "This is the best news I've ever heard—the news I've been longing to hear for years." She yawned and her eyelids drooped. "Excuse me," she said.

"You need a younger man to squire you around now," said George. "I'm getting old—and you'll never get old."

"I'll never know another man as ardent and thoughtful as you, as handsome as you, as brilliant as you," said Jenny. She meant it. She yawned again. Her eyelids drooped some more. "Excuse me," she said. "Good luck, Angel," she mumbled. Her eyes closed all the way. "Good night, Sweetheart," she said. She was asleep. Her battery was dead.

"Dream a little dream of me," whispered George.

I ducked out of sight as George brushed away a tear and left the van forever.

THE EPIZOOTIC

While new young widows in extraordinary numbers paraded their weeds for all to see, no official had yet acknowledged that the land was plagued. The general population and the press, long inured to a world gone mad, had not yet noticed that affairs had recently become even worse. The news was full of death. The news had always been full of death. It was the life insurance companies that noticed first what was going on, and well they might have. They had insured millions of lives at rates based on a life expectancy of sixty-eight years. Now, in a six-month period, the average age at death for married American males with more than twenty thousand dollars in life insurance had dropped to an appalling forty-seven years.

"Dropped to forty-seven years—and still dropping," said the president of the American Reliable and Equitable Life and Casualty Company of Connecticut. The president himself was only forty-six, very young to be heading the eighth-largest insurance company in the country. He was a humorless, emaciated, ambitious young man who had been described by the previous president as "gruesomely capable." His name was Millikan.

The previous president, who had been kicked upstairs to chairmanship of the board of directors, was with Millikan now in the company's boardroom in Hartford. He was an amiable old gentleman, a lifelong bachelor named Breed.

The third person present was Dr. Everett, a young epidemiologist from the United States Department of Health and Welfare. It was Dr. Everett who gave the plague a name that stuck. He called it "the epizootic." "When you say forty-seven years—" he said to Millikan, "is that an exact figure?"

"We happen to be somewhat short of exact figures just now," said Millikan wryly. "Our chief actuary killed himself two days ago—threw himself out his office window."

"Family man?" said Dr. Everett.

"Naturally," said the chairman of the board. "And his family is very nicely taken care of now, thanks to life insurance. His debts can all be paid off, his wife is assured an adequate income for life, and his children can go to college without having to work their ways through." The old man said all this with sad, plonking irony. "Insurance is a wonderful thing," he said, "especially after it's been in effect for more than two years." He meant by that that most life insurance contracts paid off on suicide after they had been in effect for more than two years. "No family man," he said, "should be without it."

"Did he leave a note?" said Dr. Everett.

"He left two," said the chairman. "One was to us, suggesting that we replace him with a Gypsy fortune-teller. The other was to his wife and children, and it said simply, *"I love you more than anything. I have done this so you can have all the things you deserve."* He winked ruefully at Dr. Everett, the country's outstanding authority on the epizootic. "I daresay such sentiments are quite familiar to you by now."

Dr. Everett nodded. "As familiar as chicken pox to a pediatrician," he said tiredly.

Millikan brought his fist down on the table hard. "What I want to know is what is the Government going to do about this?" he said. "At the current death rate, this company will be out of business in eight months! I presume the same is true of every life insurance company. What is the Government going to do?"

"What do you *suggest* the Government do?" said Dr. Everett. "We're quite open to suggestion—almost pathetically so."

"All right!" said Millikan. "Government action number one!"

"Number one!" echoed Dr. Everett, preparing to write.

"Get this disease out in the open, where we can *fight* it! No more secrecy!" said Millikan.

"Marvellous!" said Dr. Everett. "Call the reporters at once. We'll hold a press conference right here, give out all the facts and figures—and within minutes the whole world will know." He turned to the old chairman of the board. "Modern communications are wonderful, aren't they?" he said. "Almost as wonderful as life insurance." He reached for the telephone on the long table, took it from its cradle. "What's the name of the afternoon paper?" he said.

Millikan took the telephone away from him, hung up.

Everett smiled at him in mock surprise. "I thought that was step number one. I was just going to take it, so we could get right on to step two."

Millikan closed his eyes, massaged the bridge of his nose. The young president of American Reliable and Equitable had plenty to contemplate within the violet privacy of his eyelids. After step one, which would inevitably publicize the bad condition of the insurance companies, there would be the worst financial collapse in the country's history. As for curing the epizootic: publicity could only make the disease kill more quickly, would make it cram into a few weeks of panic deaths that would ordinarily be spread over a few queasy years. As for the grander issues, as for America's becoming weak and contemptible, as for money's being valued more highly than life itself, Millikan hardly cared. What mattered to him most was immediate and personal. All other implications of the epizootic paled beside the garish, blaring fact that the company was about to go under, taking Millikan's brilliant career with it.

The telephone on the table rang. Breed answered, received information without comment, hung up. "Two more planes just crashed," he said. "One in Georgia—fifty-three aboard. One in Indiana—twenty-nine aboard."

"Survivors?" said Dr. Everett.

"None," said Breed. "That's eleven crashes this month—so far."

"All right! All right! All right!" said Millikan, rising to his feet. "Government action number one—ground all airplanes! No more air travel at all!"

"Good!" said Dr. Everett. "We should also put bars on all windows above the first floor, remove all bodies of water from centers of population, outlaw the sales of firearms, rope, poisons, razors, knives, automobiles and boats—"

Millikan subsided into his chair, hope gone. He took a photograph of his family from his billfold, studied it listlessly. In the background of the photograph was his hundred-thousand-dollar waterfront home, and, beyond that, his forty-eight-foot cabin cruiser lying at anchor.

"Tell me," Breed said to young Dr. Everett, "are you married?"

"No," said Dr. Everett. "The Government has a rule now against letting married men work on epizootic research."

"Oh?" said Breed.

"They found out that married men working on the epizootic generally died of it before they could even submit a report," said Dr. Everett. He shook his head. "I just don't understand, just don't understand. Or sometimes I do—and then I don't again."

"Does the deceased have to be married in order for you to credit his death to the epizootic?" said Breed.

"A wife *and* children," said Dr. Everett. "That's the classic pattern. A wife alone doesn't mean much. Curiously, a wife and just one child doesn't mean much, either." He shrugged. "Oh, I suppose a few cases where a man has been unusually devoted to his mother or some other relative, or maybe even to his college, should be classified technically as the epizootic—but cases like that aren't statistically important. To the epidemiologist who deals only in staggering figures, the epizootic is overwhelmingly a disease of successful, ambitious married men with more than one child."

Millikan took no interest in their conversation. With monumental irrelevance, he now placed the photograph of his family in front of the two bachelors. It showed a quite ordinary mother with three quite ordinary children, one an infant. "Look those wonderful people in the eye!" he said hoarsely.

Breed and Dr. Everett glanced at each other strickenly,

then did as Millikan told them. They looked at the photograph bleakly, having just confirmed for each other the fact that Millikan was mortally ill with the epizootic.

"Look those wonderful people in the eye," said Millikan, as tragically resonant as the Ancient Mariner now. "That's something *I've* always been able to do—until now," he said.

Breed and Dr. Everett continued to look into the uninteresting eyes, preferring the sight of them to the sight of a man who was going to die very soon.

"Look at Robert!" Millikan commanded, speaking of his eldest son. "Imagine having to tell that fine boy that he can't go to Andover anymore, that he's got to go to public school from now on! Look at Nancy!" he commanded, speaking of his only daughter. "No more horse, no more sailboat, no more country club for her. And look at little Marvin in his dear mother's arms," he said. "Imagine bringing a baby into this world and then realizing that you won't be able to give it any advantages at all!" His voice became jagged with self-torment and shame. "That poor little kid is going to have to fight every inch of the way!" he said. "They *all* are. When American Reliable and Equitable goes smash, there isn't a thing their father will be able to do for them! Tooth and nail all the way for them!" he cried.

Now Millikan's voice became soft with horror. He invited the two bachelors to look at his wife—a bland, lazy, plump dumpling, incidentally. "Imagine having a wonderful woman like that, a real pal who's stuck with you through thick and thin, who's borne your children and made a decent home for them," he said. "Imagine," he said after a long silence, "imagine being a hero to her, imagine giving her all the things she's longed for all her life. And then imagine tell-ing her," he whispered, "that you've lost it all."

Millikan sobbed. He ran from the boardroom into his office, took a loaded revolver from his desk. As Breed and Dr. Everett burst in upon him, he blew his brains out, thereby maturing life insurance policies in the amount of one cool million.

And there lay one more case of the epizootic, the epi-demic practice of committing suicide in order to create wealth.

"You know——" said the chairman of the board, "I used to wonder what was going to become of all the Americans like him, a bright and shiny new race that believed that life was a matter of making one's family richer and richer and richer, or it wasn't life. I often wondered what would become of them, if bad times ever came again, if the bright and shiny men sud-denly discovered their net worths going down." Breed pointed to the floor. Now he pointed to the ceiling. "Instead of up," he said.

Bad times had come—about four months in advance of the epizootic.

"The one-way men—designed for up only," said Breed.

"And their one-way wives and their one-way children," said Dr. Everett. "Dear God——" he said, going to a window and looking out over a wintry Hartford, "the principal in-dustry of this country is now dying for a living."

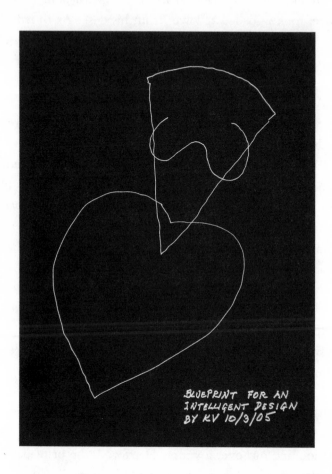

BLUEPRINT FOR AN
INTELLIGENT DESIGN
BY KV 10/3/05

HUNDRED·DOLLAR KISSES

Q: Do you understand that everything you say is going to be taken down by that stenographer over there?

A: Yes sir.

Q: And that anything you say may be used against you?

A: Understood.

Q: Your name, age, and address?

A: Henry George Lovell, Jr., thirty-three, living at 4121 North Pennsylvania Street, Indianapolis, Indiana.

Q: Occupation?

A: Until about two o'clock this afternoon, I was manager of the Records Section of the Indianapolis Office of the Eagle Mutual Casualty and Indemnity Company of Ohio.

Q: In the Circle Tower?

A: Right.

Q: Do you know me?

A: You are Detective Sergeant George Miller of the Indianapolis Police Department.

Q: Has anyone maltreated you or threatened you with maltreatment or offered you favors in order to obtain this statement?

A: Nope.

Q: Did you, at approximately two o'clock this afternoon, assault a man named Verne Petrie with a telephone?

A: I hit him on the head with the part you talk and listen in.

Q: How many times did you strike him with it?

A: Once. I hit him one good one.

Q: What is Verne Petrie to you?

A: Verne Petrie to me is what is wrong with the world.

Q: I mean, what was Verne Petrie to you in the organization of the office?

A: We were on the same junior executive level. We were in different sections. He wasn't my boss, and I wasn't his boss.

Q: You were competing for advancement?

A: No. We were in two entirely different fields.

Q: How would you describe him?

A: You want me to describe Verne with feeling, or just for the record?

Q: Any way you want to do it.

A: Verne Petrie is a big, pink, fat man about thirty-five years old. He has silky orange hair and two long upper front teeth like a beaver. He wears a red vest and chain-smokes very small cigars. He spends at least fifteen dollars a month on girlie magazines.

Q: Girlie magazines?

A: *Man About Town. Bull. Virile. Vital. Vigor. Male Valor.* You know.

Q: And you say Verne Petrie spends fifteen dollars a month on such magazines?

A: At least. The things generally cost fifty cents or more, and I never saw Verne come back from a lunch hour

when he didn't have at least one new one. Sometimes
he had three.

Q: You don't like girls?

A: Sure I like girls. I'm crazy about girls. I married one,
and I've got two nice little ones.

Q: Why should you resent it that Verne buys these
magazines?

A: I don't resent it. It just seems kind of sick to me.

Q: Sick?

A: Girlie pictures are like dope to Verne. I mean, anybody
likes to look at pin-up pictures off and on, but Verne,
he has to buy armloads of them. He spends a fortune on
them, and they're realer than anything real to him.
When it says at the bottom of a pin-up picture, "Come
play with me, Baby," or something like that, Verne
believes it. He really thinks the girl is saying that to him.

Q: He's married?

A: To a nice, pretty, affectionate girl. He's got a swell-
looking wife at home. It isn't as though he's bottled up
in the Y.M.C.A.

Q: There is never anything else in the magazines besides
pictures of girls?

A: Oh sure—there's other stuff. Haven't you ever looked
inside one?

Q: I'm asking you.

A: They're all pretty much alike. They all have at least one
big picture of a naked girl, usually right in the middle.
That's what sells the magazine, is that big picture. Then
there'll be some articles about foreign cars or decorating
a bachelor penthouse or white slavery in Hong Kong or
how to choose a loudspeaker. But what Verne wants is

the pictures of the girls. To him, looking at those pictures is just like taking the girls out on dates. Cummerbunds.

Q: Pardon me? What was that last? Cummerbunds?

A: That's another thing they generally have articles on— cummerbunds.

Q: You seem to have read these magazines rather extensively yourself.

A: I had the desk right next to Verne's. The magazines were all over the place. And every time he brought a new one back to the office, he'd rub my nose in it.

Q: Actually rub your nose in it?

A: Practically. And he always said the same thing.

Q: What was the thing he always said?

A: I don't want to say it in front of a lady stenographer.

Q: Can't you approximate it?

A: Verne would open the magazine to the picture of the girl, and he'd say, approximately, "Boy, I'd pay a hundred dollars to kiss a doll baby like that. Wouldn't you?"

Q: This bothered you?

A: After a couple of years, it was getting under my skin.

Q: Why?

A: Because it showed a darn poor sense of values.

Q: Do you think you are God Almighty, empowered to go around correcting people's sense of values?

A: I do not think I am God Almighty. I do not even think I am a very good Unitarian.

Q: Suppose you tell us what happened when you came back from lunch this afternoon?

A: I found Verne Petrie sitting at his desk with a new copy

of *Male Valor* magazine open in front of him. It was open to a two-page picture of a woman named Patty Lee Minot. She was wearing a cellophane bathrobe. Verne was listening to his telephone and looking at the picture at the same time. He had his hand over the mouthpiece. He winked at me, as though he was hearing something wonderful on the telephone. He signalled to me that I should listen in on my own telephone. He held up three fingers, meaning I should switch my phone to line three.

Q: Line three?

A: There are three lines coming into the office. And I looked around the office, and I realized that there was somebody listening in on line three on every telephone. Everybody in the office was listening in. So I listened in, and I could hear a telephone ringing on the other end.

Q: It was the telephone of Patty Lee Minot ringing in New York?

A: Yes. I didn't know it at the time, but that's what it was. Verne tried to tell me what was going on. He pointed to Patty Lee Minot's picture in the magazine, then he pointed to Miss Hackleman's desk.

Q: What was going on at Miss Hackleman's desk?

A: Miss Hackleman was out with a cold, and one of the building janitors was sitting in her chair, using her telephone. He was the one who was making the long-distance call that everybody else was listening in on.

Q: You knew him?

A: I'd seen him around the building. I knew his first name. It was stitched on the back of his coveralls. His first name was Harry. I found out later his whole name was Harry Barker.

Q: Describe him.

A: Harry? Well, he looks a lot older than he is. He looks about forty-five. Actually, I guess, he's younger than I am. He's pretty good-looking, and I think he must have been a pretty good athlete at one time. But he's losing his hair fast, and he's got a lot of wrinkles from worrying or something.

Q: So you were listening to the telephone ringing in New York?

A: Yes. And I accidentally sneezed.

Q: Sneezed?

A: Sneezed. I did it right into the telephone, and everybody jumped a mile, and then somebody said, "Gesundheit." This made Verne Petrie very sore.

Q: What did he do, exactly?

A: He got red, and he whined. He whined, "Shut up, you guys." You know. He whined like somebody who didn't want a beautiful experience spoiled by a bunch of jerks. "Come on, you guys," he whined, "either get off the line or shut up. I want to hear." And then somebody on the other end answered the telephone. It was Patty Lee Minot's maid, and the long-distance operator asked her if it was such-and-such a number, and the maid said yes it was. So the operator said, "Here's your number, sir," and the janitor named Harry started talking to the maid. Harry was all tensed up. He was making a lot of funny faces into the telephone, as though he was trying to make up his mind about how to sound. "Could I speak to Miss Melody Arlene Pfitzer, please?" he said. "Miss

Who?" said the maid. "Miss Melody Arlene Pfitzer," said Harry. "Ain't nobody here named Pfitzer," said the maid. "This Patty Lee Minot's number?" said Harry. "That's right," said the maid. "Melody Arlene Pfitzer—" said Harry, "that's Patty Lee Minot's real name." "I wouldn't know nothing about that," said the maid.

Q: Who is Patty Lee Minot?

A: Don't you know?

Q: I'm asking you for the record.

A: I just told you: she was the girl in the cellophane bathrobe in Verne's magazine. She was the girl in the middle of *Male Valor*. I guess she is what you would call a glamorous celebrity. She's in the girlie magazines all the time, and sometimes she's on television, and one time I saw her in a movie with Bing Crosby.

Q: Continue.

A: You know what it said under her picture in the magazine?

Q: What?

A: "Woman Eternal for October." That's what it said.

Q: Go on about the telephone conversation.

A: Well, the janitor named Harry was kidding around with the maid about Patty Lee Minot's real name. "Call her Melody Arlene Pfitzer sometime, and see what she says," he said. "If it's all the same to you," said the maid, "I don't believe I will." And Harry said, "Put her on, would you please? Tell her it's Harry K. Barker calling." "She know you?" said the maid. "She will if she thinks about it a minute," said Harry. "Where you know her from?" said the maid. "High school," said Harry. "I don't believe she'll want to be bothered just now, on

account of she's got a TV show tonight," said the maid.
"She isn't thinking much about high school just now,"
she said. "I used to be married to her in high school,"
Harry said. "You think that might make a difference?"
And then Verne hit me on the arm.

Q: He hit you?

A: Yes.

Q: You're claiming that he assaulted you before you
assaulted him?

A: I suppose I could, couldn't I? That's an interesting idea.
If I was to hire a shyster lawyer, I suppose that's maybe
what he'd claim. No—Verne didn't assault me. He just
hit me on the arm to get my attention, hit me hard
enough to hurt, though. And then he practically
smathered the picture of Patty Lee Minot all over my
face.

Q: Smathered?

A: Practically smeared it all around.

Q: And what did the maid say on the telephone when she
learned that Harry K. Barker had once been married to
her employer?

A: She said, "Hold on."

Q: I see.

A: And then, after she left the telephone, I said, "Hold on,"
and Verne blew up.

Q: You made a little joke on the telephone, and Verne
didn't like it?

A: I just imitated the maid, and Verne went through the
roof. He said, "All right, wise guy, shut your trap. I get
to hear your heavenly voice all day long, every day, year
in and year out. I am just about to hear the voice of

Patty Lee Minot in person, and I'll thank you kindly to keep your big yap shut. I'm paying for this call. This call is coming out of my hide. You're welcome to listen, but kindly shut up."

Q: Verne was paying for the call?

A: That's right. The call was his idea. It all started when he showed Harry the picture of Patty Lee Minot in the magazine. Verne told Harry he'd pay a hundred dollars to kiss a doll baby like that, and Harry said it was funny he should say that. Harry told Verne he used to be married to her. Verne couldn't believe it, so they bet twenty dollars on it, and then they put in the call.

Q: When Verne blew up at you, you didn't fight back in any way?

A: I just took it. He wasn't in any mood to be trifled with. It was just as though I was trying to bust up his love life. It was just as though he was having a big love affair with Patty Lee Minot, and I came along and wrecked it. I didn't say a word back to him, and then Patty Lee Minot came on the line. "Hello?" she said. "This is Harry Barker," Harry said. He was trying to be smooth and sophisticated. He was lighting a little cigar Verne had given to him. "Long time no see, Melody Arlene," he said. "Who is this really?" she said. "Is this you, Ferd?"

Q: Who is Ferd?

A: Search me. Some friend of hers who is a practical joker, I guess. Some glamorous, fun-loving New York celebrity. Harry said, "No, this is really Harry. We were married on October fourteenth, eleven years ago, Melody Arlene. Remember?" "If this is really Harry, and I don't believe it is," she said, "how come you're calling me up?" "I thought you might like to know how our daughter is, Melody Arlene," said Harry. "You never have tried to find out anything about her over all these years. I thought you might like to know how she was doing, since she is the only baby you ever had."

Q: What did she say to that?

A: She didn't say anything for a minute. Finally she said, in a very tough, twangy voice, "Who is this? Is this somebody trying to blackmail me? Because if it is, you can go straight to hell. Go ahead and give the whole story to the newspapers, if you want to. I've never tried to keep it a secret. I was married when I was sixteen to a boy named Harry Barker. We were both juniors in high school, and we had to get married on account of I was going to have a baby. Tell the whole wide world, for all I care." And then Harry said, "The baby died, Melody Arlene. Your little baby died two years after you walked out."

Q: He said what?

A: His and her baby died. Their baby died. She didn't even know it, never bothered to find out what became of her daughter. This, according to *Male Valor* magazine, was woman eternal, every red-blooded male's dream girl. And you know what she said?

Q: No.

A: Sergeant, this Woman Eternal for October said, "That's a part of my life I've blotted out completely. I'm sorry, but I couldn't care less."

Q: What was Verne Petrie's reaction when she said that?

A: No special reaction. His piggy little eyes were all glazed

over, and he was showing his teeth and kind of gnashing
them. He was off in some wild daydream about himself
and Patty Lee Minot.

Q: And then what?

A: And then nothing. She hung up, and that was that. We
all hung up, and everybody but Verne looked sick.
Harry stood up, and he shook his head. "I wish to God
I'd had more sense than to call her up," he said. "Here's
your twenty bucks, Harry," said Verne. "No thanks,"
said Harry. He was like a man in a bad dream. "I don't
want it now," he said. "It would be like money from
her." Harry looked down at his hands. "I built her
a house, a nice little house. Built it with my own
hands," he said. He started to say something else, but he
changed his mind. He shuffled out of the office, still
looking at his hands. For about the next half hour, it
was like a morgue around the office. Everybody felt
lousy—everybody but Verne. I looked over at Verne,
and he had the magazine open to the picture of Patty
Lee Minot again. He caught my eye, and he said to me,
"That lucky son of a gun."

Q: Who was a lucky son of a gun?

A: Harry Barker was a lucky son of a gun, because he'd
been married to that wonderful woman on the bed.
"That lucky son of a gun," Verne said. "Boy," he said,
"since I've heard her voice on the telephone, she's one
doll baby I'd give a thousand dollars to kiss."

Q: And then you let him have it?

A: Right.

Q: With his own telephone? On top of his head?

A: Right.

Q: Knocking him cold?

A: I knocked Verne Petrie colder than a mackerel, because it came to me all in a flash that Verne Petrie was what was wrong with the world.

Q: What is wrong with the world?

A: Everybody pays attention to pictures of things. Nobody pays attention to things themselves.

Q: Is there anything you would care to add?

A: Yes. I would like to put on the record the fact that I weigh one hundred and twenty-three pounds, and Verne Petrie weighs two hundred pounds and is a full foot taller than I am. I had no choice but to use a weapon. I stand ready, of course, to pay his hospital bill.

GUARDIAN OF
THE PERSON

"I wish there wasn't all that money," said Nancy Holmes Ryan. "I really wish it wasn't there." Nancy had been married for an hour and a half now. She was driving with her husband from Boston to Cape Cod. The time was noon, late winter. The scenery was leaden sea, summer cottages boarded up, scrub oaks still holding their brown leaves tight, cranberry bogs with frosty beards—

"That much money is embarrassing," said Nancy. "I mean it." She didn't really mean it—not very much, anyway. She was enduring the peculiar Limbo between a wedding and a wedding night. Like many maidens in such a Limbo, Nancy found her own voice unreal, as though echoing in a great tin box, and she heard that voice speaking with unreasonable intensity, heard herself expressing extravagant opinions as though they were the bedrock of her soul.

They weren't the bedrock of her soul. Nancy was bluffing—pretending to love this and hate that—dealing as best she could with the confusing fact of Limbo, of being nothing and nobody and nowhere until her new life, until her married life could truly begin.

A moment before, Nancy had launched a startlingly bitter attack on stucco houses and the people who lived in them, had made her husband promise that they would never live in a stucco house. She hadn't really meant it.

Now, out of control, not really meaning it, Nancy was wishing that her husband were poor. He was a long way from being poor. He was worth about two hundred thousand dollars.

Nancy's husband was an engineering student at M.I.T. His name was Robert Ryan, Jr. Robert was tall, quiet—pleasant and polite, but often withdrawn. He had been orphaned at the age of nine. He had been raised from then on by his aunt and uncle on Cape Cod. Like most orphaned minors with a lot of money, Robert had two guardians—one for his finances and one for his person. The Merchants' Trust Company of Cape Cod was his financial guardian. His uncle Charley Brewer was the guardian of his person. And Robert was not only going to Cape Cod to honeymoon. He was going to take full control of his inheritance as well. His wedding day was also his twenty-first birthday, and the bank's financial guardianship was legally at an end.

Robert was in a Limbo of his own. He wasn't full of talk. He was almost completely mechanical, in harmony with the automobile and little else. His responses to his pink and garrulous new bride were as automatic as his responses to the road.

On and on Nancy talked.

"I would rather start out with nothing," she said. "I wish you'd kept the money a secret from me—just left it in the bank for emergencies."

"Forget about it then," said Robert. He pushed in the cigarette lighter. It clicked out a moment later, and Robert lit a cigarette without taking his eyes from the road.

"I'm going to keep my job," said Nancy. "We'll make our

own way." She was a secretary in the admissions office at M.I.T. She and Robert had known each other for only two months before they were married. "We'll live within whatever we actually make ourselves," she said.

"Good," said Robert.

"I didn't know you had a dime when I said I'd marry you," said Nancy.

"I know," said Robert.

"I hope your uncle knows that," said Nancy.

"I'll tell him," said Robert. Robert hadn't even told his Uncle Charley that he was going to get married. That would be a surprise.

It was typical of Robert to deal in large surprises, to make his decisions in solitude. Even at the age of nine, he had found it somehow important to show very little emotional dependence on his uncle and aunt. In all the years Robert had lived with them, only one remark had been made about the way he kept his distance. His Aunt Mary had once called him her boarder.

Aunt Mary was dead now. Uncle Charley lived on, was going to meet Robert for lunch in the Atlantic House, a restaurant across the street from the bank. Charley roamed all over Cape Cod in a big, sad old Chrysler, knocking on strangers' doors. He was a straight-commission salesman of aluminum combination storm windows and screens.

"I hope your uncle likes me," said Nancy.

"He will," said Robert. "Don't worry about it."

"I worry about everything," said Nancy.

The Merchants' Trust Company of Cape Cod, as Robert's financial guardian, had certain duties to perform on Robert's twenty-first birthday. They had to get him to sign many documents, and they had to give him an accounting of their custodianship going back twelve years.

The bank was expecting him at one-thirty.

There wasn't anything in particular that Robert's other guardian, his Uncle Charley, the guardian of his person, had to do on the same day. Under law, Charley's responsibility for the boy's person simply evaporated on that day.

That was that—automatically.

But Charley couldn't let it go at that. After all, Charley had no other children, he loved Robert, and he thought that raising the boy was the best thing he and his wife had done with their lives. So Charley planned to make a sentimental little ceremony of surrendering Robert's person before the boy went into the bank.

Charley didn't know about Robert's marriage, so Charley's plan was for just two people.

Charley went into the Atlantic House a half an hour before Robert was supposed to arrive. Charley went into the bar side of the restaurant, and he picked a small table for two.

He sat down and waited.

Several people in the bar knew Charley, and they nodded to him. Those who knew Charley well were surprised to see him on the bar side, because Charley hadn't dared to take a drink for eight years. He hadn't dared to drink because he was an alcoholic. One small beer was enough to start Charley on a toot that could last for weeks.

A new waitress who didn't know Charley took his order, went over to the bar, announced the order loud and clear. "Bourbon on the rocks," she said. She said it emptily. She didn't know that she was announcing big news, announcing that Charley Brewer, after eight dry-as-dust years, was going to have a drink.

Charley got his drink.

Ned Crosby, the owner of the Atlantic House, came right along with it. When the waitress put the drink in front of Charley, Ned slipped into the chair facing him.

"Hello, Charley," said Ned, gently, watchfully.

Charley thanked the waitress for the drink, took his own sweet time in acknowledging Ned. "Hello, Ned," he said. "I'm afraid you're going to have to give up that chair pretty soon. My boy's going to walk in here any minute."

"The drink for him?" said Ned.

"For me," said Charley. He smiled serenely.

Both men were in their late forties, both were going bald, both were alcoholics. They had been boozing buddies years before. They had sworn off booze at the same time, had gone to their first meeting of Alcoholics Anonymous together.

"Today's the boy's twenty-first birthday, Ned," said Charley. "Today he is a man."

"Good for him," said Ned. He pointed to the drink. "That accounts for the celebration."

"That accounts for it," said Charley simply. He made no move to touch the drink. He wasn't going to drink it until Robert walked in.

Strangers looking at Charley and Ned would have guessed that Ned was broke and Charley was prosperous. They would have guessed exactly wrong. Ned, dumpy and humble, wearing rumpled sports clothes from plain pipe racks, took thirty thousand dollars a year out of the Atlantic House. Charley, tall and elegant, sporting a British mustache, made about a tenth that much selling storm windows and screens.

"That a new suit, Charley?" said Ned.

"It's one I've had a while," said Charley. The suit, dark, expensive, and gentlemanly, was in point of fact sixteen years old, dated back to the days when Charley had really been the rich man he seemed. Charley, like the person whose guardian he was, had inherited a lot of money, too. He had lost it all in one fantastic business enterprise after another. There had been a Venetian blind factory, a chain of frozen custard stands, a distributorship for Japanese vacuum cleaners, a ferry operating between Hyannis and Nantucket—even a scheme for harnessing steam that escaped from Italian volcanoes.

"Don't worry about the drink, Ned," said Charley.

"Did I say I was worried?" said Ned.

"Doesn't take much imagination to guess what you're thinking," said Charley. The most obvious trap that an alcoholic could fall into was a celebration, and Charley knew this perfectly well.

"That's the most flattering thing anybody's said to me all week," said Ned.

"This is no ordinary celebration," said Charley.

"They never are, Charley," said Ned.

"What I am celebrating today," said Charley, "is the one thing that really turned out well."

"Uh huh," said Ned. His face remained cheerfully quizzical. "Go on and celebrate if you want to, Charley—but not in here."

Charley closed his hand around his glass. "Yes—" he said, "in here, and pretty darn soon, too." He had been planning the dramatic gesture of the drink too long to be talked out of it now. He was fully aware of the danger the drink represented. He was scared to death of it. It represented as terrifying a test as walking a tightrope across Niagara Falls.

But the danger was the whole point.

"Ned—" said Charley, "that boy is going to watch in horror while I swallow this drink. And would you like to know what is going to happen to me?" Charley leaned forward. "*Nothing*," he said. He sat back again. "You can watch in horror," he said, "and anybody else who wants to can watch in horror, too. Sell tickets. It ought to be worth a pretty good price of admission, because Charley Brewer is going to take his first drink in eight years—swallow it right down—and that drink isn't going to touch him!

"Why?" said Charley, and he put the question so loudly that it was heard across the room.

"Why isn't this stuff poison for me today?" he said, pointing down at his glass. He answered his own question softly, sibilantly. "Because today I have nothing but a complete success to think about, Ned. This is one day my failures won't come crowding in on me, gibbering and squawking."

Charley shook his head in incredulous gratitude. "That kid—that lovely kid of mine," he said. "I can take a drink today, Ned, because today I am not a disappointed man."

Robert Ryan, Jr., parked his car in the paved lot behind the Atlantic House. It was the first stop in his married life, and his new bride was keeping track of all firsts.

"This is our very first stop," said Nancy Holmes Ryan. She pretended to memorize the place, to find love poetry in the backs of a dime store, a shoe store, a radio store, and the

Atlantic House. "I'll always remember this place as the very first place we stopped," she said.

Robert got out of the car promptly, went around to Nancy's side, opened her door.

"Wait," said Nancy. "Now that you're married, you'll have to learn how to wait a little." She turned the car mirror in order to see her own reflection in it. "You'll have to learn—" she said, "a woman can't just rush into things like a man. She's got to get ready a little."

"Sorry," said Robert.

"Especially if she's going to meet a new relative," said Nancy. She frowned at herself in the mirror—and then she tried, in quick succession, a whole series of expressions by which she might be judged. "I—I hardly know anything about him," she said.

"Uncle Charley?" said Robert.

"You haven't said much," said Nancy. "Tell me—tell me a few little things."

Robert shrugged. "Dreamer," he said.

Nancy tried to make something of this, could make very little. "Dreamer?" she echoed.

"Lost everything he had in different crazy businesses," said Robert.

Nancy nodded. "I see." She still saw very little. "Bob?"

"Hm?" said Robert.

"What does that have to do with dreams?" she said.

"Never sees things the way they really are," said Robert. His voice was just a little edgy.

"The way things really are—" he said, "that's never good enough for Uncle Charley."

The edginess increased. "Anything he's mixed up in—

he'll fancy it up in his dreams till it's the most glorious thing he ever heard of."

"That sounds like a nice way to be." Her own tone, in involuntary response to Robert's, was mildly argumentative.

"It's a lousy way to be," said Robert harshly.

"I don't see why," said Nancy.

"The poor guy bets his life again and again and again on things that are just—" he shook his head wildly, "just nothing at all! Nothing!"

Robert's bitterness startled Nancy, dismayed her. "Don't you like him, Robert?" she said.

"Sure I like him!" said Robert loudly.

Robert's tone was now so harsh, so worldly, so alone and unromantic, so unsuitable for a wedding day, that it was like a slap to Nancy. After an instant of shock, she could not hold back her tears. The tears were few, and unaccompanied by sound—but there they were in plain view, twinkling on the rims of her eyes. She turned away from Robert.

Robert turned red. His hands worked the air cumbersomely. "Sorry," he said.

"You sound so mad," said Nancy.

"I'm not," said Robert.

"You sound that way," said Nancy. "What did I say wrong?"

"Nothing—nothing to do with you," said Robert. He sighed. "You about ready?"

"No," said Nancy, "not now—not after crying."

"Take your time," said Robert.

Ned Crosby, the innkeeper, looked old. He was still at the table for two with Charley in the bar. He had been unable to wheedle his old friend out of taking a drink. With each new line of argument, Charley had become more radiant with the glamour of his plan.

Ned stood, and Charley looked up at him with amused affection.

"Going?" said Charley.

"Going," said Ned.

"I hope I've put your mind at ease," said Charley lightly.

"Sure," said Ned. He managed to smile. "Prosit, skoal, and mud in your eye," he said.

"Join the boy and me in a drink, Ned?" said Charley playfully.

"I'm tempted," said Ned, "but I'm scared to death the world wouldn't cooperate."

"What could go wrong?" said Charley.

"I don't know, and neither do you," said Ned. "But it's an awfully busy world out there, full of fast-moving people with big, fancy ideas of their own. No sooner would we get that first drink down, counting on a perfect day, and somebody would come crashing in here and say or do exactly the wrong thing."

At the end of this speech, Ned intended to take Charley's drink away from him. But he wasn't quick enough. Before he could do it, Charley was on his feet, his glass on high, saluting Robert, who stood in the doorway.

In three brave, highly ceremonious gulps, Charley drank the drink down.

Nancy Holmes Ryan watched Charley do it through the small opening between her husband's shoulder and the doorjamb. The opening widened now, until Nancy was framed alone in the doorway. Robert had gone to his uncle's side.

There was a third man with them, frowsy, worried. The third man, of course, was the innkeeper, Ned. Of the three men, only Charley looked happy.

"Don't worry—" Charley said to Robert.

"I—I'm not," said Robert.

"I'm not starting on a binge," said Charley. "I haven't taken up drinking again since you've been gone. This is a special drink." He set the glass down with melodramatic finality. "One—just one. One drink, and that's the end." He turned to Ned. "Have I shamed the Atlantic House?" he said.

"No," said Ned quietly.

"Nor am I going to," said Charley. He motioned to the chair facing him. "Sit down, person," he said to Robert.

"Person?" said Robert.

"What I've been guarding for twelve solid years," said Charley. "What'll you have?"

"Uncle Charley—" said Robert, starting to introduce Nancy.

"Sit down, sit down!" said Charley heartily. "Whatever we've got to say to each other, let's say it in comfort."

"Uncle Charley—" said Robert, "I—I'd like you to meet my wife."

"Your what?" said Charley. So far, he hadn't noticed Nancy at all. Now, when Robert nodded in her direction, Charley remained sitting, looked at her blankly.

"My wife," Robert said again, lamely.

Now Charley stood, his eyes on Nancy. His eyes were strangely empty. "How do you do?" he said.

Nancy bowed slightly. "How do you do?" she said.

"I missed your name," said Charley.

"Nancy," said Nancy.

"Nancy," said Charley.

"We were married this morning," said Robert.

"I see," said Charley. He blinked hard several times, distorting his face, as though trying to make his eyes work better. And then, realizing that the expressions might be mistaken for drunkenness, he explained loudly, "Something in my eye." He turned to Ned. "I'm not drunk, Ned," he said.

"Nobody said you were, Charley," said Ned.

"I don't suppose this table will do any longer," said Charley.

WITH HIS HAND ON THE THROTTLE

Earl Harrison was an empire builder by nature, annoyed at being shorter than most men, massively muscled, self-made, insistently the center of any gathering, unable to relax. He had calluses on his palms as tough as the back of a crocodile. He made his living building roads, and, in his middle thirties, was growing rich at it. Legions of trucks, bulldozers, graders, earth movers, rollers, asphalt spreaders, and power shovels carried his name into every corner of the state.

But Earl liked owning the equipment and watching the colossal work it did more than he liked the luxuries it could earn for him. Most of his money went right back into the business, which grew bigger and bigger and bigger, with no end in sight.

Save for good whiskey and cigars and model trains, Earl's life was Spartan. He worked with his machine operators, and dressed like them most of the time in heavy shoes and faded khaki. His house was small, and his pretty young wife, Ella, had no servants. The hobby of model railroading suited Earl perfectly—the building and controlling of a busy little world complicated with wonderful machinery. And, like his business, the empire on plywood grew as though Napoleon were running it. In his imagination he could make his model railroad as real and important as affairs in the full-scale world.

★   ★   ★

The brutish black 4-8-2, its big drivers clashing steel on steel, boomed over the quivering trestle and plunged into the tunnel mouth, whipping the chattering, screaming freight cars behind it. In another five seconds the locomotive, known along the pike as Old Spitfire, burst into the open again with the roar of a wounded devil.

It was Saturday morning, and Earl "Hotbox" Harrison was at the throttle. His gunmetal gray eyes were slits under the visor of his striped cap. His freight was behind time, eastbound on a single track, with the westbound passenger express due. Between Old Spitfire and the safety of the siding ahead was Widow's Hairpin, the most treacherous curve on the Harrisonburg and Earl City Railroad.

The passenger express whistled mournfully in the distance. Hotbox gritted his teeth. There was only one thing to do. He eased the throttle wide open as Old Spitfire shot past the water tower and into the curve.

The track writhed under the fury of the train. Suddenly, at the peak of the curve, the locomotive tottered and shook. Hotbox cried out. The locomotive leaped free of the tracks, and the train followed its crashing, rolling course down the embankment.

All was still.

"Damn!" said Earl. He shut off the power, left his stool, and went over to where Old Spitfire lay on its side.

"Bent its main rod and side rod," said Harry Zellerbach sympathetically. He and Earl had been in the basement for two hours, tirelessly shipping mythical passengers and freight back and forth between the oil burner and the water softener.

Earl set Old Spitfire on the tracks, and rolled it back

and forth experimentally. "Yeah—and dented the ashpan hopper," he said gravely. He sighed. "Old Spitfire was the first locomotive I bought when I started the pike. Remember, Harry?"

"You bet I do, Hotbox."

"And Old Spitfire is going to keep on running till I'm through with the pike."

"Till hell freezes over," said Harry with satisfaction. He had reason to be satisfied with the thought. A tall, thin, wan man, who spent most of his life in basements, he was proprietor of the local hobby shop. In terms of his own modest notions of wealth, he had struck a bonanza in Earl Harrison. There was nothing scaled to HO gauge that Earl wouldn't buy.

"Till hell freezes over," said Earl. He took a can of beer from behind a plaster mountain range, and drank to the world that was all his and still growing.

"Earl—" called his wife, Ella, from the top of the basement stairs, "lunch is getting cold, hon." Her tone was polite and apologetic, though this was the third time she'd called.

"Coming," said Earl. "On my way. Be there in two shakes."

"Please, Earl," called his mother, "Ella has a wonderful lunch, and it'll spoil if you don't come right up."

"Coming," said Earl absently, trying to straighten Old Spitfire's main rod with a screwdriver. "Please, Mom, will you two please keep your shirts on for a couple of seconds?"

The door at the top of the stairs clicked shut, and Earl exhaled with relief. "Honest to God, Harry," he said, "it's like living in a sorority house around here lately. Women, women."

"Yeah—I guess," said Harry. "Of course, you could have it worse. You could have your mother-in-law visiting you, like I do, instead of just your mother. Your mother seems like a sweet old lady."

"No question about it," said Earl. "She *is* sweet. But she still treats me like I was a little kid, and it drives me nuts. I'm not a kid anymore."

"I'll tell the world, Hotbox," said Harry loyally.

"I'm worth ten times what my old man was worth, and have a hundred times as much responsibility."

"You can say *that* again, Hotbox."

"Earl—" called Ella again. "Hotbox, honey—"

"Earl!" said his mother. "You're being rude."

"See what I mean?" said Earl to Harry. "Just like I was a kid." He turned his head toward the stairway. "Said I'd be right up, didn't I?" He returned to his work. "Old Spitfire's smashed up, but what do they care? Women are always talking about how men ought to try to understand their psychology more, but I don't think they spend ten seconds a year trying to see things from a man's point of view."

"I hear you talking, Hotbox."

"Earl—please, darn it," called Ella.

"Be up before you can say Jack Robinson," said Earl.

And twenty minutes later, Hotbox *did* come up to lunch, and lunch *was* cold. Harry Zellerbach declined Ella's halfhearted invitation to share the meal, explaining that he had to deliver some deadeyes and marlinspikes to a man who was building a model of the *Constitution* in *his* basement.

Earl removed his red neckerchief and engineer's cap, and kissed his wife and then his mother.

"Switchman's strike slow you down?" said Ella.

"He was handling a lot of rush defense shipments," said his mother. "Couldn't let our boys in the front lines down, just because lunch was getting cold." She was slight and bird-like, extremely feminine and seeming in need of protection. But she'd been blessed with six brawling sons, Earl the oldest, and had had to be as quick and clever as a mongoose to get any obedience from them. Yearning for a sweet, frilly daughter, she'd learned judo and how to play shortstop. "Cut off the troops' rail supplies, and they might have to give up the water heater and retreat to the fuse box," she said.

"Aaaaaaaaaaah," said Earl, grinning with a mixture of self-consciousness and irritation. "I guess I'm entitled to a little relaxation now and then. I don't have to apologize." It had never occured to him, before the arrival of his mother two days before, that anyone might think an apology was in order. Ella had never twitted him about the pike until now. Suddenly, it was open season on model railroaders.

"Women are entitled to a few things, too," said his mother.

"They got the vote and free access to the saloons," said Earl. "What do they want now—to enter the men's shot put?"

"Common courtesy," said his mother.

He didn't answer. Instead, he went to his file of magazines, and brought one back to the table with him. By coincidence, the magazine opened to an ad for model tanks and artillery pieces, authentic in every detail, and scaled for HO gauge layouts. He squinted at the photograph in the ad, trying to screen out the surrounding type and get the impression of realism.

"Earl—" said Ella.

"Hotbox," said his mother, "you're being spoken to by your wife, your companion for life."

"Shoot," said Earl, laying down the magazine reluctantly.

"I was wondering if maybe we couldn't all go out to dinner tonight—for a change," said Ella. "We could go to Lou's Steak House, and—"

"Not tonight, honey," said Earl. "I've got to do some troubleshooting on the block system."

"Be a sport," said his mother. "Take her out, Earl. Just the two of you go out, and I'll fix a little something for myself here."

"We go out," said Earl. "We go out together lots. Didn't we go out together last Tuesday, Ella?"

Ella nodded vaguely. "Down to the depot to see the new gas-turbine locomotive. It was on exhibit."

"Oh, that must have been nice," said Earl's mother. "Nobody ever took me to see a locomotive."

Earl felt the redness of irritation spreading over the back of his neck. "What's the big idea, you two needling me all the time lately? I work hard, and I'm entitled to play hard, I say. So I like trains. What's the matter with trains?"

"Nothing's the matter with trains, dear," said his mother. "I don't know where the world would be without trains. But there are other things, too. All week you're out on the job somewhere, and come home so tired you can hardly say hello, and then on the weekends you're down in the basement. What kind of a life is that for Ella?"

"Now, Mother—" said Ella, making the faintest of gestures to stop her.

"Who do you think I'm working for, ten, twelve hours a day?" said Earl. "Where do you suppose the money's coming from to pay for this house and this food and the cars—for clothes? I love my wife, and I work like hell for her."

"Couldn't you strike a happy medium?" said his mother. "Poor Ella—"

"Listen," said Earl, "the man in the road construction business who tries to strike a happy medium gets eaten alive."

"What a picture!" said his mother.

"Well, it's the truth," said Earl. "And I've invited Ella to play on the pike with me lots of times. She can come down and get in on the fun any time she wants. Haven't I always said that, Ella? Lots of wives take a real interest in their husbands' layouts."

"That's right," said Ella. "Harry Zellerbach's wife can lay track and wind a transformer and talk for hours about 4-6-6-4 articulated locomotives and 0-4-0 docksides."

"Well, a woman can go *too* far," said Earl. "I think Maude Zellerbach is probably a little punchy. But Ella could have a good time, if she'd just give it a chance. I gave her a Bowser M-1 4-8-2 for her birthday, and she hasn't had it out of the roundhouse once in six months."

"Ella—how could you?" said Earl's mother. "If I had a Bowser all my own, heaven knows when I'd get my housework done."

"OK, you've had your fun," said Earl. "Now let a man eat in peace. I've got a lot on my mind."

"We could go for a ride in the car this afternoon," said Ella. "We could show Mother the countryside, and you could do your thinking out in the fresh air."

The atmosphere of conspiracy made Earl stubborn. He wasn't going to be wheedled into anything. "Trouble is," he said, "Harry's expecting in a shipment of stuff this afternoon, and he's going to give me first look. With the metal shortage, the shipments are small, and everything's on a first-come, first-serve basis. You go. I'd better stay."

"It's like being mother to a dope fiend," said Earl's mother. "I didn't raise him this way."

"Aaaaaaaaaah," said Earl again. His eyes dropped to his magazine, and he scanned, ironically, an article about a man whose wife painted the scenery background for his layout, swell little barns and haystacks and snow-covered peaks and clouds and birds and everything.

"Earl," said his mother, "Ella hasn't been out to a movie or to supper with you for four months. You *should* take her out tonight."

"Never mind, Mother," said Ella.

Earl abandoned the magazine. "Mother," he said evenly, "I love you dearly, as a good son should. But I'm not your little boy anymore. I'm a grown man, entitled to make up my own mind, not to have my life run by you. Everything is fine between Ella and me, and we go out whenever I can possibly spare the time. Isn't that right, Ella?"

"Yes," said Ella. And then she spoiled it. "I guess."

"Now, there's this shipment coming in this afternoon, and the block system is all balled up, so, I'm sorry, but—"

"She could help you with the block system," said Earl's mother. "Ella could help you this afternoon, and then tonight would be free."

"I would, Earl," said Ella.

"Well, you see—" said Earl. "That is, I mean—" He shrugged. "OK."

★   ★   ★

Ella worked hard and gamely in the basement. Her slender fingers were clever, and she learned the knack of splicing and soldering wires after one demonstration from Earl.

"By golly, Ella," said Earl, "we should have tried this before. A circus, isn't it?"

"Yup," said Ella, dropping a bead of solder onto a connection.

Earl, as he moved busily about the edge of the layout, hugged Ella ardently every time he passed her. "See? You never know till you try, eh?"

"Nope."

"And, when you get that last circuit done there, then the real fun begins. We'll get the trains rolling, and see how the system works."

"Anything you say," said Ella. "There—the circuit's done."

"Wonderful," said Earl. Together, they hid the block system's wires under the roadbeds.

Then Earl put his arm around Ella, and gave her a long, now poetic, now philosophic, now technical lecture on the operation of a layout. Grandly, he seated her on the stool and guided her hand to the throttle. He put his engineer's cap on her head, where it came to rest on level with her ears. Her large, dark eyes were all but hidden by the visor, glittering like the eyes of an animal at bay in a shallow hole.

"OK," said Earl judiciously, "let's see, what'll we have for a situation?"

"You'd go a long way before you found a more unlikely one than this one," said Ella, looking bleakly over the miniature landscape, awaiting instructions.

Earl was deep in thought. "That's the difference between a kid's toy railroad and an honest-to-gosh pike," he said. "A kid will just run his train around and around in circles. This thing is set up to do hauling jobs just like the real thing."

"I'm glad there's a difference," said Ella.

"OK, I've got the situation," said Earl. "Let's say a big load of frozen beef has just been brought in to the Earl City yards for shipment to Harrisonburg."

"Lord!" said Ella helplessly.

"Don't get panicky. That's the thing—keep your head and think it out," said Earl affectionately. "Just take that Baldwin diesel switcher, pick up those reefers in the hold yard, run 'em over to the loading platform, then back to the icing plant, then over the hump track to the southbound classification yard. Then pick 'em up with your Bowser in the roundhouse, hook on whatever's in the forwarding yard, and off you go."

"I do?"

"Here," said Earl, "I'll give you a hand on this one." He stood behind Ella, his arms enveloping her as he pushed buttons and switches.

Hours later, the two of them were still in the basement, now side by side on stools before the control panel.

Ecstatic, fresh as a daisy, Earl closed a circuit, and a snub-nosed diesel-electric grumbled out of a siding, picked up a string of hopper cars, and labored up a long plaster grade to a coal loader. *Dingadingadingading!* went a warning bell at a crossing, and a little robot popped out of his shack to wave a lantern.

Exhausted, but sticking grimly to her post, Ella drove her

passenger express through an underpass, beneath the diesel-electric.

Earl pressed a button, Ella pressed another, and the two locomotives whistled cheerily at each other.

"Ella—" called Earl's mother from the top of the stairs. "If you and Earl are going out to supper, you'd better get dressed."

"Seemed like minutes, didn't it?" laughed Earl. "Whole afternoon gone like that!" He snapped his fingers.

Ella took his hand, and seemed to come alive again, like a fish freed from a hook and thrown back into deep, cold water. "Let's go," she said. "What'll I wear? Where'll we go? What'll we do?"

"You go on up," said Earl. "I'll be up in two shakes, soon as I get the equipment back in the yards."

Earl and Ella, as a grand finale to their companionable afternoon in the basement, had put almost every piece of rolling stock into service on the little countryside, so Earl had a big job on his hands, restoring order to the pike while Ella took a shower and dressed. He might have picked up the trinkets and set them down again where he wanted them, and been done with the job in a minute or two. But he would have stolen from the poor box before he would have done such a thing. Under their own power, creeping at scale speeds, the trains made their way to their proper destinations, and were there broken up by switchers.

Signals winked on and off, road barriers dipped and rose, bells tinkled—and euphoria and pride filled the being of Hotbox Harrison, who had this much of the universe precisely as he would have it, under his thumb.

Over the tiny din he heard the outside door of the basement open and close. He turned to see Harry Zellerbach, who grinned and hugged a long, heavy parcel to his chest.

"Harry!" said Earl. "By golly, I thought you'd forgotten me. Been waiting for you to call all afternoon."

"I'll forget you when I forget my own name, Hotbox," said Harry. He looked meaningfully at the box he was carrying, and winked. "The stuff that came through was mostly junk, or stuff you already had, so I didn't bother calling. But there's one thing, Hotbox—" He looked at the box again, coyly. "You'll be the first one to see it, next to my wife. Nobody else even knows I got it."

Earl clapped him on his arm. "There's a friend for you!"

"I try to be, Hotbox," said Harry. He laid the box on the edge of the layout, and lifted the lid slowly. "First one in the state, Hotbox." There in the box, twinkling like a tiara, lay a long, sleek locomotive, silver, orange, black, and chromium.

"The Westinghouse gas-turbine job," said Earl huskily, awed.

"And only sixty-eight forty-nine," said Harry. "That's practically cost for me, and I got it at a steal. It's got a whine and a roar built in."

Reverently, Earl set it on the tracks, and gently fed power to it. Without a word, Harry took over the controls, and Earl stalked about the layout, spellbound, watching the dream locomotive from all angles, calling out to Harry whenever the illusion of reality was particularly striking.

"Earl—" called Ella.

He didn't answer.

"Hotbox!"

"Hmm?" he said dreamily.

"Come on, if we're going to get any supper."

"Listen," called Earl, "put on another plate, will you? Harry's going to stay for supper." He turned to Harry. "You will, won't you? You'll want to be here when we find out just what this baby can do."

"Pleasure, Hotbox."

"We're going out for supper," said Ella.

Earl straightened up. "Oh—for gosh sakes. That's right, we were."

"Listen to this," said Harry, and the locomotive blew its horn, loud and dissonant.

Earl shook his head in admiration. "Monday," he called to Ella. "We'll go out Monday. Something big has just come up, Sweetheart. Wait'll you see."

"Earl, we haven't got anything much in the house for supper," said Ella desolately.

"Sandwiches, soup, cheese—anything at all," said Earl. "Don't knock yourself out on our account."

"Now, get a load of the reserve power, Hotbox," said Harry. "She's taking that grade without any trouble at half-throttle. Now watch what happens."

"Whooooooooey!" said Earl. He felt a hand on his shoulder. "Oh—hi Mom." He pointed at the new locomotive. "What do you think of that, eh? That's the new era in railroading you see there, Mom. Turbine job."

"Earl, you can't do that to Ella," she said. "She was all dressed up and excited, and then you let her down like this."

"Didn't you hear me give her a rain check?" said Earl. "We're going out on Monday instead. Anyway, she's nuts about the pike now. She understands. We had a whale of a time down here, this afternoon."

"I've never been so disappointed in anyone in all my life," said his mother evenly.

"It's just something you aren't in a position to understand."

She turned her back without another word, and left.

Ella brought Earl and Harry sandwiches, soup, and beer, for which they thanked her gallantly.

"You wait until Monday," said Earl, "and we're going out and have us a time, Sweetheart."

"Fine," said Ella spiritlessly. "Good. Glad."

"You and Mom going to eat upstairs?"

"Mom's gone."

"Gone? Where?"

"I don't know. She called a cab and went."

"She's always been like that," said Earl. "Gets something in her head, and the next thing you know, *bing*, she's gone ahead and done it. Any crazy darn thing. No holding her. Independent as hell."

The telephone rang, and Ella excused herself to answer it.

"For you, Harry," she called down. "It's your wife."

When Harry Zellerbach returned, he was smiling broadly. He put his arm around Earl's shoulder, and, to Earl's surprise, he sang "Happy Birthday" to him.

"Happy birthday, dear Hotbox," he concluded, "happy birthday ta-hoo yooooooooou."

"That's sweet," said Earl, "but it's nine months off."

"Oh? Huh. That's funny."

"What's going on?"

"Well—your mother was just over at the hobby shop, and bought you a present. Told my old lady it was for your birthday. Maude called me so I could be the first to congratulate you."

"What'd she buy?" said Earl.

"Guess I better not tell you, Hotbox. Supposed to be a surprise. I've said too much already."

"Scaled to HO?" wheedled Earl.

"Yeah—she made sure about that. But that's all I'm going to tell you."

"Here she comes now," said Earl. He could hear the swish of wheels through the gravel of the driveway. "She's a sweet old lady, you know, Harry?"

"She's your mother, Hotbox," said Harry soberly.

"She used to have a heck of a temper, and she could run like the wind, and every so often she used to catch me and wallop me a good one. But, you know, I had it coming to me every time—in spades."

"Mum knows best, Hotbox."

"Mother," said Ella at the top of the stairs, "what on earth have you got? For heaven's sakes, what are you going to do? Mother—"

"Quick," Earl whispered to Harry, "let's be fooling around with the pike, so she won't know we know something special is going on. Let her surprise us."

The two busied themselves with the trains, as though they didn't hear the footsteps coming down the stairs. "OK," said Earl, "let's try this for a situation, Harry. There's a big Shriners' convention in Harrisonburg, see, and we've got to put on a couple of specials to—" He let the sentence die. Harry was looking in consternation at the foot of the basement steps.

The air was rent with a bloodcurdling cry.

Earl, the hair on the back of his neck standing on end, faced his mother.

She loosed the cry again. *"Eeeeeeeeeeeeeooooowwwwrrrr!"*

Earl gasped and recoiled. His mother was glaring at him through the goggles of an aviator's helmet. She held a model H-36 at arm's length, and, with terrifying sound effects, was making it dive and climb.

"Mother! What are you doing?"

"Hobby? *Hrrrrrrrowowowow.* Pilot to bombardier. Bombardier to pilot. Roger. Wilco. *Rumrumrumrum.*"

"Have you lost your mind?"

She circled the oil burner noisily, putting the ship through loops and barrel rolls. "Roger. Wilco. *Owrrrr. Rattattattatt!* Got 'em!"

Earl switched off the power to the layout, and waited limply for his mother to emerge from behind the furnace.

She appeared with a roar, and, before Earl could stop her, she climbed onto the layout with amazing agility, and put one foot on a mirror lake, the other in a canyon. The plywood quaked under her.

"Mother! Get off!"

"Bombs away!" she cried. She whistled piercingly, and kicked a trestle to splinters. *"Kaboom!"*

The plane was in a climb again. *"Yourrrowrrrourrrrrr.* Pilot to bombardier. Got the A-bomb ready?"

"No, no, no!" begged Earl. "Mother, please—I surrender, I give up!"

"Not the A-bomb," said Harry, aghast.

"A-bomb ready," she said grimly. The bomber's nose

dropped until it pointed at the roundhouse. "*Mmmmm-meeeeeeeeeewwwwtttrr!* There she goes!"

Earl's mother sat with all her might on the roundhouse. "*Blamme!*"

She stepped down from the table, and before Earl could order his senses, his mother was upstairs again.

When Earl finally came upstairs, shocked and weary, he found only his wife, Ella, who sat on the couch, her feet thrust straight out. She looked dazed.

"Where's Mom?" said Earl. There was no anger in his voice—only awe.

"On her way to a movie," said Ella, not looking at Earl but at a blank place on the wall.

"She had the cab waiting outside."

"Blitzkrieg," said Earl, shaking his head. "When she gets sore, she gets sore."

"She isn't sore anymore," said Ella. "She was singing like a lark when she came upstairs."

Earl mumbled something and shuffled his feet.

"Hmm?" said Ella.

He reddened, and squared his shoulders. "I said, I guess I had it coming to me." He mumbled again.

"Hmm?"

He cleared his throat. "I said, I'm sorry about the way I double-crossed you tonight. Sometimes my mind doesn't work too hot, I guess. We've still got time for a show. Would you go out with me?"

"Hey, Hotbox!" cried Harry Zellerbach, hurrying into the room. "It's the nuts. It's terrific!"

"What is?"

"It really looks like it's been bombed. No kidding. You photograph it the way it is, and show people the picture, and they'd say, "Now *there's* a battlefield." I'll go down to the shop and get some gun turrets from model airplane kits, and tonight we can convert a couple of your trains into armored trains, and camouflage 'em. And I've got a half-dozen HO Pershing tanks I could let you have."

Earl's eyes grew bright with excitement, like incandescent lamps burning out, and then dimmed again. "Let's run up white flags, Harry, and call it a night. You know what Sherman said about war. I'd better see what I can do about making an honorable peace."

GIRL POOL

My good, beloved wife, née Amy Lou Little, came to me from the girl pool. And there's an enchanting thought for lonely men—a pool of girls, teeming, warm, and deep.

Amy Lou Little was a pretty, confident, twenty-year-old girl from Birmingham, Alabama. When my wife-to-be graduated from secretarial school in Birmingham, the school said she was fast and accurate, and a recruiter from the Montezuma Forge and Foundry Company, way up north, offered her a very good salary if she would come to Pittsburgh.

When my wife-to-be got to Pittsburgh, they put her in the Montezuma Forge and Foundry Company's girl pool, with earphones and a Dictaphone and an electric typewriter. They put her at a desk next to Miss Nancy Hostetter, leader of section C of the girl pool, who had been in the girl pool for twenty-two years. Miss Hostetter was a great elk of a woman, righteous, healthy and strong, and inconceivably fast and accurate. She said Amy was to look upon her as a big sister.

I was in the Montezuma Forge and Foundry Company, too, a rootless pleaser of unseen customers. The customers wrote to the company, and twenty-five of us replied, genially, competently. I never saw the customers, and the customers never saw me, and no one suggested that we exchange snapshots.

All day long, I talked into a Dictaphone, and messengers carried off the records to the girl pool, which I'd never seen.

There were sixty girls in the girl pool, ten to a section. Bulletin boards in every office said the girls belonged to anyone with access to a Dictaphone, and almost any man would have found a girl to his taste among the sixty. There were maidens like my wife-to-be, worldly women made up like showgirls, moon-faced matrons, and erect and self-sufficient spinsters, like Miss Hostetter.

The walls of the girl pool were eye-rest green, and had paintings of restful farm scenes on them, and the air was a rhapsody of girls' perfumes and the recorded music of André Kostelanetz and Mantovani. From morning until night, the voices of Montezuma's men, transcribed on Dictaphone records, filled the girls' ears.

But the men sent only their voices, never their faces, and they talked only of business. And all they ever called a girl was "operator."

"Molybdenum, operator," said a voice in Amy's ear, "spelled m-o-l-y-b-d-e-n-u-m."

The nasal Yankee voice hurt Amy's ears—sounded, she said, like somebody beating a cracked bell with a chain. It was my voice.

"Clangbang," said Amy to my voice.

"The unit comes with silicone gaskets throughout," said my voice. "That's s-i-l-i-c-o-n-e, operator."

"Oh, you don't have to spell silicone for me," said Amy. "Isn't anything I don't know about silicones after six months in this bughouse."

"Yours truly," said my voice, "Arthur C. Whitney, Jr., Customer Relations Section, Boiler Sales Department, Heavy

Apparatus Division, Room 412, Building 77, Pittsburgh Works."

"ACW:all," Amy typed at the bottom of the letter. She separated the letter and copies from the carbon paper, dropped them into her out-basket, and slipped my record from the spindle of her Dictaphone.

"Why don't you bring your face around to the girl pool sometime, Arthur?" said my wife-to-be to my record. "We'd treat you like Clark Gable, just any man at all." She put another record from her in-basket onto her spindle. "Come on, you old devil, you," she said to the new record, "thaw out this half-frozen Alabama girl. Make me swoon."

"Five carbons, operator," said a new, harsh voice in Amy's ear. "To Mr. Harold N. Brewster, Thrust-Bearing Division, Jorgenson Precision Engineering Products Corporation, Lansing 5, Michigan."

"You *are* a hot-blooded old thing, aren't you?" said Amy. "What makes you men up here so passionate—the steam heat?"

"Did you say something to me, Amy?" said Miss Hostetter, removing her earphones. She was a tall woman, without ornaments, save for her gold twenty-year-service pin. She looked at Amy with bleak reproach. "What's the trouble now?"

Amy stopped her Dictaphone. "I was talking to the gentleman on the record," she said. "Got to talk to somebody around here, or go crazy."

"There are lots of nice people to talk to," said Miss Hostetter. "You're so critical of everything, when you haven't really had time to find out what everything's about."

"You tell me what this is about," said my wife-to-be, including the girl pool in a sweep of her hand.

"There was a very good cartoon about that in the *Montezuma Minutes,*" said Miss Hostetter. The *Montezuma Minutes* was the company's weekly newspaper for employees.

"The one with the ghost of Florence Nightingale hovering over a stenographer?" said Amy.

"That was a good one," said Miss Hostetter. "But the one I had in mind showed a man with his new Thermolux furnace, and there were thousands of women all around him and the furnace, kind of ghostly. 'He doesn't send orchids, but he should,' the caption said, 'to the ten thousand women behind every dependable Montezuma product.'"

"Ghosts, ghosts, ghosts," said my wife-to-be. "Everybody's ghosts up here. They come out of the smoke and the cold in the morning, and they rush around and worry about boilers and silicone gaskets and molybdenum all day, then they disappear at five, plain fade away without a word. I don't know how anybody up here ever gets married or falls in love or finds anything nice to laugh about, or anything. Back home in high school—"

"High school isn't life," said Miss Hostetter.

"God help women, if this is life—cooped up all together, with a floor all to themselves," said my wife-to-be.

The two women faced each other with antipathies they'd been honing to razor sharpness for six months. The little blades glinted in their eyes, while they smiled politely.

"Life is what you make it," said Miss Hostetter, "and ingratitude is one of the worst sins. Look around you! Pictures on the walls, carpets on the floor, beautiful music, hospitalization and retirement, the Christmas party, fresh flowers on our desks, coffee hours, our own cafeteria, our own recreation room with television and ping-pong."

"Everything but life," said my wife-to-be. "The only sign of life I've heard of up here is that poor Larry Barrow."

"Poor Larry Barrow!" said Miss Hostetter, shocked. "Amy—he killed a policeman!"

Amy opened her top desk drawer, and looked down at the picture of Larry Barrow on the front page of the *Montezuma Minutes*. Barrow, a handsome young criminal, had shot a policeman in a Pittsburgh bank holdup two days before. He had last been seen climbing over a fence to hide somewhere in the vast Montezuma works. There were plenty of places where he could hide.

"He could be in the movies," said Amy.

"As a killer," said Miss Hostetter.

"Not necessarily," said Amy. "He looks like a lot of nice boys I knew in high school."

"Don't be childish," said Miss Hostetter. She dusted her big hands briskly. "Well, we aren't getting any work done, are we? Ten minutes to go until morning coffee break. Let's make the most of them."

Amy turned on her Dictaphone. "Dear Mr. Brewster," said the voice, "your request for estimates on modernization of your present heating plant with DM-114 Thermolux conversion condensers has been forwarded by company teletype to our Thermolux specialist in your district, and..."

Amy, as her fingers danced expertly over the keys, was free to think about whatever she pleased, and, with her top drawer still open, with Larry Barrow's picture still in view, she thought about a man, wounded, freezing, starving, hated, hunted, and alone, somewhere out in the works.

"Considering the thermal conductivity of the brick walls of the buildings to be heated," said the voice in Amy's ear, "as

five Btu—that's abbreviation for British thermal unit, operator, with a capital *B*—per square foot per hour per degree
Fahrenheit—capitalize Fahrenheit, operator—per inch..."

And my wife-to-be saw herself in the clouds of pink tulle
she'd worn on the June night of the high school graduation
dance, and, on her arm, limping, healing, free, was Larry
Barrow. The scene was in the South.

"And, taking the thermal diffusivity—d-i-f-f-u-s-i-v-i-t-y,
operator—as, k over w," said the voice in Amy's ear, "it seems
safe to say that..."

And my wife-to-be was helplessly in love with Larry Barrow. The love filled her life, thrilled her, and nothing else
mattered.

"Ting-a-ling," said Miss Hostetter, looking at the wall
clock and removing her earphones. There was a coffee break
in the morning, and another in the afternoon, and Miss
Hostetter greeted each as though she were a cheery little bell
connected to the clock. "Ting-a-ling, everybody."

Amy looked at Miss Hostetter's craggy, loveless, humorless
face, and her dream fell to pieces.

"A penny for your thoughts, Amy," said Miss Hostetter.

"I was thinking about Larry Barrow," said Amy. "What
would you do if you saw him?"

"I'd keep right on walking," said Miss Hostetter primly.
"I'd pretend I hadn't recognized him, and I'd keep right on
walking until I could get help."

"What if he suddenly grabbed you, and made you a prisoner?" said Amy.

Miss Hostetter reddened over her high cheekbones.
"That's quite enough of *that* kind of talk," she said. "That's
how panic gets started. I understand that some of the girls in

the Wire and Cable Department got each other so upset about this man they had to be sent home. That isn't going to happen here. The girls in the girl pool are a cut above that."

"Even so—" said Amy.

"He isn't anywhere near this part of the works," said Miss Hostetter. "He's probably dead by now, anyway. They said there was blood in that office he broke into last night, so he isn't in any condition to go around grabbing people."

"Nobody really knows," said Amy.

"What you need," said Miss Hostetter, "is a cup of hot coffee, and a fast game of ping-pong. Come on. I'm going to beat you."

"Dear Sir:" said a voice in the pretty ear of my wife-to-be that afternoon, "We would very much like to have you as our guest at a demonstration of the entire line of Thermolux heating equipment in the Bronze Room of the Hotel Gresham at four-thirty, Wednesday . . ." The letter was not to one man, but to thirty. Each of the thirty was to get an individually typed invitation.

By the tenth time Amy had typed the same letter, she felt as though she were drowning. She put the project aside, temporarily, and, for the sake of variety, slipped another record from her in-box onto her Dictaphone spindle.

She rested her fingers on the keyboard, on *a, s, d,* and *f,* on *j, k, l,* and *;,* awaiting orders from the record. But the only sound from the record was a shushing sound, like the sound of the sea in a seashell.

After many seconds, a soft, deep, sweetly wheedling voice spoke in Amy's ear, spoke from the record.

"I read about you girls on the bulletin board," said the

voice. "Says you girls belong to anybody with access to a Dictaphone." The voice laughed quietly. "*I* got access to a Dictaphone."

The record scratched on in another long silence.

"I'm cold and sick and lonely and hungry, Miss," said the voice at last. There was a cough. "I'm feverish, and I'm dying, Miss. Guess everybody will be real glad when I'm dead."

Another silence, another cough.

"All I ever did wrong was not let anybody push me around, Miss," said the voice. "Somewhere, somewhere, maybe there's a girl who thinks a boy shouldn't be shot or starved or locked up like an animal. Somewhere, maybe there's a girl who's got a heart left inside her.

"Somewhere," said the voice, "maybe there's a girl with a heart, who'd bring this boy something to eat, and some bandages, and give him a chance to live a little while longer.

"Maybe," said the voice, "she's got a heart of ice, and she'll go tell the police, so they can shoot this boy, and she can be real proud and happy.

"Miss," said the voice to my wife-to-be, "I'm going to tell you where I've been and where I'll be when you hear this. You can do anything you want with me—save me or get me killed, or plain let me die. I'll be in building 227." The voice laughed quietly again. "I'll be back of a barrel. Isn't much of a building, Miss. You won't have any trouble finding me in it."

The record ended.

Amy imagined herself cradling Larry Barrow's curly head in her round, soft arms.

"There, there," she murmured. "There, there." Tears filled her eyes.

A hand dropped on Amy's shoulder. It was Miss Hostetter's hand. "Didn't you hear me say ting-a-ling for the coffee break?" she said.

"No," said Amy.

"I've been watching you, Amy," said Miss Hostetter. "You've just been listening. You haven't been typing. Is there something strange about that record?"

"Perfectly ordinary record," said Amy.

"You looked so upset."

"I'm all right. I'm fine," said Amy tensely.

"I'm your big sister," said Miss Hostetter. "If there's anything—"

"I don't *want* a big sister!" said Amy passionately.

Miss Hostetter bit her lip, turned white, and stalked into the recreation room.

Furtively, Amy wrapped Larry Barrow's record in face tissues, and hid it in the bottom drawer of her desk, with her hand cream, face cream, lipstick, powder, rouge, perfume, nail polish, manicure scissors, nail file, nail buffer, eyebrow pencil, tweezers, bobby pins, vitamin tablets, needle and thread, eyedrops, brush, and comb.

She closed the drawer, and looked up to see the baleful eyes of Miss Hostetter, who watched her through a screen of milling girls in the doorway of the recreation room, watched her over a cup of steaming coffee and a saucer with two little cookies on it.

Amy smiled at her glassily, and went into the recreation room. "Ping-pong, anybody?" said Amy, fighting to keep her voice even.

She received a dozen merry challenges, and, during the recreation period, she daydreamed to the took-took of the ping-pong ball instead of the tack-tack of her typewriter.

★ ★ ★

At five, whistles blew triumphantly in the works and all over Pittsburgh.

My wife-to-be had spent the afternoon in a suppressed frenzy of fear, excitement, and love. Her wastebasket was stuffed with mistakes. She hadn't dared to play Barrow's record again, or even to exchange a glance with Miss Hostetter, for fear of giving away her terrible secret.

Now, at five, André Kostelanetz and Mantovani and the blowers of the heating system were turned off. The mail girls came into the girl pool with trays of cylinders to be transcribed first thing in the morning. They emptied withered flowers from the vases on the desks. They would bring fresh flowers from the company hothouse in the morning. The girl pool became whirlpools around a dozen coatracks. In separate whirlpools, Amy and Miss Hostetter pulled on their cloth coats.

The girl pool became a river, flowing down the fireproof iron stairway into the company street. At the very end of the river was my wife-to-be.

Amy stopped, and the river left her behind, in the little cyclones of fly ash, in the canyon walled by numbered building façades.

Amy returned to the girl pool. The only light now came from the orange fires of furnaces in the distance.

Trembling, she opened the bottom drawer of her desk, and found the record gone.

Stunned and angry, she opened Miss Hostetter's bottom drawer. The record was there. The only other objects in the green steel bin were a bottle of Mercurochrome and a clipping from the *Montezuma Minutes,* entitled, "Creed of a Woman of Montezuma." "I am a Woman of Montezuma," the creed began, "hand in hand with Men, marching to a Better Tomorrow under the three banners of God, Country, and Company, bearing the proud shield of Service."

Amy wailed in anguish. She ran out of the girl pool, down the iron stairway, and down the company street to the main gate, to the headquarters of the company police. She was sure Miss Hostetter was there, proudly telling the police what she'd learned from the record.

The headquarters of the company police were in one corner of a great reception room by the main gate. Around the walls of the room were exhibits of the company's products and methods. In its center was a stand, where a fat concessionaire sold candy, tobacco, and magazines.

A tall woman in a cloth coat was talking animatedly to the policeman on duty.

"Miss Hostetter!" said Amy breathlessly, coming up behind her.

The woman turned to look curiously at my wife-to-be, and then returned her attention to the policeman. She was not Miss Hostetter. She was a visitor, who had taken a tour of the works and lost her purse inside.

"It could have been lost or stolen just anywhere," said the woman, "where all that terrible noise was, with all the hot steel and sparks; where that big hammer came crashing down; where that scientist showed us his whatchamacallit in his laboratory—anywhere! Maybe that killer who's running around wild in there snatched it while I wasn't looking."

"Lady," said the policeman patiently, "it's almost sure he's dead. And he isn't after purses, if he is alive. He's after something to eat. He's after life." He smiled grimly. "But he isn't going to get it—not for long."

The corners of my wife-to-be's sweet red mouth pulled down involuntarily.

Somewhere out in the works, dogs bayed.

"Hear that?" said the policeman with satisfaction. "They got dogs looking for him now. If he's got your purse, lady, which he doesn't, we'll have it back in jig time."

Amy looked around the big room for Miss Hostetter. Miss Hostetter wasn't there. Helplessness weakened Amy, and she sat down on a hard bench before a display entitled, "Can Silicones Solve Your Problems?"

Depression settled over Amy. She recognized it for what it was—the depression she always felt when a good movie ended. The theater lights were coming on, taking from her elation and importance and love she really had no claim to. She was only a spectator—one of many.

"Hear them dogs?" said the concessionaire to a customer behind Amy. "Special kind, I heard. Bloodhounds are the gentlest dogs alive, but the ones they've got after Barrow are half coonhound. They can teach that kind to be tough—to take care of the tough customers."

Amy stood suddenly, and went to the candy counter. "I want a chocolate bar," she said, "the big kind, the twenty-five-cent kind. And a Butterfinger and a Coconut Mounds bar, and one of those caramel things—and some peanuts."

"Yes, ma'am!" said the concessionaire. "Going to have yourself a real banquet, aren't you? Just watch out you don't hurt that complexion with too much sweets—that's all."

★ ★ ★

Amy hurried back into the works, and squeezed into a crowded company bus. She was the only girl on the bus. The rest were men on the evening shift. When they saw my wife-to-be, they grew heavily polite and attentive.

"Could you please let me out at building 227?" said Amy to the driver. "I don't know where it is."

"Don't know as I know where it is, either," said the driver. "Don't get much call for that one." He took a dog-eared map of the works down from the sun visor.

"You don't get *any* call for that one," said a passenger. "Nothing in 227 but a bunch of lanterns, some barrels of sand, and maybe a potbellied stove. You don't want 227, Miss."

"A man called the girl pool for a stenographer to work late," said Amy. "I thought he said 227." She looked at the driver's map, and saw the driver's finger pointing to a tiny square all by itself in the middle of the railroad yard, building 227. There was a big building fairly near to it, on the edge of the yard, building 224. "He might have said building 224," said Amy.

"Oh sure!" said the driver happily. "Shipping Department. That's the one you want."

All on board sighed with relief, and looked with affectionate pride at the pretty little Southern girl they were taking such good care of.

Amy was now the last passenger on the bus. The bus was crossing the wasteland between the heart of the works and the railroad yard, a tundra of slag heaps and rusting scrap. Out in the wasteland, away from the street, was a constellation of dancing flashlight beams.

"The cops and the dogs," said the driver to Amy.

"Oh?" said Amy absently.

"Started from the office where he broke in last night," said the driver. "The way the dogs are talking it up, they must be pretty close to him."

Amy nodded. My wife-to-be was talking to Miss Hostetter in her imagination. "If you've told the police," she was saying, "you've killed him, just as sure as if you'd aimed a gun at him and pulled the trigger. Don't you understand? Don't you care? Haven't you got an ounce of womanhood in you?"

Two minutes later, the driver let Amy off at the Shipping Department.

When the bus was gone, Amy walked out into the night, and stood on the edge of the railroad yard, a sea of cinders sprinkled with twinkling red, green, and yellow signal lights, and streaked with glinting rails.

As Amy's eyes grew used to the night, her heart beat harder, and from the many hulking forms she chose one, a small, squat building that was almost certainly building 227—where a dying man had said he'd be waiting for a girl with a heart.

The world dropped away, and the night seemed to snatch Amy up and spin her like a top, and she was running across the cinders to the building. The building loomed, and my wife-to-be stopped against its weathered clapboards, panting, and trying to listen above the roaring of blood at her temples.

Someone moved inside, and sighed.

Amy worked her way along the outside wall to the door. The padlock and hasp had been pried from the old wood.

Amy knocked on the door. "Hello," she whispered, "I brought you something to eat."

Amy heard an intake of breath, nothing more.

She pushed open the door.

In the wedge of frail gray light let in by the door stood Miss Hostetter.

Each woman seemed to look through the other, to wish her out of existence. Their expressions were blank.

"Where is he?" said Amy at last.

"Dead," said Miss Hostetter, "dead—behind the barrels."

Amy began an aimless, shuffling walk about the room, and stopped when she was as far from Miss Hostetter as she could get, her back to the older woman. "Dead?" she murmured.

"As a mackerel," said Miss Hostetter.

"Don't talk about him that way!" said my wife-to-be.

"That's how dead he is," said Miss Hostetter.

Amy turned to face Miss Hostetter angrily. "You had no business taking my record."

"It was anybody's record," said Miss Hostetter. "Besides, I didn't think you had the nerve to do anything about it."

"Well, I *did*," said Amy, "and I thought the least I could expect was to be alone. I thought you'd gone to the police."

"Well, I *didn't*," said Miss Hostetter. "You should have expected me to be here—you of all people."

"Nothing ever surprised me more," said Amy.

"You sent me here, dear," said Miss Hostetter. Her face looked for a moment as though it would soften. But her muscles tightened, and the austere lines of her face held firm. "You've said a lot of things about my life, Amy, and I heard them all. They all hurt, and here I am." She looked down at her hands, and worked her fast and accurate fingers slowly. "Am I still a ghost? Does this crazy trip out here to see a dead man make me not a ghost anymore?"

Tears filled the eyes of my wife-to-be. "Oh, Miss Hostetter," she said, "I'm so sorry if I hurt you. You're not a ghost, really you're not. You never were." She was overwhelmed with pity for the stark, lonesome woman. "You're full of love and mercy, Miss Hostetter, or you wouldn't be here."

Miss Hostetter gave no sign that the words moved her. "And what brought *you* here, Amy?"

"I loved him," said Amy. The pride of a woman in love straightened her back and colored her cheeks and made her feel beautiful and important again. "I loved him."

Miss Hostetter shook her homely head sadly. "If you loved him," she said, "take a look at him. He has a lovable knife in his lovable lap, and a lovable grin that will turn your hair white."

Amy's hand went up to her throat. "Oh."

"At least we're friends now, aren't we, Amy?" said Miss Hostetter. "That's something, isn't it?"

"Oh, yes, yes," said Amy limply. She managed a wan smile. "That's a great deal."

"We'd better leave," said Miss Hostetter. "Here come the men and the dogs."

The two left building 227 as the men and the dogs zigzagged across the wasteland a quarter of a mile away.

The two caught a company bus in front of the Shipping Department, and said nothing to each other during the long, dead trip back to the main gate.

At the main gate, it was time for them to part, each to her own bus stop. With effort, they managed to speak.

"Goodbye," said Amy.

"See you in the morning," said Miss Hostetter.

"It's so hard for a girl to know what to do," said my wife-to-be, swept by longing and a feeling of weakness.

"I don't think it's supposed to be easy," said Miss Hostetter. "I don't think it ever was easy."

Amy nodded soberly.

"And Amy," said Miss Hostetter, laying her hand on Amy's arm, "don't be mad at the company. They can't help it if they want their letters nicely typed."

"I'll try not," said Amy.

"Somewhere," said Miss Hostetter, "a nice young man is looking for a nice young woman like you, and tomorrow's another day.

"What we both need now," said Miss Hostetter, fading, ghost-like, into the smoke and cold of Pittsburgh, "is a good, hot bath."

When Amy scuffed through the fog to her bus stop, ghost-like, she found me standing there, ghost-like.

With dignity, we each pretended that the other was not there.

When suddenly, my wife-to-be was overwhelmed with the terror that she'd held off so long, she burst into tears and leaned against me, and I patted her back.

"My gosh," I said, "another human being."

"You'll never know how human," she said.

"Maybe I will," I said. "I could try."

I did try, and I do try, and I give you the toast of a happy man: May the warm springs of the girl pool never run dry.

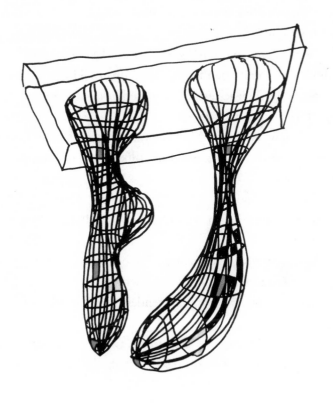

RUTH

The two women nodded formally across the apartment's threshold. They were lonely women, widows; one middle-aged and the other young. Their meeting now—ostensibly to defeat their loneliness—only emphasized how solitary each was.

Ruth, the young woman, had travelled a thousand miles for this meeting with a stranger; had endured the clatter and soot and itch of a railroad coach from springtime in an Army town in Georgia to a factory town in a still-frozen New York valley. Now she wondered why it had seemed so right, so imperative that she come. This heavy, elderly woman, who blocked the door and smiled only with difficulty, had seemed in her letters to want this, too.

"So you're the woman who married my Ted," said the older woman coolly.

Ruth tried to imagine herself with a married son, and supposed she might have phrased the question in the same way. She set her bags down in the hall. She had expected to sweep into the apartment amid affectionate greetings, warm herself by a radiator, freshen up, and then begin to talk of Ted. Instead, her husband's mother seemed intent on examining her before letting her in. "Yes, Mrs. Faulkner," said Ruth, "we had five months together before he went overseas." Under the woman's critical stare, she found herself adding, almost defensively, "A happy five months."

"Ted was all I had," said Mrs. Faulkner. She said it as though it were a reproach.

"He was a fine man," said Ruth uneasily.

"My little boy," said Mrs. Faulkner. It was an aside to an unseen, sympathetic audience. She shrugged. "You must be cold. Do come in, Miss Hurley." Hurley was Ruth's maiden name.

"I could just as easily stay at a hotel," said Ruth. The woman's gaze made her feel foreign, self-conscious about her drawling speech, about her clothes, which were insubstantial, better suited to a warmer climate.

"I wouldn't hear of your staying anywhere but here. We have so much to talk about. When is Ted's child to be born?"

"In four months." Ruth slid her suitcase just inside the door, and sat, with an air of temporariness, on the edge of a sofa covered with slippery chintz. The only illumination in the overheated room came from a lamp on the mantel, its frail light muddled by a tortoiseshell shade. "Ted told me so much about you, I've been dying to meet you," said Ruth.

On the long train ride, Ruth had pretended for hours at a time that she was talking to Mrs. Faulkner, winning her affection from the first. She had rehearsed and polished her biography a dozen times in anticipation of Mrs. Faulkner's saying, "Now tell me something about yourself." She was ready with her opening line: "Well, I have no relatives, I'm afraid—no close ones, anyway. My father was a colonel in the cavalry, and..." But Ted's mother didn't put the opening question.

Silent and thoughtful, Mrs. Faulkner poured two tiny glasses of sherry from an expensive-looking decanter. "The personal effects—" she said at last, "they told me they were sent to you."

Ruth was puzzled for a moment. "Oh, the things he had with him overseas? Yes, I have them. It's customary, I think—I mean, it's a matter of routine to send them to the wife."

"I suppose it's all done automatically by machines in Washington," said Mrs. Faulkner ironically. "A general just pushes a button, and—" She left the sentence unfinished. "Could I have the things, please?"

"They're mine," said Ruth, and thought how childish that must sound. "I think he wanted me to have them." She looked down at the absurdly small glass of sherry, and wished for twenty more to take the edge off the ordeal.

"If it comforts you to think so, go right on thinking of them as yours," said Mrs. Faulkner patiently. "I simply want to have everything in one place—what little is left."

"I'm afraid I don't understand."

Mrs. Faulkner turned her back, and spoke softly, piously. "Having it all together makes him just a little nearer." She turned a switch on a floor lamp, suddenly filling the room with white brilliance. "These things will mean nothing to you," she said. "If you were a mother, you might understand how utterly priceless they are to me." She dabbed at a speck of dust on the ornate, glass-faced cabinet that squatted on lions' paws against the wall. "You see? I've left room in the cabinet for the things I knew you had."

"It's very sweet," said Ruth. She wondered what Ted might have thought of the cabinet—with its baby shoes, the book of nursery rhymes, the penknife, the Boy Scout badge . . . Apart from its cheap sentimentality, Ted, too, would have sensed something unwholesome, sick about it. Mrs. Faulkner stared at the trinkets wide-eyed, unblinking, bewitched.

Ruth spoke to break the spell. "Ted told me you were doing awfully well at your shop. Is business as good as ever?"

"I've given it up," said Mrs. Faulkner absently.

"Oh? Then you're giving all your time to your club activities?"

"I've resigned."

"I see." Ruth fidgeted, taking off her gloves and putting them on again. "Ted said you were an awfully clever decorator, and I see he was right. He said you liked to do this place over every year or two. What sort of changes do you plan for next time?"

Mrs. Faulkner turned away from the shelf reluctantly. "Nothing will ever be changed again." She held out her hand. "Are the things in your suitcase?"

"There isn't much," said Ruth. "His billfold—"

"Cordovan, isn't it? I gave it to him in his junior year in high school."

Ruth nodded. She opened a suitcase, and dug into its bottom. "A letter to me, two medals, and a watch."

"The watch, please. The engraving on the back, I believe, says that it was a gift from me on his twenty-first birthday. I have a place ready for it."

Resignedly, Ruth held out the objects to her, cupped in her hands. "The letter I'd like to keep."

"You can certainly keep the letter and the medals. They have nothing to do with the boy I want to remember."

"He was a man, not a boy," said Ruth mildly. "He'd want to be remembered that way."

"That's your way of remembering him," said Mrs. Faulkner. "Respect mine."

"I'm sorry," said Ruth, "I do respect it. But you should be proud of him for being brave and—"

"He was gentle and sensitive and intelligent," interrupted Mrs. Faulkner passionately. "They should never have sent him overseas. They may have tried to make him hard and cheap, but at heart he was still my boy."

Ruth stood, and leaned against the cabinet, the shrine. Now she understood what was going on, what was behind Mrs. Faulkner's hostility. To the older woman, Ruth was one of the shadowy, faraway conspirators who had taken Ted.

"For heaven's sake, dear, look out!"

Startled, Ruth jerked her shoulder away from the cabinet. A small object tottered from an open shelf and smashed into white chips on the floor. "Oh!—I'm *so* sorry."

Mrs. Faulkner was on her knees, brushing the fragments together with her fingers. "How could you? How *could* you?"

"I'm awfully sorry. Can I buy you another one?"

"She wants to know if she can buy me another one," quavered Mrs. Faulkner, again to an unseen audience. "Where is it you can buy a candy dish made by Ted's little hands when he was seven?"

"It can be mended," said Ruth helplessly.

"Can it?" said Mrs. Faulkner tragically. She held the fragments before Ruth's face. "Not all the king's horses and all the king's men—"

"Thank heaven there were two of them," said Ruth, pointing to a second clay dish on the shelf.

"Don't touch it!" cried Mrs. Faulkner. "Don't touch anything!"

Trembling, Ruth backed away from the cabinet. "I'd better be going." She turned up the collar of her thin cloth coat. "May I use your phone to call a cab—please?"

Mrs. Faulkner's aggressiveness dissolved instantly into an expression of pitiability. "No. You can't take my boy's child away from me. Please, dear, try to understand and forgive me. That little dish was sacred. Everything that's left of my little boy is sacred, and that's why I behaved the way I did." She gathered a bit of Ruth's sleeve in her hand and held it tightly. "You understand, don't you? If there's an ounce of mercy in you, you'll forgive me and stay."

Ruth drove the air from her lungs with pent-up exasperation. "I'd like to go right to bed, if you don't mind." She wasn't tired, was so keyed up, in fact, that she expected to spend the night staring at the ceiling. But she didn't want to exchange another word with this woman, wanted to hide her humiliation and disappointment in the white oblivion of bed.

Mrs. Faulkner became the perfect hostess, respectful and solicitous. The small guest room, tasteful, crisp, barren, like all guest rooms implied an invitation to make oneself at home, and at the same time admitted that it was an impossibility. The room was cool, as though the radiators had only been turned on an hour or so before, and the air was sweet with the smell of furniture polish.

"And this is for the baby and me?" said Ruth. She had no intention of staying beyond the next morning, but felt forced to make conversation as Mrs. Faulkner lingered in the doorway.

"This is for you alone, dear. I thought the baby would be more comfortable in my room. It's larger, you know. I hardly know where you'd put a crib in here." She smiled primly. "Now, you *will* forgive me, won't you, dear?" She turned without waiting for an answer, and went to her room, humming softly.

Ruth lay wide-eyed for an hour between the stiff sheets. Her thoughts came in disconnected pulses of brilliance—glimpses of this moment and that. Ted's long, contemplative face appeared again and again. She saw him as a lonely child—as he had first come to her; then as a lover; then as a man. The shrine—commemorating a child, ignoring a man—made a pathetic kind of sense. For Mrs. Faulkner, Ted had died when he'd loved another woman.

Ruth threw back the covers, and walked to the window, needing the refreshment of a look at the outdoors. There was only a brick wall a few feet away, chinked with snow. She tiptoed down the hall, toward the big living room windows that framed the blue Adirondack foothills. She stopped.

Mrs. Faulkner, her gross figure silhouetted through a thin nightgown, stood before the shelf of souvenirs, talking to it. "Good night, darling, wherever you are. I hope you can hear me and know that your mother loves you." She paused, and appeared to be listening, and looked wise. "And your child will be in good hands, darling—the same hands that cradled you." She held up her hands for the shelf to see. "Good night, Ted. Sleep tight."

Ruth stole back to bed. A few moments later, bare feet padded down the hall, a door closed, and all was still.

★ ★ ★

"Good morning, Miss Hurley." Ruth blinked up at Ted's mother. The brick wall outside the guest room window glared, the snow gone. The sun was high. "Did you sleep well, my child?" The voice was cheerful, intimate. "It's almost noon. I have breakfast for you. Eggs, coffee, bacon, and biscuits. Would you like that?"

Ruth nodded and stretched, and drowsily doubted the nightmare of their meeting the night before. Sunlight was splashed everywhere, dispelling the funereal queasiness of their first encounter.

The table in the kitchen was aromatic with the peace and plenty of a leisurely breakfast.

As Ruth returned Mrs. Faulkner's smile across her third cup of coffee, she was at her ease, content with starting a new life in these warm surroundings. The night before had been no more than a misunderstanding between two tired, nervous women.

Ted wasn't mentioned—not at first. Mrs. Faulkner talked wittily about her early days as a businesswoman in a man's world, made light of what must have been desperate years after her husband's death. And then she encouraged Ruth to talk about herself, and she listened with flattering interest. "And I suppose you'll be wanting to go back to the South to live someday."

Ruth shrugged. "I have no real ties there—or anywhere else, for that matter. Father was an Army regular, and I've lived on practically every post you can name."

"Where would you most like to make your home?" Mrs. Faulkner coaxed.

"Oh—this is a pleasant enough part of the country."

"It's awfully cold," said Mrs. Faulkner with a laugh. "It's the world headquarters for sinus trouble and asthma."

"Well, I suppose Florida would be more easy going. I guess, if I had my choice, I'd like Florida best."

"You have your choice, you know."

Ruth set down her cup. "I plan to make my home here—the way Ted wanted me to."

"I meant after the baby is born," said Mrs. Faulkner. "Then you'd be free to go wherever you liked. You have the insurance money, and with what I could add to that you could get a nice little place in St. Petersburg or somewhere like that."

"What about you? I thought you wanted to have the child near you."

Mrs. Faulkner reached into the refrigerator. "Here, you poor dear, you need cream, don't you." She set the pitcher before Ruth. "Don't you see how nicely it would work out for both of us? You could leave the child with me, and be free to lead the life a young woman should lead." Her voice became confiding. "It's what Ted wants for both of us."

"I'm darned if it is!"

Mrs. Faulkner stood. "I think I'm the better judge of that. He's with me every minute I'm in this house."

"Ted is dead," said Ruth incredulously.

"That's just it," said Mrs. Faulkner impatiently. "To you he *is* dead. You can't feel his presence or know his wishes now, because you hardly knew him. One doesn't get to know a person in five months."

"We were man and wife!" said Ruth.

"Most husbands and wives are strangers till death does them part, dear. I hardly knew my husband, and we had several years together."

"Some mothers try to make their sons strangers to every woman but themselves," said Ruth bitterly. "Praise be to God, you failed by a hair!"

Mrs. Faulkner strode man-like into the living room. Ruth listened to the springs creaking in the chair before the sacred cabinet. Again the whispered dialogue with silence drifted down the hall.

In ten minutes, Ruth was packed and standing in the living room.

"Child, where are you going?" said Mrs. Faulkner, without looking at her.

"Away—South, I guess." Ruth's feet were close together, her high heels burrowing in the carpet as she shifted petulantly from one foot to the other. She had a great deal to say to the older woman, and she waited for her to face her. A hundred vengeful phrases had sprung to mind as she packed—just, unanswerable.

Mrs. Faulkner didn't turn her head, continued to stare at the mementos. Her big shoulders were hunched, her head down—an attitude of stubborn mass and wisdom. "What are you, Miss Hurley, some sort of goddess who can give or take away the most precious thing in a person's life?"

"You asked me to give a great deal more than you have any right to ask." Ruth imagined how a small boy might have felt, standing on this spot while the keen bully of a woman decided what, exactly, he was to do next.

"I ask only what my son asks."

"That isn't so."

"She's wrong, isn't she, dear?" said Mrs. Faulkner to the cabinet. "She doesn't love you enough to hear you, but your mother does."

Ruth slammed the door, ran into the wet street, and flagged a puzzled motorist to a stop.

"I ain't no cab, lady."

"Please, take me to the station."

"Look, lady, I'm going uptown, not downtown." Ruth burst into tears. "All right, lady. For heaven's sakes, all right. Get in."

"Train number 427, the Seneca, arriving on track four," said the voice in the loudspeaker. The voice seemed intent on shattering any illusions passengers might have of their destinations' being better than what they were leaving. San Francisco was droned as cheerlessly as Troy; Miami sounded no more seductive than Knoxville.

Thunder rolled across the ceiling of the waiting room. The pillar by Ruth trembled. She looked up from her magazine to the station clock. Her train would be next, southbound.

When she bought her ticket, checked her baggage through, and settled on a hard bench to read away the dead minutes, her movements had been purposeful, quick, her walk almost a swagger. The motions had been an accompaniment to a savage dialogue buzzing in her head. In her imagination she had lashed out at Mrs. Faulkner with merciless truths, had triumphantly wrung from that rook of a woman apologies and tears.

For the moment, the vengeful fantasy left Ruth satisfied, forgetful of her recent tormentor. She felt only boredom and incipient loneliness. To dispel these two, she looked from group to group in the waiting room, reading in faces and clothes and luggage the commonplace narratives that had brought each person to the station.

A tall, baby-faced private chatted stiffly with his well-dressed mother and father: yanked out of gray flannels and college by the draft... nothing but a marksman's medal... bright, lots of money... father uncomfortable about son's rank and overparking...

A racking cough cut into Ruth's thoughts. An old man, cramped against the armrest at the end of a completely vacant bench, was doubled by a coughing fit. He waited for the coughing to subside, so that he could take another puff on the cigarette butt between his dirty fingers.

A frail, bright-eyed old woman handed a redcap a dollar, and demanded his polite attention as she gave precise instructions as to how her luggage was to be handled: on her annual expedition to criticize her children and spoil her grandchildren...

Again the agonized coughing. Now Ruth caught the stench of the dirty man's breath, brought to her nostrils by a sudden gust from the door. The cough worsened, tearing the breath from him. The cigarette dropped.

Ruth twisted around on the bench so that her gaze wouldn't naturally fall on him. A winded fat man, his red face determinedly cheerful beneath a homburg, begged to be let in at the first of the ticket line: salesman... ball bearings or boilers or something like that...

Again the agonized coughing. Irritated that so disagreeable a sight should make demands on her attention, Ruth glanced once more at the old man. He had slumped over the arm of the bench, twisted, quaking.

The fat salesman looked down at the old man, and then straight ahead again, keeping his place in line.

The old lady, still instructing the redcap, raised her voice to be heard above the interruption.

The young soldier and his correct parents weren't so vulgar as to acknowledge that something unsightly was at hand.

A newsboy burst into the station, started to stride down the aisle between Ruth and the old man, stopped a few feet short, and headed for the other end of the waiting room, shouting news of a tragedy a thousand miles away. "Read all about it!"

Another train rumbled overhead. Everyone was moving toward the ramp now, avoiding the aisle in which the old man lay, giving no sign that it was anything but luck that made them choose another route to the train.

"*Buffalo, Harrisburg, Baltimore, and Washington,*" said the voice in the loudspeaker.

Ruth realized that it was her train, too. She stood without looking again at the old man. He was no more than disgustingly drunk, she told herself. He deserved to lie there, sleeping it off. She tucked her magazine and purse under her arm. Someone—the police or some charity or whoever's job it was—would be along to pick him up.

"*Board!*"

Ruth skirted the man and strode toward the ramp. The hiss and chilling dampness from the track level billowed down the ramp to envelop her. Pale lights, wreathed in steam, stretched away in seeming infinity—unreal, offering nothing to compete with her thoughts.

And her thoughts nagged, making her imagine an annoying, repetitive sound—a man's cough. Louder and louder it grew in her mind, seeming to echo and amplify in a vast stone vault.

"Board!"

Ruth turned, and ran back down the ramp. In seconds she was leaning over the old man, loosening his collar, rubbing his wrists. She laid his slight frame out at full length, and placed her coat under his head.

"Redcap!" she shouted.

"Yes'm?"

"This man is dying. Call an ambulance!"

"Yes ma'am!"

Horns honked as Ruth walked against the light. She took no notice, busily upbraiding in her mind the insensitive men and women in the railroad station. The ambulance had taken the old man away, and now Ruth, having missed her train, had four more hours to spend in Ted's hometown.

"Just because he was ugly and dirty, you wouldn't help him," she told the imagined crowd. "He was sick and needed help, and you all went your selfish ways rather than touch him. Shame on you." She looked challengingly at persons coming down the sidewalk toward her, and had her look returned with puzzlement. "You'd pretend there was nothing serious wrong with him," she murmured.

Ruth killed time in a woman's way, pretending to be on a shopping errand. She looked critically at window displays, fingered fabrics, priced articles, and promised salesgirls she would be back to buy after looking in one or two more shops. Her activity was almost fully automatic, leaving her thoughts to go their righteous, self-congratulatory way. She was one of the few, she told herself, who did not run away from the untouchables, from unclean, sick strangers.

It was a buoyant thought, and Ruth let herself believe that

Ted was sharing it with her. With the thought of Ted came the image of his formidable mother. The buoyance grew as Ruth saw how selfish Mrs. Faulkner was by comparison. The older woman would have sat in the waiting room oblivious to everything but the tragedy in her own narrow life. She would have muttered to a ghost while the old man hacked his life away.

Ruth relived her bitter, humiliating few hours with the woman, the bullying and wheedling in the name of a nightmarish notion of motherhood and an armful of trinkets. Disgust and the urge to get away came back full strength. Ruth leaned against a jewelry counter, and came face-to-face with herself in a mirror.

"Can I help you, madam?" said a salesgirl.

"What? Oh—no, thank you," said Ruth. The face in the mirror was vindictive, smug. The eyes had the same cold glaze as the eyes that had looked at the old man in the station and seen nothing.

"You look a little ill. Would you like to sit down for a moment?"

"No, really—there's nothing wrong," said Ruth absently.

"There's a doctor on duty in the store."

Ruth looked away from the mirror. "This is silly of me. I felt unsteady there for just a minute. It's passed now." She smiled uncertainly. "Thanks very much. I've got to be on my way."

"A train?"

"No," said Ruth wearily. "A terribly sick old woman needs my help."

WHILE MORTALS SLEEP

If Fred Hackleman and Christmas could have avoided each other, they would have. He was a bachelor, a city editor, and a newspaper genius, and I worked for him as a reporter for three insufferable years. As nearly as I could tell, he and the Spirit of Christmas had as little in common as a farm cat and the Audubon Society.

And he was like a farm cat in a lot of ways. He was solitary, deceptively complacent and lazy, and quick with the sharp claws of his authority and wit.

He was in his middle forties when I worked for him, and he had seemingly lost respect not just for Christmas but for government, matrimony, business, patriotism, and just about any other important institution you could name. The only ideals I ever heard him mention were terse leads, good spelling, accuracy, and speed in reporting the stupidity of mankind.

I can remember only one Christmas during which he radiated, faintly, anything like joy and goodwill. But that was a coincidence. A jailbreak happened to take place on December twenty-fifth.

I can remember another Christmas when he badgered a rewrite girl until she cried, because she'd said in a story that a man had passed on after having been hit by a freight train.

"Did he get up, dust himself off, giggle, and pass on to

wherever he was headed before his little misunderstanding with the locomotive?" Hackleman wanted to know.

"No." She bit her lip. "He died, and—"

"Why didn't you say so in the first place? He died. After the locomotive, the tender, fifty-eight loaded freight cars and the caboose rolled over him, he died. That we can tell our readers without fear of contradiction. First-rate reporting—he died. Did he go to Heaven? Is that where he passed on to?"

"I—I don't know."

"Well, your story says we do know. Did the reporter say he had definite information that the dead man is now in Heaven—or en route? Did you check with the man's minister to see if he had a ghost of a chance of getting in?"

She burst into tears. "I hope he did!" she said furiously. "I tried to say I hoped he did, and I'm not sorry!" She walked away, blowing her nose, and paused by the door to glare at Hackleman. "Because it's Christmas!" she cried, and she left the newspaper world forever.

"Christmas?" said Hackleman. He seemed baffled, and looked around the room as though hoping someone would translate the strange word for him. "Christmas." He walked over to the calendar on the wall, and ran his finger along the dates until he came to the twenty-fifth. "Oh—that's the one with the red numbers. Huh."

But the Christmas season I remember best is the last one I spent with Hackleman—the season in which the great crime was committed, the robbery proclaimed by Hackleman, gleefully, as the most infamous crime in the history of the city.

It must have been on about the first of December that I heard him say, as he went over his morning mail, "Goddamn it, how much glory can come to a man in one short lifetime?"

He called me over to his desk. "It isn't right that all of the honors that pour into these offices every day should be shared only by management," he said. "It's to you, the working stiffs, that the honors really belong."

"That's very kind of you," I said uneasily.

"So, in lieu of the raise which you richly deserve, I am going to make you my assistant."

"Assistant city editor?"

"Bigger than that. My boy, you are now assistant publicity director of the Annual Christmas Outdoor Lighting Contest. Bet you thought I wasn't even aware of the brilliant, selfless job you've been doing for the paper, eh?" He shook my hand. "Well, here's your answer. Congratulations."

"Thanks. What do I do?"

"The reason executives die young is that they don't know how to delegate authority," said Hackleman. "This should add twenty years to my life, because I hereby delegate to you my full authority as publicity director, just tendered me by the Chamber of Commerce. The door of opportunity is wide open. If your publicity makes this year's Annual Christmas Outdoor Lighting Contest the biggest, brightest one yet, there'll be no ceiling on how high you can rise in the world of journalism. Who's to say you won't be the next publicity director of National Raisin Week?"

"I'm afraid I'm not very familiar with this particular art form," I said.

"Nothing to it," said Hackleman. "The contestants dangle colored electric lights all over the fronts of their houses, and the man whose meter goes around fastest wins. That's Christmas for you."

★   ★   ★

As a dutiful assistant publicity director, I boned up on the history of the event, and learned that the contest had been held every year, except for the war years, since 1938. The first winner won with a two-story Santa Claus, outlined in lights on the front of his house. The next winner had a great pair of plywood bells, outlined in lights and hung from the eaves, which swung back and forth while a loudspeaker concealed in the shrubbery went ding-dong.

And so it went: each winner bettered the winner of the year before, until no entrant had a prayer of winning without the help of an electrical engineer, and the Power and Light Company had every bit of its equipment dangerously over-loaded on the night of the judging, Christmas Eve.

As I said, Hackleman wanted nothing to do with it. But, unfortunately for Hackleman, the publisher of the paper had just been elected president of the Chamber of Commerce, and he was annoyed to learn that one of his employees was squirming out of a civic duty.

The publisher rarely appeared in the city room, but his visits were always memorable—particularly the visit he made two weeks before Christmas to educate Hackleman on his twofold role in the community.

"Hackleman," he said, "every man on this staff is not only a newspaper man, he's an active citizen."

"I vote," said Hackleman. "I pay my taxes."

"And there it stops," said the publisher reproachfully. "For ten years you've been city editor, and for ten years you've been ducking the civic duties that come to a man in such a position—foisting them off on the nearest reporter." He pointed at me. "It's a slap in the face of the community, sending out kids like this to do work that most citizens would consider a great honor."

"I haven't got time," said Hackleman sullenly.

"Make the time. Nobody asks you to spend eighteen hours a day in the office. That's your idea. It isn't necessary. Get out with your fellow men once in a while, Hackleman, especially now. It's the Christmas season, man. Get behind this contest and—"

"What's Christmas to me?" said Hackleman. "I'm not a religious man and I'm not a family man, and eggnog gives me gastritis, so the hell with Christmas."

The publisher was stunned. "The hell with Christmas?" he said, hollowly, hoarsely.

"Certainly," said Hackleman.

"Hackleman," said the publisher evenly, "I order you to take part in running the contest—to get into the swing of Christmas. It'll do you good."

"I quit," said Hackleman, "and I don't think that will do you much good."

And Hackleman was right. His quitting did the paper no good. It was a disaster, for in many ways he *was* the paper. However, there was no wailing or gnashing of teeth in the paper's executive offices—only a calm, patient wistfulness. Hackleman had quit before, but had never managed to stay away from the paper for more than twenty-four hours. His whole life was the paper, and his talking of quitting it was like a trout's talking of quitting a mountain stream to get a job clerking in a five-and-ten.

Setting a new record for an absence from the paper, Hackleman returned to his desk twenty-seven hours after quitting. He was slightly drunk and surly, and looked no one in the eye.

As I passed his desk, quietly and respectfully, he mumbled something to me.

"Beg your pardon?" I said.

"I said Merry Christmas," said Hackleman.

"And a Merry Christmas to you."

"Well, sir," he said, "it won't be long now, will it, until old soup-for-brains with the long white beard will come a-jingling over our housetops with goodies for us all."

"No—guess not."

"A man who whips little reindeer is capable of anything," said Hackleman.

"Yes—I suppose."

"Bring me up to date, will you, kid? What's this goddamn contest all about?"

The committee that was supposed to be running the contest was top-heavy with local celebrities who were too busy and important to do a lick of work on the contest—the mayor, the president of a big manufacturing company, and the chairman of the Real Estate Board. Hackleman kept me on as his assistant, and it was up to us and some small fry from the Chamber of Commerce to do the spadework.

Every night we went out to look at entries, and there were thousands of them. We were trying to make a list of the twenty best displays from which the committee would choose a winner on Christmas Eve. The Chamber of Commerce underlings scouted the south side of town, while Hackleman and I scouted the north.

It should have been pleasant. The weather was crisp, not

bitter; the stars were out every night, bright, hard, and cold against a black velvet sky. Snow, while cleared from the streets, lay on yards and rooftops, making all the world seem soft and clean; and our car radio sang Christmas carols.

But it wasn't pleasant, because Hackleman talked most of the time, making a bitter indictment against Christmas.

One time, I was listening to a broadcast of a children's choir singing "Silent Night," and was as close to heaven as I could get without being pure and dead. Hackleman suddenly changed stations to fill the car with the clangor of a jazz band.

"Wha'd you do that for?" I said.

"They're running it into the ground," said Hackleman peevishly. "We've heard it eight times already tonight. They sell Christmas the way they sell cigarettes—just keep hammering away at the same old line over and over again. I've got Christmas coming out of my ears."

"They're not selling it," I said. "They're just happy about it."

"Just another form of department store advertising."

I twisted the dial back to the station carrying the children's choir. "If you don't mind, I'd enjoy hearing this to the end," I said. "Then you can change it again."

"Sleee-eeep in heav-en-ly peace," piped the small, sweet voices. And then the announcer broke in. "This fifteen-minute interlude of Christmas favorites," he said, "has been brought to you by Bullard Brothers Department Store, which is open until ten o'clock every evening except Sunday. Don't wait until the last minute to do your Christmas shopping. Avoid the rush."

"There!" said Hackleman triumphantly.

"That's a side issue," I said. "The main thing is that the Savior was born on Christmas."

"Wrong again," said Hackleman. "Nobody knows when he was born. There's nothing in the Bible to tell you. Not a word."

"You're the last man I'd come to for an expert opinion on the Bible," I said heatedly.

"I memorized it when I was a kid," said Hackleman. "Every night I had to learn a new verse. If I missed a word, by God, the old man knocked my block off."

"Oh?" This was an unexpected turn of events—unexpected because part of Hackleman's impressiveness lay in his keeping to himself, in his never talking about his past or about what he did or thought when he wasn't at work. Now he was talking about his childhood, and showing me for the first time an emotion more profound than impatience and cynicism.

"I didn't miss a single Sunday School session for ten years," said Hackleman. "Rain or shine, sick or well, I was there."

"Devout, eh?"

"Scared stiff of my old man's belt."

"Is he still alive—your father?"

"I don't know," said Hackleman without interest. "I ran away when I was fifteen, and never went back."

"And your mother?"

"Died when I was a year old."

"Sorry."

"Who the hell asked you to be sorry?"

We were pulling up before the last house we planned to look at that night. It was a salmon-pink mansion with a spike fence, iron flamingos, and five television aerials—combining in one monster the worst features of Spanish architecture, electronics, and sudden wealth. There was no Christmas lighting display that we could see—only ordinary lights inside the house.

We knocked on the door, to make sure we'd found the right place, and were told by a butler that there was indeed a lighting display, on the other side of the house, and that he would have to ask the master for permission to turn it on.

A moment later, the master appeared, fat and hairy, and with two prominent upper front teeth—looking like a groundhog in a crimson dressing gown.

"Mr. Fleetwood, sir," said the butler to his master, "these gentlemen here—"

The master waved his man to silence. "How have you been, Hackleman?" he said. "It's rather late to be calling, but my door is always open to old friends."

"Gribbon," said Hackleman incredulously, "Leu Gribbon. How long have you been living here?"

"The name is Fleetwood now, Hackleman—J. Sprague Fleetwood, and I'm strictly legitimate. There was a story the last time we met, but there isn't one tonight. I've been out for a year, living quietly and decently."

"Mad Dog Gribbon has been out for a year, and I didn't know it?" said Hackleman.

"Don't look at me," I said. "I cover the School Board and the Fire Department."

"I've paid my debt to society," said Gribbon.

Hackleman toyed with the visor of a suit of armor guarding the entrance into the baronial living room. "Looks to me like you paid your debt to society two cents on the dollar," he said.

"Investments," said Gribbon, "legitimate investments in the stock market."

"How'd your broker get the bloodstains out of your money to find out what the denominations were?" said Hackleman.

"If you're going to abuse my hospitality with rudeness, Hackleman, I'll have you thrown out," said Gribbon. "Now, what do you want?"

"They wish to see the lighting display, sir," said the butler.

Hackleman looked very sheepish when this mission was announced. "Yeah," he mumbled, "we're on a damn fool committee."

"I thought the judging was to take place Christmas Eve," said Gribbon. "I didn't plan to turn it on until then—as a pleasant surprise for the community."

"A mustard gas generator?" said Hackleman.

"All right, wise guy," said Gribbon haughtily, "tonight you're going to see what kind of a citizen J. Sprague Fleetwood is."

It was a world of vague forms and shades of blue in the snowy yard of J. Sprague Fleetwood, alias Mad Dog Gribbon. It was midnight and Hackleman and I stamped our feet and blew on our hands to keep warm, while Gribbon and three servants hurried about the yard, tightening electrical connections and working over what seemed to be statues with screwdrivers and oil cans.

Gribbon insisted that we stand far away from the display in order to get the impact of the whole, whenever it was ready to be turned on. We couldn't tell what it was we were about to see, and were particularly tantalized by what the butler was doing—filling an enormous weather balloon from a tank of gas. The balloon arose majestically, captive at the end of a cable, as the butler turned the crank of a winch.

"What's that for?" I whispered to Hackleman.

"Sending for final instructions from God," said Hackleman.

"What'd he get sent to prison for?"

"Ran the numbers in town for a while, and had about twenty people killed so he could keep his franchise. So they put him away for five years for not paying his income taxes."

"Lights ready?" bawled Gribbon, standing on a porch, his arms upraised, commanding a miracle.

"Lights ready," said a voice in the shrubbery.

"Sound ready?"

"Sound ready, sir."

"Balloon ready?"

"Balloon aloft, sir."

"Let 'er go!" cried Gribbon.

Demons shrieked from the treetops.

Suns exploded.

Hackleman and I cowered, instinctively threw our arms across our faces.

We uncovered our eyes slowly, fearfully, and saw stretching before us, in blinding, garish light, a life-sized nativity scene. Loudspeakers on every side blared earsplitting carols. Plaster cattle and sheep were everywhere, wagging their heads, while shepherds raised and lowered their right arms like railroad-crossing gates, jerkily pointing into the sky.

The Virgin Mary and Joseph looked down sweetly on the child in the manger, while mechanical angels flapped their wings and mechanical wise men bobbed up and down like pistons.

"Look!" cried Hackleman above the din, pointing where the shepherds pointed, where the balloon had disappeared into the sky.

There, over the salmon-pink palace of Mad Dog Gribbon, hung in the Christmas heavens from a bag of gas, shone an imitation of the star of Bethlehem.

Suddenly, all was black and still again. My mind was numb. Hackleman stared blankly at the place where the star had been, speechless.

Gribbon trotted toward us. "Anything else in town that can touch it?" he panted proudly.

"Nope," said Hackleman bleakly.

"Think it'll win?"

"Yup," murmured Hackleman. "Unless somebody's got an atomic explosion in the form of Rudolph the Red-nosed Reindeer."

"People will come from miles around to see it," said Gribbon. "Just tell 'em in the newspaper story to follow the star."

"Listen, Gribbon," said Hackleman, "you know there isn't any money that goes with the first prize, don't you? Nothing but a lousy little scroll worth maybe a buck."

Gribbon looked offended. "Of course," he said. "This is a public service, Hackleman."

Hackleman grunted. "Come on, kid, let's call it a night, eh?"

It was a real break, our finding the certain winner of the contest a week before the judging was to take place. It meant that the judges and assistants like myself could spend most of Christmas Eve with our families, instead of riding around town for hours, trying to decide which was the best of twenty or so equally good entries. All we had to do now was to drive to Gribbon's mansion, be blinded and deafened, shake his hand and give him his scroll, and return home in time to trim the tree, fill the stocking, and put away several rounds of eggnog.

As thoughts of Christmas made Hackleman's neurotic staff gentle and sentimental, and the preposterous rumor that he had a heart of gold gained wide circulation, Hackleman behaved in typical holiday fashion, declaring that heads were going to roll because Mad Dog Gribbon had been out of prison and back in town for a year without a single reporter's finding out about it.

"By God," he said, "I'm going to have to go out on the street again, or the paper'll fold up for want of news." And, during the next two days, the paper would have done just that, if it hadn't been for news from the wire services, because Hackleman sent out almost everybody to find out what Gribbon was up to.

Desperate as Hackleman made us, we couldn't find a hint of skulduggery in Gribbon's life since he'd left prison. The only conclusion to draw was that crime paid so well that Gribbon could retire in his early forties, and live luxuriously and lawfully for the rest of his days.

"His money really does come from stocks and bonds," I told Hackleman wearily at the end of the second day. "And he pays his taxes like a good boy, and never sees his old friends anymore."

"All right, all right, all right," said Hackleman irritably.

"Forget it. Never mind." He was more nervous than I'd ever seen him be before. He drummed on his desk with his fingers, and jumped at unexpected sounds.

"You have something special against him?" I asked. It wasn't like Hackleman to go after anyone with such zeal. Ordinarily, he never seemed to care whether justice or crime won out. What interested him were the good news stories that came out of the conflict. "After all, the guy really is going straight."

"Forget it," said Hackleman. Suddenly, he broke his pencil in two, stood up, and strode out, hours before his usual departure time.

The next day was my day off. I would have slept till noon, but a paper boy was selling extras under my bedroom window. The headline was huge and black, and spelled one terrible word: KIDNAPPED! The story below said that plaster images of Jesus, Mary, and Joseph had been stolen from Mr. J. Sprague Fleetwood, and that he had offered a reward of one thousand dollars for information leading to their return before the judging of the Annual Christmas Outdoor Lighting Contest on Christmas Eve.

Hackleman called a few minutes later. I was to come to the office at once to help trace down the clues that were pouring in.

The police complained that, if there were any clues, hordes of amateur detectives had spoiled them. But there was no pressure at all on the police to solve the robbery. By evening the search had become a joyful craze that no one escaped—that no one wanted to escape. And the search was for the people to make, not for the police.

Throngs went from door to door, asking if anyone had seen the infant Jesus.

Movie theaters played to empty houses, and a local radio giveaway program said mournfully that nobody seemed to be home in the evenings to answer the telephone.

Thousands insisted on searching the only stable in the city, and the owner made a small fortune selling them hot chocolate and doughnuts. An enterprising hotel bought a full-page ad, declaring that if anyone found Jesus and Mary and Joseph, here was an inn that would make room for them.

The lead story in every edition of the paper dealt with the search and every edition was a sellout.

Hackleman remained as sarcastic and cynical and efficient as ever.

"It's a miracle," I told him. "By taking this little story and blowing it up big, you've made Christmas live."

Hackleman shrugged apathetically. "Just happened to come along when news was slow. If something better comes along, and I hope it will, I'll drop this one right out of sight. It's about time somebody was running berserk with an automatic shotgun in a kindergarten isn't it?"

"Sorry I opened my mouth."

"Have I remembered to wish you a merry Saturnalia?"

"Saturnalia?"

"Yeah—a nasty old pagan holiday near the end of December. The Romans used to close the schools, eat and drink themselves silly, say they loved everybody, and give each other gifts." He answered the phone. "No, ma'am, we haven't found Him yet. Yes, ma'am, there'll be an extra if He turns up. Yes, ma'am, the stable's already been checked pretty carefully. Thank you. Goodbye."

★　★　★

The search was more a spontaneous, playful pageant than an earnest hunt for the missing figures. Realistically, the searchers didn't have much of a chance. They made a lot of noise, and went only where they thought it would be pleasant or interesting to go. The thief, who was apparently a nut, would have had little trouble keeping his peculiar loot out of sight.

But the searchers were so caught up in the allegory of what they were doing that a powerful expectation grew of its own accord, with no help from the paper. Everyone was convinced that the holy family would be found on Christmas Eve.

But on that eve, no new star shone over the city save the five-hundred-watt lamp hung from a balloon over the mansion of J. Sprague Fleetwood, alias Mad Dog Gribbon, the victim of the theft.

The mayor, the president of a big manufacturing company, and the chairman of the Real Estate Board rode in the back seat of the mayor's limousine, while Hackleman and I sat on the jump seats in front of them. We were on our way to award the first-prize scroll to Gribbon, who had replaced the missing figures with new ones.

"Turn down this street here?" said the chauffeur.

"Just follow the star," I said.

"It's a light, a goddamn electric light that anybody can hang over his house if he's got the money," said Hackleman.

"Follow the goddamn electric light," I said.

Gribbon was waiting for us, wearing a tuxedo, and he opened the car door himself. "Gentlemen—Merry Christmas." His eyes down, his hands folded piously across his round belly, he led us down a path, bounded by ropes, that led around the display and back to the street again. He passed by the corner of the mansion, just short of the point where we would be able to see the display. "I like to think of it as a shrine," he said, "with people coming from miles around, following the stars." He stepped aside, motioning us to go ahead.

And the dumbfounding panorama dazzled us again, looking like an outdoor class in calisthenics, with expressionless figures bobbing, waving their arms, flapping their wings.

"Gangster heaven," whispered Hackleman.

"Oh, my," said the mayor.

The chairman of the Real Estate Board looked appalled, but cleared his throat and recovered gamely. "Now, there's a display," he said, clinging doggedly to his integrity.

"Where'd you get the new figures?" said Hackleman.

"Wholesale from a department-store supply house," said Gribbon.

"What an engineering feat," said the manufacturer.

"Took four engineers to do it," said Gribbon proudly. "Whoever swiped the figures left the neon halos behind, thank God. They're rigged so I can make 'em blink, if you think that'd look better."

"No, no," said the mayor. "Mustn't gild the lily."

"Uh . . . do I win?" said Gribbon politely.

"Hmmm?" said the mayor. "Oh—do you win? Well, we have to deliberate, of course. We'll let you know this evening."

No one seemed able to think of anything more to say, and we shuffled back to the limousine.

"Thirty-two electric motors, two miles of wire, nine

hundred and seventy-six lightbulbs, not counting neon," said Gribbon as we pulled away.

"I thought we were going to just hand him the scroll right then and there," said the real estate man. "That was the plan, wasn't it?"

"I just couldn't bring myself to do it then," sighed the mayor. "Suppose we could stop somewhere for a stirrup cup."

"He obviously won," said the manufacturer. "We wouldn't dare give the prize to anyone else. He won by brute force— brute dollars, brute kilowatts, no matter how terrible his taste is."

"There's one more stop," said Hackleman.

"I thought this was a one-stop expedition," said the manufacturer. "I thought we'd agreed on that."

Hackleman held up a card. "Well, it's a technicality. The official deadline for entries was noon today. This thing came in by special delivery about two seconds ahead of the deadline, and we haven't had a chance to check it."

"It certainly can't match this Fleetwood thing," said the mayor. "What could? What's the address?"

Hackleman told him.

"Shabby neighborhood out on the edge of town," said the real estate man. "No competition for our friend Fleetwood."

"Let's forget it," said the manufacturer. "I've got guests coming in, and . . ."

"Bad public relations," said Hackleman gravely. It was startling to hear the words coming from him, enunciated with respect. He'd once said that the three most repellent forms of life were rats, leeches, and public relations men . . . in descending order.

To the three important men in the back seat, though, the

words were impressive and troubling. They mumbled and fidgeted, but didn't have the courage to fight.

"Let's make it quick," said the mayor, and Hackleman gave the driver the card.

Stopped by a traffic signal, we came abreast of a group of cheerful searchers, who called to us, asking if we knew where the holy family was hidden.

Impulsively, the mayor leaned out of the window. "You won't find them under that," he said, waggling his finger at the light over Gribbon's house.

Another group crossed the street before us, singing:

For Christ is born of Mary,
And gathered all above,
While mortals sleep, the angels keep
Their watch of wondering love.

The light changed, and we drove on, saying little as we left the fine homes behind, as the electric lamp over Gribbon's mansion was lost behind black factory chimneys.

"You sure the address is right?" said the chauffeur uncertainly.

"I guess the guy knows his own address," said Hackleman.

"This was a bad idea," said the manufacturer, looking at his watch. "Let's call up Gribbon or Fleetwood or whatever his name is, and tell him he's the big winner. The hell with this."

"I agree," said the mayor. "But, as long as we're this far along, let's see it through."

The limousine turned down a dark street, banged over a chuckhole, and stopped. "This is it gentlemen," said the chauffeur.

We were parked before an empty, leaning, roofless house, whose soundest part was its splintered siding, a sign declaring it to be unfit for human habitation.

"Are rats and termites eligible for the contest?" said the mayor.

"The address checks," said the chauffeur defensively.

"Turn around and go home," said the mayor.

"Hold it," said the real estate man. "There's a light in the barn in back. My God, I came all this way to judge and I'm going to judge."

"Go see who's in the barn," said the mayor to the chauffeur.

The chauffeur shrugged, got out, and walked through the snow-covered rubbish to the barn. He knocked. The door swung open under the impact of his fist. Silhouetted by a frail, wavering light from within, he sank to his knees.

"Drunk?" said Hackleman.

"I don't think so," murmured the mayor. He licked his lips. "I think he's praying—for the first time in his life." He got out of the car, and we followed him silently to the barn. When we reached the chauffeur, we went to our knees beside him.

Before us were the three missing figures. Joseph and Mary sheltered against a thousand drafts the sleeping infant Jesus in his bed of straw. The only illumination came from a single oil lantern, and its wavering light made them live, alive with awe and adoration.

On Christmas morning, the paper told the people where the holy family could be found.

All Christmas Day the people streamed to the cold, lonely barn to worship.

A small story inside announced that Mr. Sprague Fleetwood had won the Annual Christmas Outdoor Lighting Contest with thirty-two electric motors, two miles of wire, and nine hundred and seventy-six lightbulbs, not counting neon, and an Army surplus weather balloon.

Hackleman was on the job at his desk, critical and disillusioned as ever.

"It's a great, great story," I said.

"I'm good and sick of it," said Hackleman. He rubbed his hands. "What I'm looking forward to is January when the Christmas bills come in. A great month for homicides."

"Well, there's still got to be a follow-up on the Christmas story. We still don't know who did it."

"How you going to find out who did it? The name on the entry blank was a phony, and the guy who owns the barn hasn't been in town for ten years."

"Fingerprints," I said. "We could go over the figures for fingerprints."

"One more suggestion like that, and you're fired."

"Fired?" I said. "What for?"

"Sacrilege!" said Hackleman grandly, and the subject was closed. His mind, as he said, was on stories in the future. He never looked back.

Hackleman's last act with respect to the theft, the search, and Christmas was to send me out to the barn with a photographer on Christmas night. The mission was routine and trite, and it bored him.

"Get a crowd shot from the back, with the figures facing the camera," said Hackleman. "They must be pretty damn dusty by now, with all the sinners tramping through. Better go over 'em with a damp cloth before you make the shot."

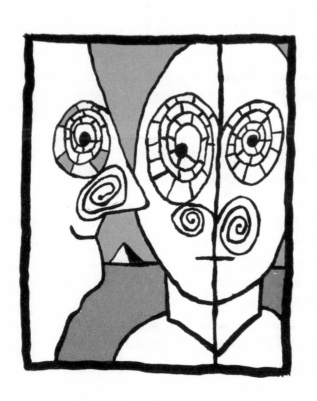

OUT, BRIEF CANDLE

Annie Cowper thought of the letters from Schenectady as having come like a sweet, warm wind at the sunset of her life. The truth was that she was only in her middle forties when they started to come, and the sunset of her life was still far away. She had all of her teeth and needed her steel-rimmed spectacles only for reading.

She felt old because her husband, Ed, who really was old, had died and left her alone on the hog farm in northern Indiana. When Ed died, she had sold the livestock, rented the flat, black, rich land to neighbors, read her Bible, watered her houseplants, fed her chickens, tended her small vegetable garden, or simply rocked—waiting patiently and without rancor for the Bright Angel of Death. Ed had left her plenty of money, so she wasn't goaded into doing anything more, and the people in the area, the only area Annie knew, made her feel that she was doing the right thing, the customary thing, the only thing.

Though she was without relatives, she wasn't without callers. Farm wives came often for an hour or two of stifled pity over cakes and coffee.

"If my Will went, I just don't know what I'd do," said one. "In the city, I don't think folks really know what it is to be one flesh. They just change husbands as often as they please, and one's as good as another one."

"Yes," said Annie, "I certainly wouldn't care for that. Have another peach surprise, Doris June."

"I mean, in the city a man and woman don't really need each other except to—" Delicately, Doris June left the sentence unfinished.

"Yes, that's true," said Annie. One of her duties as a widow, she had learned, was to provide dramatic proof to the neighboring wives that, bad as their husbands might be at times, life without them would be worse.

Annie didn't spoil this illusion for Doris June by telling her about the letters—telling her what she had discovered so late in life about womanly happiness, telling her about one man, at least, who could make her happy from as far away as Schenectady.

Sometimes other women's husbands came to the farm, too, gruff and formal, to perform some man's chore that their wives had noticed needed doing—patching a roof, putting a new packing in the pump, greasing the idle machinery in the barn. They knew she was a virtuous widow, and respected her severely for it. They hardly spoke.

Sometimes Annie wondered how the husbands would act if they knew about the letters. Maybe they would think she was a loose woman, then, and accept her formal invitations for coffee which were meant to be declined. They might even make remarks with double meanings and full of shy flirtation—the sort of remarks they made to the shameless girl behind the coffee counter in the diner in town.

If she'd shown the men the letters, they would have read something dirty into them, she thought, when the letters weren't at all like that, really. They were spiritual, they were poetry, and she didn't even know or care what the man who wrote them looked like.

Sometimes the minister came for a visit, too, a bleak, flesh-less, dust-colored old man, who was overjoyed by her death-like peace and moral safety.

"You make me want to go on, Mrs. Cowper," he said. "I wish you could talk to our young people sometime. They don't believe it's possible for a person to live a Christian life in this modern day and age."

"That's very kind of you," said Annie. "I think all young people are kind of wild, and settle down later. Have another raspberry delight, won't you? They'll only spoil, and I'll have to throw them away."

"You were never wild, were you, Mrs. Cowper?"

"Well—of course I married Ed when I was just a little bet-ter than sixteen. I didn't have much chance for running around."

"And you wouldn't have, if you'd had the chance," said the minister triumphantly.

Annie felt a strange impulse to argue with him and tell him proudly about the letters. But she fought the wicked im-pulse, and nodded gravely.

A few would-be lovers called, too, with honorable inten-tions and a powerful lust for her land. But, while these callers spoke clumsy poetry about her fields, not one made her feel that she was anything more than what she saw of herself in the mirror—a tall, lean woman, as unornamental as a tele-phone pole, with coarse, work-swollen hands, and a long nose whose tip had been bitten to a permanent red by frost. Like Ed, they never tried.

The moment a would-be lover left after a chilly visit, mumbling about weather and crops and twisting his hat, Annie would feel a great need for the letters from Schenectady. She would lock the door, pull the blinds, lie on her bed, and read and reread the letters until hunger or sleep or a knock on the door forced her to hide them again until another time.

Ed died in October, and Annie got along without him and without the letters, too, until the next spring—or what should have been spring. It was in early May, when a sudden, bitter frost killed the daffodil sprouts, that Annie had written:

"Dear 5587: This is the first time I have ever written to a total stranger. I just happened to be waiting in the drugstore to get a prescription for my sinus trouble filled, and I picked up a copy of Western Romance Magazine. I don't usually read magazines like that. I think they are silly. But I just happened to turn to the pen pals section, and I saw your letter, and I read where you are lonely and could sure use a pen pal." She smiled at her foolishness. "I will tell you a little about myself," she wrote. "I am fairly young still, and I have brown hair, green eyes, and..."

In a week, a reply had come, and the code number used by the magazine became a name: Joseph P. Hawkins, of Schenectady, New York.

"My dear Mrs. Cowper:" Hawkins had written, "I have received many replies to my plea for pen pals, but none has moved me more deeply than yours. A meeting of kindred spirits, such as I believe ours to be, is a rare thing, indeed, in this vale of tears, and is fuller of true bliss than the most perfect of physical matings. I see you now as an angel, for the voice I hear in your letters is the voice of an angel. The instant the angel appeared, loneliness fled, and I knew I was not really alone on this vast and crowded planet after all..."

Annie had giggled nervously as she read the first letter, and felt guilty about having led the poor man on so, and she had been a little shocked, too, by the ardent tone of the letter. But she'd found herself rereading the letter several times a day, each time with increased pity. At last, in a fever of compassion, she had given the poor man his wish, and painstakingly tried to create another angel for him.

From then on there had been no turning back, no will to turn back.

Hawkins was eloquent and poetic—but most of all he was exquisitely sensitive to a woman's moods. He sensed it when Annie was depressed, though she never told him she was, and he would say just the right thing to cheer her. And when she was elated, he nourished her elation, and kept it alive for weeks instead of fleeting minutes.

She tried to do the same for him, and her fumbling efforts seemed to sit surprisingly well with her pen pal.

Never once did Hawkins say a vulgar thing, nor did he harp on the fact of his being a man and her a woman. That was unimportant, he said vehemently. The important thing was that their spirits would never be lonely again, so splendidly were they matched. It was a very high-level correspondence—on such a high level, in fact, that Annie and Hawkins went for an entire year without mentioning anything as down-to-earth as money, work, age, physical appearances, organized religion, or politics. Nature, Fate, and the undefinable sweet aches of the spirit were subject matter enough to keep them both writing on and on and on and on and on. The second winter without Ed seemed no worse than a chilly May to Annie, because, for the first time in her life, she had discovered what true friendship was like.

When the correspondence finally came down to earth, it wasn't Joseph P. Hawkins who brought it down—it was Annie. When spring came again, she was writing to him, as he had written to her, about the millions of tender little shoots poking their heads up, and about the mating songs of the birds and the budding of the trees, and the bees carrying pollen from one plant to the next—when she suddenly felt compelled to do what Hawkins had forbidden her to do.

"Please," he had written, "let us not descend to the vulgarity of, as I believe the phrase goes, 'exchanging snaps.' No photographer, save in Heaven, could ever take a picture of the angel that rises from your letters to blind me with adoration."

But one heady, warm spring night, Annie enclosed a snapshot anyway. The picture was one Ed had taken at a picnic five years before, and, at the time, she'd thought it was a terrible likeness. But now, as she studied it before sealing her letter, she saw a great deal in the woman in the picture that she had not seen before—a haze of spiritual beauty that softened every harsh line.

The next two days of waiting were nightmares. She hated herself for having sent the picture, and told herself that she was the ugliest woman on earth, that she had ruined everything between herself and Hawkins. Then she would try to calm herself by telling herself that the picture couldn't possibly make any difference—that the relationship was purely spiritual, that she might as well have enclosed a blank sheet of paper, for all the difference the picture, beautiful or ugly, could make. But only Joseph P. Hawkins could say what the effect of the picture was.

He did so by special-delivery airmail. "Bright angel, adieu!" he wrote, and Annie burst into tears.

But then she forced herself to read on. "Frail, wispish counterfeit of my mind's eye, stand aside, dethroned by warm and earthly, vibrant bride of my mind—my Annie as she really is! Adieu, ghost! Make way for life, for I live and Annie lives, and it is spring!"

Annie was jubilant. She hadn't spoiled anything with the picture. Hawkins had seen the haze of spiritual beauty, too.

It wasn't until she sat down to write that she understood how changed the relationship was. They had admitted that they were not only spirit but flesh, and Annie's skin tingled at the thought—and the pen that once had wings did not budge. Every phrase that came to Annie's mind seemed foolish, inflated, though phrases like them had seemed substantial enough in the past.

And then the pen began to move with a will of its own. It wrote two words that said more than Annie had said in the hundred pages that had gone before:

"I come."

She was blind with love, gloriously out of control.

Hawkins's reply, a telegram, was almost as short: "PLEASE DON'T. AM DEATHLY ILL."

That was his last communication. Annie's telegrams and special-delivery letters brought no more response from Joseph P. Hawkins. A long-distance call revealed that Hawkins had no telephone. Annie was shattered, able to think of nothing but the gentle, lonely man, wasting away without a soul to care for him, *really care,* seven hundred miles from the vibrant bride of his mind.

After one agonized week of Hawkins's profound silence, Annie strode from the Schenectady railroad station, flushed with love, suffocating in her new girdle, tormented by her savings, which crackled and scratched in her stocking-tops and spare bosom. She carried a small suitcase and her knitting bag, into which she'd swept the entire contents of her medicine cabinet.

She wasn't afraid, not even rattled, though she'd never been on a train before, and had never seen anything remotely like the clouds of smoke and clanging busyness of Schenectady. She was numbed by duty and love, impressively tall and long-striding, leaning forward aggressively.

The cabstand was empty, but Annie told a redcap Hawkins's address, and he directed her to a bus that would take her there.

"You just ask the bus driver where you should get off," said the redcap.

And Annie did—at two-minute intervals. She sat right behind the driver, her modest luggage on her lap.

As the bus picked its way through mazes of noisy, fuming factories and slums and jounced over chuckholes and railroad tracks, Annie could see Hawkins, thin and white, tall, delicate, and blue-eyed, wasting away on a hard narrow bed in a tenement room.

"Is this the place where I get off?"

"No, ma'am. Not yet. I'll let you know."

The factories and slums dropped away, and pleasant little houses on neat, green, postage-stamp lots took their place. Peering into the windows as the bus passed, Annie could imagine Hawkins lying abed in his small, shipshape bachelor's quarters, once husky, now wan, his body ravished by disease.

"Is this where I get off?"

"A good ways, yet, ma'am. I'll let you know."

The small houses gave way to larger ones, and these gave way to mansions, the largest homes Annie had ever seen. She was the only passenger aboard now, awed by a new image of Hawkins, a dignified old gentleman with silver hair and a tiny mustache, languishing in a bed as big as her vegetable garden.

"Is this the neighborhood?" said Annie incredulously.

"Right along here somewhere." The bus slowed, and the driver looked out at the house numbers. At the next corner, he stopped the bus and opened the door. "Somewhere in that block, lady. I was looking for it, but I guess I missed it."

"Maybe it's in the next block," said Annie, who'd been watching too, with a quaking heart, as the house numbers came closer and closer to the one she knew so well.

"Nope. Got to be in this one. Nothing up ahead but a cemetery, and that goes for six blocks."

Annie stepped out into the quiet, shaded street. "Thank you very much."

"You're certainly welcome," said the driver. He started to close the door, but hesitated.

"You know how many people are dead in that cemetery up there?"

"I'm a stranger in town," said Annie.

"All of 'em," said the driver triumphantly. The door clattered shut, and the bus grumbled away.

An hour later, Annie had rung every doorbell and been barked at by every dog in the block.

No one had ever heard of Joseph P. Hawkins. Everyone agreed that, if there were such an address, it would be a tombstone in the next block.

Desolately, her big feet hurting, Annie trudged along the grass outside the iron-spiked cemetery fence. There were only stone angels to return her bewildered, searching gaze. She came at last to the stone arch that marked the cemetery entrance. Defeated, she sat down on her suitcase to wait for the next bus.

"Looking for somebody?" said a gruff voice behind her.

She turned to see a dwarfed old man standing under the cemetery arch. One eye was blind and white as a boiled egg, and the pupil of the other eye was bright and cunning, and roamed restlessly. He carried a shovel clotted with fresh earth.

"I—I'm looking for Mr. Hawkins," said Annie. "Mr. Joseph P. Hawkins." She stood, and tried to conceal her horror.

"Cemetery business?"

"He works here?"

"Did," said the dwarf. "Dead now."

"No!"

"Yep," said the dwarf without feeling. "Buried this morning."

Annie sank down, until she was seated on the suitcase again, and then she cried softly. "Too late, too late."

"A friend of yours?"

"The dearest friend a woman ever had!" said Annie passionately, brokenly. "Did you know him?"

"Nope. They just put me on the job out here when he took sick. From what I hear, he was quite a gentleman, though."

"He was, he was," said Annie. She looked up at the old man, and contemplated his shovel uneasily. "Tell me," she said, "He wasn't a—a grave-digger, was he?"

"Landscape architect and memorial custodian."

"Oh," said Annie, smiling through her tears, "I'm so glad." She shook her head. "Too late, too late. What can I do now?"

"I hear he liked flowers pretty well."

"Yes," said Annie, "he said they were the friends who always came back and never disappointed him. Where could I get some?"

"Well, it's supposed to be against the law, but I guess maybe it'd be all right if you picked some of those crocuses inside the gate there, just as long as nobody saw you. And there are some violets over there by his house."

"His house?" said Annie. "Where's his house?"

The old man pointed through the arch to a small, squat stone building, matted with ivy.

"Oh—the poor man," said Annie.

"It's not so bad," said the old man. "I live there now, and it's all right. Come on. You get the flowers, and then I'll drive you over to where he's buried in the truck. It's a long walk, and you'd get lost. He's in the new part we're just opening up. First one there, in fact."

The cemetery's little pickup truck followed ribbons of asphalt through the still, cool, forest of marble, until Annie was lost. The seat of the truck was jammed forward, so that the old man's short legs could reach the pedals. Annie's long legs, as a consequence, were painfully cramped by the dashboard. In her lap was a bouquet of crocuses and violets.

Neither spoke. Annie couldn't bear to look at her companion, and could think of nothing to say to him, and he, in turn, didn't seem particularly interested in her—was simply performing a routine and tiresome chore.

They came at last to an iron gate that barred the way into mud ruts leading into a wood.

The old man unlocked the gate. He put the truck into low gear, and it pushed into the twilight of the woods, with briars and branches scratching at its sides.

Annie gasped. Ahead was a peaceful, leafy clearing, and there, in a patch of sunlight, was a fresh grave.

"Headstone hasn't come yet," said the dwarf.

"Joseph, Joseph," whispered Annie. "I'm here."

The dwarf stopped the truck, limped around to Annie's side, and opened her door with a courtly gesture. He smiled for the first time, baring a ghastly set of dead-white false teeth.

"Could I be alone?" said Annie.

"I'll wait here."

Annie laid her flowers on the grave, and sat beside it for an hour, reciting to herself all the wonderful, tender things Joseph had said to her.

The chain of thought might have gone on for hours more, if the little man hadn't broken it with a polite cough.

"We'd better go," he said. "The sun will be going down soon."

"It's like tearing my heart out, leaving him here alone."

"You can come back another time."

"Yes," said Annie, "I will."

"What kind of a man was he?"

"What kind?" said Annie, standing reverently. "I never saw him. We just wrote to each other. He was a good, good man."

"What did he do that was good?"

"He made me feel pretty," said Annie. "I know what that's like now."

"You know what he looked like?"

"No. Not exactly."

"He was tall and broad shouldered, I hear. He had blue eyes and curly hair. That the way you imagined him?"

"Oh, yes!" said Annie happily. "Exactly. I could tell."

The sun was setting when the one-eyed gnome drove into the cemetery, after having warned Annie about strangers and put her on the train. Tombstones cast long shadows across his way as he went once more to the lonely poet's grave in the woods.

He took Annie's bouquet from the grave with a sigh.

He drove back to his stone house, and put the flowers in water, in a vase on his desk. He touched off the fire laid in the fireplace, to drive out the early spring evening's dampness, made himself a cup of coffee, and sat down to write, leaning forward to sniff Annie's flowers as he did so.

"My dear Mrs. Draper:" he wrote. "How strange that you, my pen pal and soul's dearest friend, should be on a chicken farm in British Columbia, a beautiful land that I shall probably never see. No matter what you say about life in British Columbia, it must be very beautiful, for hasn't it produced you? Please, please, please," he wrote, and he grunted emphatically as he underlined the three words, "let us not descend to the vulgarity of, as I believe the phrase goes, 'exchanging snaps.' No photographer, save in Heaven, could ever take a picture of the angel that rises from your letters to blind me with adoration."

TANGO

Every job application form I fill out asks for a tabulation, with dates, of what I've done with my adult life so far, and tells me sternly to leave no periods unaccounted for. I would give a great deal for permission to leave out the last three months, when I served as a tutor in a village called Pisquontuit. Anyone writing my former employer there for an appraisal of my character would get his ears burnt off.

On each application form there is a small blank section entitled *remarks,* where I might tell my side of the Pisquontuit story. But there seems little chance of anyone's understanding my side if he hasn't seen Pisquontuit. And the chances of an ordinary man's seeing Pisquontuit are about the same as his chances for being dealt two spade royal flushes in a row.

Pisquontuit is an Indian word said to mean "shining waters," and is pronounced *Ponit* by the few privileged to know that the village exists. It is a secret assemblage of mansions by the sea. The entrance is unmarked, an unpromising lane leading from the main road into a forest of scrub pine. A guard lives in the forest by a turnaround on the lane, and he makes all cars that do not belong in Pisquontuit turn around and go back where they came from. The cars that belong in Pisquontuit are either very big ones or very little ones.

I worked there as a tutor for Robert Brewer, an amiable, mildly fogbound young man who was preparing to take college entrance examinations and needed help.

I think I can say without fear of contradiction that Pisquontuit was the most exclusive community in America. While I was there, a gentleman sold his house on the grounds that his neighbors were "a pretty stuffy bunch." He went back to where *he* came from, Beacon Hill in Boston. My employer, Robert's father, Herbert Clewes Brewer, spent most of his time between sailboat races writing indignant letters to Washington. He was indignant because every mansion in the village was shown on United States Geodetic Survey maps, which could be bought by just anybody.

It was a quiet community. Its members had paid a handsome price for peace, and small ripples looked like tidal waves. At the heart of my troubles there was nothing more violent or barbaric than the tango.

The tango, of course, is a dance of Spanish-American origin, usually in four-four time, and is distinguished by low dips and twisting steps on the toes. One Saturday night, at the weekly dance of the Pisquontuit Yacht Club, young Robert Brewer, my student, who had never even seen the tango performed in his eighteen years of life, began to dip lowly and twist his toes. His movements were tentative at first, as involuntary as shudders. Robert's mind and face were blank when it happened. The heady Latin music wandered in through his ears, found nobody at home under his crew cut, and took command of his long, thin body.

Something clicked, locking Robert in the machinery of the music. His partner, a plain, wholesome girl with three million dollars and a low center of gravity, struggled in embarrassment, and then, seeing the fierce look in Robert's eyes, succumbed. The two became as one, a fast-moving one.

It simply was not done in Pisquontuit.

Dancing at Pisquontuit was an almost imperceptible shifting of weight from one foot to the other, with the feet remaining in place, from three to six inches apart. This seemly shifting of weight was all things to all music, samba, waltz, gavotte, fox-trot, bunny hug, or hokeypokey. No matter what new dance craze came along, Pisquontuit overpowered it easily. The ballroom could have been filled with clear gelatin to shoulder height without hampering the dancers. It could have been filled to a point just below the dancers' nostrils, for that matter, for agreement on every subject was so complete that discussion had been reduced to a verbal shorthand resembling asthma.

And there was Robert crossing and recrossing the ballroom floor like a Chris-Craft.

No one paid the slightest attention to Robert and his partner as they careered and careened. This indifference was equivalent to breaking a man on the wheel or throwing him down the oubliette in other times and places. Robert had put himself in the same class with the poor devil in Pisquontuit history who put lampblack on the bottom of his sailboat, another who found out too late that no one *ever* went swimming before eleven in the morning, and another who could not break the habit of saying okey dokey on the telephone.

When the music was over, Robert's partner, flushed and rattled, excused herself, and Robert's father joined him by the bandstand.

When Mr. Brewer was angry, he thrust his tongue between his teeth and talked around it, withdrawing it only to make *s* sounds. "Good Lord, Bubs!" he said to Robert. "What do you think you are, a gigolo?"

"I don't know what happened," said Robert, crimson. "I never did a dance right before, and I just kind of went crazy. Like flying."

"Consider yourself shot down in flames," said Mr. Brewer. "This isn't Coney Island, and it isn't going to become Coney Island. Now go apologize to your mother."

"Yessir," said Robert, shaken.

"Looked like a damn flamingo playing soccer," said Mr. Brewer. He nodded, pulled in his tongue, closed his teeth with a clack, and stalked away.

Robert apologized to his mother and went straight home.

Robert and I shared a suite, bathroom, sitting room, and two bedrooms, on the third floor of what was known as the Brewer cottage. Robert seemed to be asleep when I got home shortly after midnight.

But at three in the morning I was awakened by soft music from the sitting room, and by the sounds of someone striding around in agitation. I opened my door and surprised Robert in the act of tangoing by himself. In the instant before he saw me, his nostrils were flaring and his eyes were narrowed, the smoldering eyes of a sheik.

He gasped, turned off the phonograph, and collapsed on the couch.

"Keep it up," I said. "You were doing fine."

"I guess nobody's as civilized as he'd like to think," said Robert.

"Lots of nice people tango," I said.

He clenched and unclenched his hands. "Cheap, asinine, grotesque!"

"It isn't supposed to look good," I said. "It's supposed to feel good."

"It isn't done in Pisquontuit," he said.

I shrugged. "What's Pisquontuit?"

"I don't mean to be impolite," he said, "but you couldn't possibly understand."

"I've been around long enough to see the sort of thing they get exercised about around here," I said.

"It's very easy for you to make comments," said Robert. "It's easy to make fun of anything, if you don't have any responsibilities."

"Responsibilities?" I said. "You've got responsibilities? For what?"

Robert looked about himself moodily. "This—all this. Someday I'll be taking all this over, presumably. You, you're free as the air, to come and go as you please and laugh all you like."

"Robert!" I said. "It's just real estate. If it depresses you, why, when you take it over, sell it."

Robert was shocked. "Sell it? My grandfather built this place."

"Fine bricklayer," I said.

"It's a way of life that's rapidly disappearing all over the world," said Robert.

"Farewell," I said.

"If Pisquontuit goes under," said Robert gravely, "if we all abandon ship, who's going to preserve the old values?"

"What old values?" I said. "Being grim about tennis and sailing?"

"Civilization!" he said. "Leadership!"

"What civilization?" I said. "That book your mother

keeps saying she's going to read someday, if it kills her? And who around here leads anything anywhere?"

"My great-grandfather," said Robert, "was lieutenant governor of Rhode Island."

For want of a reply to this thunderclap, I started the phonograph, filling the room with the tango once more.

There was a gentle knock on the door, and I opened it to find Marie, the young and beautiful upstairs maid, standing outside in her bathrobe.

"I heard voices," she said. "I thought maybe there were prowlers." Her shoulders were moving gently in time with the music.

I took her easily in my arms, and we tangoed together into the sitting room. "With every step," I said to her, "we betray our lower-middle-class origins and drive the stake deeper into the heart of civilization."

"Huh?" said Marie, her eyes closed.

I felt a hand on my shoulder. Robert, breathing shallowly and quickly, was cutting in.

"After us the deluge," I said, loading the record changer.

Thus began Robert's secret vice—and Marie's, and mine. Almost every night the ritual was repeated. We would start the phonograph, Marie would come to investigate, and Marie and I would dance, with Robert looking on sullenly. Then Robert would rise painfully from his couch, like an arthritic old man, and take her from me wordlessly. It was the Pisquontuit equivalent of the Black Mass.

In three weeks' time, Robert was an excellent dancer and hopelessly in love with Marie.

"How did it happen?" he said to me. "How *could* it?"

"You are a man and she is a woman," I said.

"We're utterly different," he said.

"Vive la utter difference," I said.

"What'll I do, what'll I do?" he said heartbrokenly.

"Proclaim your love," I said.

"For a maid?" he said incredulously.

"Royalty's all gone or spoken for, Robert," I said. "The descendants of the lieutenant governor of Rhode Island have no choice but to marry commoners. It's like musical chairs."

"You're not very funny," said Robert bitterly.

"Well, you can't marry anybody in Pisquontuit, can you?" I said. "There's been a guard in the woods for three generations, and now all the people inside are at least second cousins. The system carries the seeds of its own destruction, unless it's willing to start mixing in chauffeurs and upstairs maids."

"There's new blood coming in all the time," said Robert.

"He left," I said. "He went back to Beacon Hill."

"Oh? I didn't know that," said Robert. "I don't notice much of anything anymore but Marie." He laid his hand on his chest. "This force," he said, "it just does with you what it wants to do with you, makes you feel what it wants to make you feel."

"Steady, boy, steady," I said, and I went to question Marie rather sharply as to whether she loved Robert or not.

Over the noise of the vacuum cleaner, she gave me coy, equivocal answers. "I feel like I'd kind of created him," she said, "starting with nothing."

"He says you've showed him the savage in himself," I said.

"That's what I mean," she said. "I don't think there *was* any savage to begin with."

"What a pity," I said, "after they've gone to so much

expense keeping the savages out. If you married him, you'd have a very rich savage, you know."

"It's just an incubator baby now," she said wickedly.

"Life is losing all meaning for Robert," I said. "You don't know what you're doing to him. He's stopped caring if he wins or loses at tennis and sailing."

As I spoke of another's love and looked into the wide, blue windows of her soul, a rich, insistent yearning flooded my senses. "He can't even manage a smile anymore when somebody pronounces Pisquontuit the way it's spelled," I murmured, my voice trailing off at the end.

"I'm very sorry, I'm sure," she said bewitchingly.

I lost my head. I seized her by the wrist. "Do you love me?" I whispered hoarsely.

"I might," she said.

"Do you or don't you?"

"It's hard," she said, "for a girl who's been brought up to be friendly and affectionate to tell. Now let an honest girl get about her work."

I told myself that I had never seen such an honest and pretty girl in all my life, and went back to Robert a jealous rival.

"I can't eat, I can't sleep," he said.

"Don't cry on my shoulder," I snapped. "Go talk to your father about it. Let *him* sympathize."

"God no!" he said. "What an idea!"

"Have you ever talked to him about *anything*?" I said.

"Well, for a while there, there was what he called *getting to know the boy,*" said Robert. "He used to set aside Wednesday nights for that, when I was little."

"All right," I said, "you've got a precedent for talking to

him. Recreate the spirit of those days." I wanted him to get off the couch so *I* could lie down and stare at the ceiling.

"Oh, we didn't talk exactly," said Robert. "The butler would come up to my room and set up a motion-picture projector, and then father would come up and run off Mickey Mouse for an hour. We just sat in the dark with the thing grinding away."

"As thick as thieves!" I said. "What brought an end to these emotional binges?"

"A combination of things," said Robert. "The war mostly. He was chief air-raid warden of Pisquontuit, in charge of the siren and all, and it took a lot out of him. And I got the hang of feeding the film through the spools and all myself."

"Kids mature early around here," I said, contemplating a nice dilemma. It was my duty as tutor to make Robert a mature individual. Yet, his immaturity gave me my biggest advantage over him in our rivalry for Marie. After much thought, I devised a plan that promised to make Robert a man and deliver Marie into my arms free and clear.

"Marie," I said, catching her in the hall, "is it Robert or is it me?"

"Shhhhh!" she said. "Keep your voice down. There's a cocktail party downstairs, and sound carries right down the stairway."

"Wouldn't you like to be taken away from all this?" I whispered.

"Why?" she said. "I like the smell of furniture polish, I make more money than my girlfriend at the airplane factory, and I meet a very high class of people."

"I'm asking you to marry me, Marie," I said. "*I'd* never be ashamed of you."

She took a step backward. "Now, what made you say a mean thing like that? Who's ashamed of me, I want to know?"

"Robert," I said. "He loves you, but his shame is bigger than his love."

"He's glad enough to dance with me," she said. "We have a lovely time."

"In private," I said. "Do you think, for all your charms, he'd dance one step with you at the Yacht Club? In a pig's eye."

"He would," she said slowly, "if I wanted him to, if I really wanted him to."

"He'd rather die," I said. "You've heard of closet drinkers? Well, you've got yourself a closet lover."

I left her with this annoying thought, and was gratified to see a challenging look in her eye when she came to dance late that night. She did nothing unusual, however, until Robert cut in. Ordinarily, she transferred from me to Robert without opening her eye or missing a step. This time she stopped, her eyes open wide.

"What is this?" said Robert, dipping lowly and twisting his toes, while she stood as rigid as an iron post. "Something wrong?"

"No," said Marie in a brittle tone. "Why would you think there was something wrong?"

Reassured, Robert started to dip and twist some more, but again failed to budge Marie.

"There *is* something wrong," he said.

"Do you think I'm at all attractive, Robert?" said Marie coolly.

"Attractive?" said Robert. "Attractive? Lord yes! I should say. I'll tell the world."

"As attractive as any girl my age in Pisquontuit?"

"More!" said Robert heartily, starting to dance again, and again getting nowhere. "Much more, much, much more," he said, his movements subsiding.

"And do I have good manners?"

"The best!" said Robert, puzzled. "Absolutely the best, Marie."

"Then why don't you take me to the next Yacht Club dance?" she said.

Robert became as rigid as Marie. "To the Yacht Club?" he said. "To the *Pisquontuit* Yacht Club?"

"That's the one," said Marie.

"What she's asking, Robert," I said helpfully, "is, are you a man or a mouse? Are you going to take her to the Yacht Club dance, or does she go out of your life forever and into the airplane factory?"

"They need a good girl at the airplane factory," said Marie.

"I never saw a better one," I said.

"They're not ashamed of their girls over at the airplane factory," said Marie. "They have picnics and Christmas parties and wedding showers and all kinds of things, and the foremen and the vice presidents and the works manager and the comptroller and all come to the parties and dance with the girls and have a fine time. My girlfriend gets taken out regularly everywhere by the comptroller."

"What's the comptroller?" said Robert, fighting for time.

"I don't know," said Marie, "except he *works* for a living, and he isn't any closet lover."

Robert was stung speechless.

"Man or mouse?" I said, bringing the issue back into focus.

Robert chewed his lip, and at last murmured something we couldn't understand.

"What was that?" said Marie.

"Mouse," said Robert with a sigh. "I said mouse."

"Mouse," said Marie softly.

"Don't say it *that* way," said Robert desolately.

"What other way is there to say mouse?" said Marie. "Good night."

I followed her out into the hall. "Well," I said, "it's been rough on him, but—"

"Marie—" said Robert, appearing in the doorway, wan. "You wouldn't like it. You'd hate it. You'd have a terrible time. Everybody has a terrible time. That's why I said mouse."

"As long as there's music," said Marie, "and the gentleman is proud of his lady, nothing else matters."

"Um," said Robert. He disappeared into the sitting room again, and we heard the couch springs creak.

"You were saying—?" said Marie.

"I was saying it was a rough thing to put him through," I said to Marie, "but it'll do him a world of good in the long run. This will eat into him for years, and there's a good chance he'll become the first rounded human being in Pisquontuit history. A long, slow, profound double take."

"Listen," said Marie. "He's talking to himself. What's he saying?"

"Mouse, mouse, mouse," said Robert. "Mouse, mouse—"

"We've lit the fuse," I whispered, "on a spiritual time bomb."

"Mouse, man, mouse, man—" said Robert.

"Couple of years from now," I said, "*kaboom!*"

"Man!" shouted Robert. "Man, man, man!" He was on his feet, charging out into the hall. "Man!" he said savagely, and he bent Marie over backwards, kissing her hotly. He straightened her up and pulled her after him down the stairs to the second floor.

I followed them down, appalled.

"Robert," gasped Marie. "Please, what's going on?"

Robert pounded on his parents' bedroom door. "You'll see," he said. "I'm going to tell all the world you're mine!"

"Robert—listen," I said, "maybe you ought to cool off first, and—"

"Aha! The great mouse exposer!" he said wildly. He knocked me down. "How was that for a mouse tap?" He pounded on the door again. "Out of the sack in there!"

"I don't want to be yours," said Marie.

"We'll go out West somewhere," said Robert, "and raise Herefords or soybeans."

"I just wanted to go to a Yacht Club dance," piped Marie fearfully.

"Don't you understand?" said Robert. "I'm yours!"

"But I'm his," said Marie, pointing to me. She twisted away from Robert and ran upstairs to her room, with Robert on her heels. She slammed her door and locked it.

I stood slowly, rubbing my bruised cheek.

Mr. and Mrs. Brewer's bedroom door opened suddenly. Mr. Brewer stood in the doorway, glaring at me, his tongue between his teeth. "Well?" he said.

"I uh—up wupp," I said. I smiled glassily. "Never mind, sir."

"Never mind!" he bellowed. "You beat on the door like the world's coming to an end, and now you say never mind. Are you drunk?"

"Nossir."

"Well, neither am I," he said. "My mind's clear as a bell, and you're fired." He slammed the door.

I went back to Robert's and my suite and began packing. Robert was lying on the couch again, staring at the ceiling.

"She's packing, too," he said.

"Oh?"

"I guess you'll be getting married, eh?"

"Looks that way. I'll have to find another job."

"Count your blessings," he said. "Here, but for the grace of God, lie you."

"Calmed down, have you?" I said.

"I'm still through with Pisquontuit," he said.

"I think you're wise," I said.

"I wonder," he said, "if you and Marie would do me a little favor before you leave?"

"Name it."

"I'd kind of like to dance her down the steps." Robert's eyes grew narrow and smoldered again, as they had when I'd surprised him tangoing by himself. "You know," he said, "like Fred Astaire."

"You bet," I said. "I wouldn't miss it for the world."

The volume of the phonograph was turned up high, and all twenty-six rooms of the Brewer cottage pulsed at dawn with the rhythm of the tango.

Robert and Marie, a handsome couple, dipped lowly and twisted their toes as they descended the spiral staircase. I followed with Marie's and my luggage.

Again Mr. Brewer burst from his bedroom, his tongue between his teeth. "Bubs! What does this mean?"

Robert's reply to his father's question, I realize with each job application form I fill out, was unnecessarily heroic. Had we left it unsaid, Mr. Brewer's attitude toward me might have softened in time. But now, when I write his name down as my last employer, I smear it with the ball of my thumb, hoping that prospective employers will take my honest smile as reference enough.

"It means, sir," said Robert, "that you should thank my two friends here for raising your son from the dead."

BOMAR

There were no windows in the Stockholders' Records Section of the Treasurer's Department of the American Forge and Foundry Company. But the soft, sweet music from the loudspeaker on the green wall by the clock, music that increased the section's productivity by 3 percent, kept pace with the seasons, and provided windows of a sort for the staff—Bud Carmody and Lou Sterling, and Nancy Daily.

The loudspeaker was playing spring songs when Carmody and Sterling left the sixty-four-year-old Miss Daily in charge, and went out for morning coffee.

Both were lighthearted, unhaunted by ambition as they sauntered along the factory street to the main gate, outside of which was the Acme Grille. It had been made clear to both of them that they didn't have the priceless stuff of which executives were made. So, unlike so many wide-eyed and hustling men all around them, they were free to dress comfortably and inexpensively, and go out for coffee as often as they pleased.

They also had a field of humor that was closed to those with big futures in the organization. They could make jokes about the American Forge and Foundry Company, its products, its executives, and its stockholders.

Carmody, who was forty-five, was theoretically in charge

of the section, of young Sterling, Miss Daily, and the files. But he was spiritually an anarchist, and never gave orders. He was a tall, thin dreamer, who prided himself on being creative rather than domineering, and his energies went into stuffing the suggestion box, decorating the office for holidays, and collecting limericks, which he kept in a locked file in his desk.

Carmody had been lonely and a little sour, as wave after wave of enterprising young men passed him on the ladder of success. But then the twenty-eight-year-old Sterling, also tall, thin, and dreamy, had joined the section after unappreciated performances in other departments, and life in the section had become vibrant. Carmody and Sterling stimulated each other to new peaks in creativity—and out of the incredibly fruitful union of their talents had come many things, the richest being the myth of Bomar Fessenden III.

There really was a Bomar Fessenden III, and he was a stockholder of the company, but neither Carmody nor Sterling knew anything about him save the number of shares he owned, one hundred, and his home address, 5889 Seaview Terrace, Great Neck, Long Island, New York. But Bomar's splendid name had caught Sterling's fancy. He started talking knowingly about the debauched life Fessenden led with the dividends the section mailed to him, claiming Fessenden as an old friend, a fraternity brother who wrote regularly from fleshpots around the world—Acapulco, Palm Beach, Nice, Capri...Carmody had been charmed by the myth, and had contributed heavily to it.

"Some day!" said Carmody, as they walked through the main gate. "Too bad Bomar Fessenden III isn't here to see it."

"That's one of the many reasons I would never trade

places with Bomar," said Sterling. "Not for all his wealth and comfort and beautiful women. He never gets to see the seasons come and go."

"Cut off from life, that's what Bomar is," said Carmody. "He might as well be dead. When winter comes, what does he do?"

"Bomar runs away from it," said Sterling. "Pathetic. He runs away from everything. I just got a card from him saying he's pulling out of Buenos Aires because of the dampness."

"And all the time, what Bomar is really running away from is himself, the futility of his whole existence," said Carmody, sliding into a booth in the Acme Grille. "But his hollowness still pursues him as certainly as his dividend checks."

"Two crumb-buns and draw two, black," said Sterling to the waitress.

"By golly," said Carmody, "I wonder what old Bomar wouldn't give to be here with us right now, making plain, wholesome talk with plain, wholesome people over plain, wholesome food?"

"Plenty," said Sterling. "I can read that between the lines in his letters. There Bomar is, wherever he is, spending a fortune every day on liquor and beautiful women and expensive playthings, when he could find peace of mind right here with us, for a mere twenty cents."

"That'll be twenty-five apiece," said the waitress.

"Twenty-five!" said Carmody incredulously.

"Coffee's done went up a nickel," said the waitress.

Carmody smiled wanly. "So, for peace of mind, Bomar's got to pay a nickel more." He threw a quarter down on the table. "Damn the expense!"

"This is our day to howl," said Sterling. "Have another crumb-bun."

"Who's Bomar?" said the waitress. "All the time you talk about Bomar."

"Who is Bomar?" said Sterling. He looked at her pityingly. "Bomar? Bomar Fessenden III? Ask anybody!"

"Ask Miss Daily," said Carmody gleefully. "If you really want to get an earful about Bomar, ask Miss Daily. She can't think about anything else."

"Ask her what she thinks of Bomar's latest girlfriend," said Sterling.

Carmody pursed his lips in imitation of Miss Daily, and imitated her voice. "That hussy from the Copacabana!"

Poor Miss Daily, who had been with the company for thirty-nine years, had been assigned to the Stockholders' Records Section only a month before, and believed everything Sterling and Carmody told her about Bomar.

Carmody continued his expert imitation of Miss Daily. "There ought to be laws against somebody like Bomar having all that money, and throwing it around like it was water, with so many people going hungry everywhere," he said indignantly. "If I were a man, I'd go to wherever Bomar was, push his stuck-up old butler aside, and give him the thrashing of his life."

"What's the butler's name?" said Sterling.

"Dawson?" said Carmody. He shook his head. "Redfield? No, no, not Redfield."

"Come on, man—think," said Sterling. "You made him up."

"Perkins? Nope, no. Slipped my mind completely." He smiled and shrugged. "No matter. Miss Daily will remember.

She hasn't forgotten a shred of the whole ugly story that is the life of Bomar Fessenden III."

"Oh," said Carmody vaguely, displaying his leadership, as he and Sterling returned to the basement office after coffee. "They're here. Guess we might as well fall to, huh?"

The office was filled with cardboard boxes containing the spring dividend checks, which the section would compare with the most up-to-date information on the whereabouts of and number of shares held by the company's thousands of owners. Miss Daily, tiny and shy, bright-eyed as a chicken, was sorting through the contents of one of the boxes.

"We don't have to go over them all, Miss Daily," said Carmody. "Just the ones with recent changes of address or changes in holdings."

"I know," said Miss Daily. "I've got the list on my desk."

"Good. Fine," said Carmody. "I see you're already in 'F.' Do you mean to say that in the short time Mr. Sterling and I have been gone, you've gotten that far?"

"I was looking up our fine Mr. Bomar Fessenden III," said Miss Daily grimly.

"Everything square with my old pal?" said Sterling.

Miss Daily was white with resentment. "Yes," she said crisply, "quite. Two hundred and fifty dollars."

"Spit in the ocean," said Sterling. "I doubt if Bomar even knows he owns a piece of this company, it's such a little piece. The big money comes in from Standard Oil, DuPont, General Motors, and all that."

"A hundred shares!" said Miss Daily. "You call that a little piece?"

"Well, that's only worth ten thousand dollars, after all," said Carmody patiently, "take or leave a hundred. The necklace he gave to Carmella down in Buenos Aires cost more than that."

"You mean Juanita," said Miss Daily.

"I beg your pardon," said Carmody. "I meant Juanita."

"Carmella was the bullfighter's daughter in Mexico City," said Miss Daily. "She got the Cadillac."

"Of course," said Sterling to Carmody, reproachfully, "how could you get Carmella and Juanita confused?"

"Stupid of me," said Carmody.

"They're not at all alike," said Miss Daily.

"Well, he's through with Juanita anyway," said Sterling. "He's left Buenos Aires. It got damp."

"Mercy me—damp!" said Miss Daily with bitter sarcasm. "It's more than a body can put up with!"

"What else has Bomar got to say for himself?" said Carmody.

"Oh—he's in Monte Carlo now. Flew up. Got a new girl now. Fifi. Met her while he was playing roulette. He says he dropped five thousand watching her instead of keeping his mind on the game," said Sterling.

Carmody chuckled appreciatively. "What a card, Bomar."

Miss Daily snorted.

"Now, now, Miss Daily, you mustn't get mad at Bomar," said Sterling. "He's just playful and high-spirited is all. We'd all live high, if we could."

"Speak for yourself," said Miss Daily hotly. "It's the wickedest thing I ever heard of. That nasty boy—and here we are, sending him more money, money he won't even notice, so he can throw it away. It isn't Christian. I wish I were already retired, so I wouldn't have to face doing this."

"Grit your teeth, the way Mr. Sterling and I do," said Carmody.

"Bite the bullet, Miss Daily," said Sterling.

Two weeks later, Carmody and his protégé, Sterling, were in the Acme Grille, with Carmody speaking to Sterling sternly for the first time in their relationship.

"Man, you've killed the goose that laid the golden eggs," said Carmody. "You're weak. You succumbed to temptation."

"You're right, you're right," said Sterling miserably. "I can see that now. I over-did. I wasn't myself. Twenty-four-hour flu."

"Overdid!" said Carmody. "You had Bomar charter the *Queen Elizabeth*."

"Madcap Bomar," said Sterling ruefully. "When she doubted it, I tried to turn it into a joke."

"You turned the whole thing into a joke. When she started cross-examining you about everything we'd ever told her about Bomar, you went all to pieces."

"It was a lot of material to keep track of," said Sterling. "What can I say, after I've said I'm sorry? What gets me is how hard it hit her."

"Of course it hit her hard. She's humiliated, and it takes a big piece out of her life. The lonely old soul took to Bomar like a cannibal to a fat Baptist missionary. She loved Bomar, he made her feel so righteous. Now you've taken Bomar from her—and from us, boy."

"I didn't admit we'd made the whole thing up."

"It was plain enough. The only thing that would convince her now would be for Bomar to show up in the flesh."

Sterling stirred his coffee thoughtfully. "Well—is that *utterly* inconceivable?"

"Not utterly," Carmody admitted.

"There—you see?" said Sterling. "It's always darkest before the dawn. Think of what it would mean to Miss Daily to be able to square off Bomar Fessenden III, to his face! In three more months she retires after forty years of service. What a way to wind it up!"

Carmody nodded interestedly, and chewed. "Your crumb-bun taste a little funny?"

"Order a crumb-bun, you get a crumb-bun," said Sterling. "Now, about Bomar: he should be fat and dissipated, short and insolent—"

"With a sports coat down to his knees," said Carmody, "a tie like the flag of Liberia, and gum-soles as thick as fruit-cakes."

Miss Daily was absent from the office when Carmody and Sterling returned after an extensive search for a replica of the Bomar Fessenden III of their imaginations. They'd found their man in a supply room of the Research and Development Laboratory, and bought his services for five dollars. His name was Stanley Broom, and, as Bomar, he was perfect.

"He doesn't have to *act* worthless," said Sterling happily, "he *is* worthless."

"Shh!" said Carmody, and Miss Daily walked in.

She looked terribly upset. "You're making fun of me again," she said.

"Why would we do that?" said Carmody.

"You two made it all up—about Bomar."

"Made it up?" said Sterling incredulously. "My dear Miss Daily, Bomar is going to be in this very office before twenty-four hours have passed. I just received a telegram. He's stopping off here on his way from Monte Carlo to Catalina."

"Please, please," said Miss Daily, "you've done too much already. You don't know what you've done."

"Miss Daily, it most certainly isn't a joke," said Sterling. "He'll be here tomorrow, and you can see him for yourself. Pinch him, even. He's real, all right." He watched her closely, puzzled by the importance she seemed to attach to Bomar. "If Bomar were a joke—what difference would that make?"

"He is real? You promise?" she said.

"You'll see him tomorrow," said Carmody.

"You swear he's done everything you say he's done?" said Miss Daily.

"I made that up about the *Queen Elizabeth,*" said Sterling. "The rest is true?"

"Oh, Bomar's a wild one, Miss Daily," said Carmody.

Unaccountably, Miss Daily seemed vastly relieved. She sank down in her chair, and managed to smile. "It *is* true," she said faintly. "Thank the Lord. If it had all been made up, oh, I—" She shook her head, and left the sentence unfinished.

"If it had all been made up, you what?" said Carmody.

"Never mind, never mind," said Miss Daily absently. "If it's all true, I have no regrets."

"What sort of regrets might you have had?" said Carmody.

"Never you mind, never you mind," she crooned. "So, tomorrow I come face-to-face at last with Master Fessenden. Good!"

★ ★ ★

At the Acme Grille, shortly after eight the next morning, Sterling and Carmody rehearsed Stanley Broom for the drama he was about to enact before Miss Daily in the Stockholders' Records Section.

Broom was dressed flamboyantly, and wore an insolent sneer that seemed to invite all the world to slap his fat face. "This can't take long," he said, "or I'll get canned."

"Fifteen minutes at the outside," said Sterling. "We walk in together, see—and I introduce you to Carmody and Miss Daily casually. You're stopping off to see me, your old college buddy, on your way from Monte Carlo to Catalina. Got it?"

"Check," said Broom. "Listen, she isn't going to take a swat at me or anything, is she?"

"Couldn't hurt a flea," said Sterling. "She isn't even five feet tall, and she weighs under a hundred."

"She could still be *wiry,*" said Broom.

"Naaaah. Now listen, what's the name of your yacht?"

"*The Golden Eagle,* and it's anchored at Miami Beach," said Broom. "I may have the crew bring it around through the canal to the West Coast."

"Who you in love with now?" said Sterling.

"Fifi. I met her at Monte Carlo, and she's going to follow me to Catalina in a few days, at my expense. She's got to shake off a count she was engaged to."

"What have you given her so far?" said Sterling.

"Uh—emerald and a blue mink."

"*Silver—*blue mink," said Carmody. "OK, I'd say we're in pretty good shape. I'll go on back to the office, and make sure Miss Daily is there for Bomar's grand entrance."

★ ★ ★

Miss Daily was pink with excitement as she sat in the office, waiting for Bomar, and her breathing was shallow. She shuffled papers nervously, accomplishing nothing. Her lips moved, but made no sounds.

"Eh?" said Carmody. "What was that, Miss Daily?"

"I wasn't speaking to you," said Miss Daily politely. "I was getting things straight in my mind."

"That's the stuff. Really going to give him a piece of your mind, eh?"

"Bomar, you old dog!" said Sterling in the hall, just outside the office door. "You're a sight for sore eyes!"

Miss Daily snapped the point on her pencil in a nervous spasm, and Sterling and Broom walked in.

Broom puffed on a preposterously big and foul cigar, and took in the office in a withering glance. "Steerage," he said. "How can you bear it? I've been in here ten seconds, and it's driving me mad."

Miss Daily was white and trembling, but as yet speechless, fascinated.

"Do you mean to say that people really live like this?" said Broom.

"They do," said Miss Daily in a small voice, "if they're not too lazy or spoiled to help do the world's work."

"I suppose that's an insult," said Broom, "but not a very good one, since most of the world's work isn't worth doing. Besides, someone has to give his full attention to the finer things in life, or there'd be no civilization."

"Fifi?" said Miss Daily. "Carmella? Juanita? Amber? Collette?"

"You *do* keep track of the stockholders down here, don't you?" said Broom.

"I've told her a little about you, Bomar," said Sterling.

"I just found out I owned stock in this thing the other day," said Broom, "but apparently Miss Pry here has known about me all along."

"My name is Miss Daily," said Miss Daily, "Miss Nancy Daily."

"Well, get off your high horse, Miss Daily," said Broom. "I haven't done anything to hurt the lower classes."

"You're what's wrong with the world," said Miss Daily bravely, her back straight, her lips trembling. "And now that I've met you, and seen that you're worse than I ever imagined you to be, I'm not sorry at all I did what I did. I'm glad."

"Huh?" said Broom, his stride broken. He looked questioningly at Carmody and Sterling, who in turn looked uneasily at Miss Daily.

"Your last dividend check, Mr. Fessenden," said Miss Daily. "I signed your name on the back, and sent it to the Red Cross."

Carmody and Sterling exchanged glances full of horror.

"I did it single-handed," said Miss Daily. "Mr. Carmody and Mr. Sterling know nothing about it. It was only two hundred and fifty dollars, so you won't miss it—and it's in better hands than if you'd given it to that shameless Fifi."

"Um," said Broom, completely at sea.

"Well, aren't you going to call the police?" said Miss Daily. "I'm quite ready to go, if it would satisfy you to prefer charges."

"Well, I—uh—" mumbled Broom. He got no help with his lines from Carmody and Sterling, who were thunderstruck. "Easy come, easy go," he said at last. "Isn't that right, Sterling?"

Sterling roused himself. "Root of all evil," he said desolately.

Broom tried to think of something more to say, but failed.

"Well, off to Monte Carlo," he said. "Ta ta."

"Catalina," said Miss Daily. "You just came from Monte Carlo."

"Catalina," said Broom.

"Don't you feel much better, Mr. Fessenden?" said Miss Daily. "Doesn't it make you happy to have done something unselfish for a change?"

"Yup," said Broom, nodding gravely, and he left.

"He took it like a little gentleman," said Miss Daily to Carmody and Sterling.

"Oh, it's easy enough for Bomar," said Carmody bleakly, looking with loathing at Sterling, the Frankenstein who'd invented the monster. A new check would have to be made out to the real Bomar, and Carmody could think of no graceful way of explaining to the powers upstairs what had happened to the old one. Carmody, Sterling, and Miss Daily were through at American Forge and Foundry. The monster had turned on them savagely, and destroyed all three.

"I think Mr. Fessenden learned something today," said Miss Daily.

Carmody laid his hand on Miss Daily's shoulder. "Miss Daily, there's something you'd better know," he said grimly. "We're in quite a mess, Miss Daily. That was not Bomar Fessenden III who was just in here, and nothing we've said about Bomar is true."

"A joke," said Sterling bitterly.

"Well, I must say it wasn't a very funny joke," said Miss Daily. "It was quite unkind, treating me like an idiot."

"No—it wasn't funny at all, the way it turned out," said Carmody.

"Not as funny as my joke about forging the check," said Miss Daily.

"That was a joke?" said Carmody.

"Certainly," said Miss Daily sweetly. "Aren't you going to smile, Mr. Carmody? Not even a little snicker, Mr. Sterling? Heavens—it really *is* time to retire. No one seems to be able to laugh at himself anymore."

THE MAN WITHOUT
NO KIDDLEYS

"I done ate twelve barium meals in my time," said Noel Sweeny. Sweeny had never felt really well, and now, on top of everything else, he was ninety-four years old. "Twelve times Sweeny's stomach's been x-rayed. Reckon that's some kind of a world's record."

Sweeny was on a bench by a shuffleboard court in Tampa, Florida. He was talking to another old man, a stranger who shared the bench with him.

The stranger had plainly just begun a new way of life in Florida. He wore black shoes, black silk socks, and the trousers of a blue serge business suit. His sports shirt and fighter-pilot cap were crackling, glossy new. A price tag was still stapled to the hem of his shirt.

"Um," said the stranger to Sweeny, without looking at him. The stranger was reading the *Sonnets* of William Shake-speare.

"From fairest creatures we desire increase,/That thereby beauty's rose might never die," Shakespeare said to the stranger.

"How many times *you* had *your* stomach x-rayed?" Sweeny said to the stranger.

"Um," said the stranger.

"Music to hear, why hear'st thou music sadly?" said Shake-speare. *"Sweets with sweets war not, joy delights in joy."*

"I ain't got no spleen," said Sweeny. "You believe it?"

The stranger did not respond.

Considerately, Sweeny moved closer to the stranger and yelled in his ear. "Sweeny ain't had no spleen since nineteen hundred and forty-three," he yelled.

The stranger dropped his book and almost fell off the bench. He cowered and covered his ringing ears. "I'm not deaf," he said, full of pain.

Firmly, Sweeny pulled one of the stranger's hands away from his ear. "I didn't think you *heard* me," he said.

"I heard you," said the stranger, trembling. "I heard it all: barium meals, gallstones, tired blood, and sleepy liver bile. I heard every word of what Dr. Sternweiss said about your gastric sphincter. Has Dr. Sternweiss thought of setting it to music?"

Sweeny picked up the book of sonnets and put it on the opposite end of the bench, out of the stranger's reach. "You want to make that little bet now?" he said.

"What bet?" said the stranger, very pale.

"See?" said Sweeny, beaming bleakly. "I was right—you *wasn't* listening! A while back I asked you did you want to bet how many kiddleys we got between us, and you said, 'Um.'"

"How many *kiddies*?" said the stranger. His expression softened—was cautiously interested! He liked children, and thought the bet was a charming one. "Do we count children and grandchildren—or how do we do it?" he said.

"Not *kiddies*," said Sweeny. "Kiddleys."

"Kiddleys?" said the stranger, puzzled.

Sweeny put his hands over the spots where his kidneys were—or had been. "Kiddleys," he said. His error was one of such long standing that it had the ring of authority.

The stranger was disappointed and annoyed. "If you don't mind, I don't want to think about kidneys," he said. "Please—could I have my book back?"

"After we bet," said Sweeny craftily.

The stranger sighed. "Would a dime be enough?" he said.

"Fine," said Sweeny. "The money's just to make it a little more interesting."

"Oh," said the stranger emptily.

Sweeny studied him for a long time. "I guess we got three kiddleys between us," he said at last. "How many you guess?"

"I guess none," said the stranger.

"None?" said Sweeny, amazed. "If there wasn't *no* kiddleys between us, we'd both be dead. A man can't live without *no* kiddleys. You got to guess two, three, or four."

"I have lived happily since eighteen hundred and eighty-four without a *trace* of a kiddley," said the stranger. "I gather that you *do* have a kiddley, which makes one kiddley between us. Therefore the bet ends in a tie, with no money changing hands. Now, please, sir—would you kindly hand me my book?"

Sweeny held up his hands, barring all access to the book. "How dumb you think I am?" he said challengingly.

"I've gone as deeply as I care to into that subject," said the stranger. "Please, sir—the book."

"If you ain't got no kiddleys," said Sweeny, "just tell me one thing."

The stranger rolled his eyes. "Can't we change the subject?" he said. "I used to have a garden up north. I'd like to start a little vegetable garden down here. Do people have little vegetable gardens down here? Do you have a garden?"

Sweeny would not be deflected. He stabbed the stranger

in the chest with his finger. "How you eliminate waste?" he said.

The stranger hung his head. He stroked his face in helpless exasperation. He made soft raspberry sounds. He straightened up to smile benignly at a pretty girl jiggling by. "Look at those trim ankles, Mr. Sweeny—those rosy heels," he said. "Oh to be young—or to *pretend* to be young, dreaming here in the sunshine." He closed his eyes, dreamed.

"I guessed right, didn't I?" said Sweeny.

"Um," said the stranger.

"We only got three kiddleys between us, and now you're trying to change the subject and mix me up so's you can get out of paying off," said Sweeny. "Well—I don't mix up so easy."

The stranger dug a dime from his pocket without opening his eyes. He held it out to Sweeny.

Sweeny did not take it. "I ain't gonna take it till I know for sure I'm entitled to it," he said. "I gave you my word of honor I don't got but one kiddley. Now you got to give me your word of honor how many kiddleys you got."

The stranger bared his teeth dangerously in the sunshine. "I swear by all that's holy," he said tautly. "I have no kiddleys."

"What happened to 'em?" said Sweeny. "Bright's disease?"

"Sweeny's disease," said the stranger.

"Same name as me?" said Sweeny, surprised.

"Same name as you," said the stranger. "And a *horrible* disease it is."

"What's it like?" said Sweeny.

"Anybody who suffers from Sweeny's disease," snarled the

stranger, "mocks beauty, Mr. *Sweeny;* invades privacy, Mr. *Sweeny;* disturbs the peace, Mr. *Sweeny;* shatters dreams, Mr. *Sweeny;* and drives all thoughts of love, Mr. *Sweeny,* away!"

The stranger stood. He put his face inches from Sweeny's. "Anyone suffering from Sweeny's disease, sir, makes life of the spirit impossible by reminding all around him that men are nothing but buckets of guts!"

The stranger made barking sounds of frantic indignation. He snatched up his book of sonnets, strode to another bench twenty feet away, and sat down with his back to Sweeny. He snuffled and snorted and turned the pages roughly.

"The forward violet thus did I chide:" Shakespeare said to him, *"Sweet thief, whence didst thou steal thy sweet that smells,/If not from my love's breath?"* The excitement of battle began to subside in the stranger.

"The purple pride/Which on thy soft cheek for complexion dwells/In my love's veins thou hast too grossly dy'd," said Shakespeare, still chiding the violet.

The stranger tried to smile in pure, timeless, placeless pleasure. The smile, however, would not come. The almighty here-and-now was making itself too strongly felt.

The stranger had come to Tampa for only one reason— that his old bones had betrayed him. No matter how much his home in the North meant to him, no matter how little Florida meant to him—his old bones had cried out that they couldn't stand another winter in the snow and cold.

He had thought of himself, as he accompanied his old bones down South, as a silent, harmless cloud of contemplation.

He found himself instead, only hours after his arrival in

Tampa, the author of a savage attack on another old man. The back that he'd turned to Sweeny saw far more than his eyes. His eyes had gone out of focus. His book was a blur.

His back sensed keenly that Sweeny, a kind and lonely man of simpleminded pleasures, was all but destroyed. Sweeny, who'd wanted to go on living, even if he had only half a stomach and one kidney, Sweeny, whose enthusiasm for life hadn't diminished an iota after he'd lost his spleen in nineteen hundred and forty-three—now Sweeny didn't want to live anymore. Sweeny didn't want to live anymore, because an old man he'd tried to befriend had been so savage and mean.

It was a hideous discovery for the stranger to make—that a man at the end of his days was as capable of inflicting pain as the rawest, loudest youth. With so little time left, the stranger had added one more item to his long, long list of regrets.

And he ransacked his mind for elaborate lies that would make Sweeny want to live again. He settled, finally, on an abject, manly, straightforward apology as the only thing to do.

He went to Sweeny, held out his hand. "Mr. Sweeny," he said, "I want to tell you how sorry I am that I lost my temper. There was no excuse for it. I'm a tired old fool, and my temper's short. But the last thing in my heart I want to do is hurt you."

He waited for some fire to return to Sweeny's eyes. But not even the faintest spark returned.

Sweeny sighed listlessly. "Never mind," he said. He didn't take the stranger's hand. Plainly, he wanted the stranger to go away again.

The stranger kept his hand extended, prayed to God for

the right thing to say. He himself would lose the will to live if he abandoned Sweeny like this.

His prayer was answered. He became radiant even before he spoke, he was so sure his words were going to be the right ones. One regret, at least, was going to be wiped off the slate.

The stranger raised his proferred hand to a position of solemn oath. "Mr. Sweeny," he said, "I give you my solemn word of honor that I have two kiddleys. If you have one kiddley, that makes three kiddleys between us."

He handed Sweeny a dime. "So you win, Mr. Sweeny."

Sweeny was restored to health instantly. He jumped up, shook the stranger's hand. "I knowed you was a two-kiddley man by looking at you," he said. "You couldn't be nothing *but* a two-kiddley man."

"I just don't know what got into me to pretend I was ever anything else," said the stranger.

"Well," said Sweeny cheerfully, "nobody likes to lose." He looked at the dime one last time before pocketing it. "Anyways—you got a lesson cheap. Don't never bet nobody down here at his own game." He nudged the stranger, winked confidingly. "What's your game?"

"My game?" said the stranger. He thought awhile, amiably. "Shakespeare, I suppose."

"Now you see," said Sweeny, "if you was to come up to me and make me a little bet about Shakespeare—" Sweeny shook his head craftily. "I just wouldn't bet you. I wouldn't even listen."

Sweeny nodded and walked away.

MR. Z

George was the son of a country minister and the grandson of a country minister. He was in the Korean War. When that was over, he decided to become a minister, too.

He was an innocent. He wanted to help people in trouble. So he went to the University of Chicago. He didn't study just theology. He studied sociology and psychology and anthropology, too. He went to school the year around, and, during one summer session, there was a course offered in criminology.

George didn't know anything about criminals, so he took it.

And he was told to go to the county jail to interview a prisoner named Gloria St. Pierre Gratz. She was the wife of Bernard Gratz, who was said to be a killer for hire and a thief. Ironically, Gratz remained at large and unhunted, since nothing could be proved against him. His wife was in jail for possessing stolen goods, goods almost certainly stolen by him. She had not implicated him—neither had she given a reasonable account of where else the diamonds and fur coats might have come from. She was serving a year and a day. Her sentence was just about up when George went to see her. George was interviewing her not simply because of her criminality, but because she had an astoundingly high I.Q. She told George that she preferred to be addressed by her maiden name, the name she had used during her days as an exotic dancer. "I never learned how to answer to the name of Mrs. Gratz," she said. "That's nothing against Bernie," she said. "I just never learned." So George called her Miss St. Pierre.

He talked to Miss St. Pierre through a screen at the jail. It was the first jail George had ever been in. He had written down the bare bones of her biography in a loose-leaf notebook. Now he was double-checking the information.

"Let's see—" he said to her, "you left high school in the middle of your junior year, and you changed your name from Francine Pefko to Gloria St. Pierre. You stopped seeing Mr. F, and you became a carhop outside of Gary. And it was there that you met Mr. G?"

"Arny Pappas," she said.

"Right—" said George, "Arny Pappas—Mr. G. Is *carhop* one word or two?"

"Two words, one word—" she said, "who ever wrote it down before?" She was a tiny girl—a trinket brunette, very pretty, very pale, and hard as nails. She was bored stiff with George and his questions. She yawned a lot, not bothering to cover her velvet mouth. And her responses were bewilderingly derisive. "A smart college kid like you ought to be able to make *ten* words out of it," she said.

Gamely, George went on trying to sound professional and brisk. "Well now," he said, "was there some reason for your discontinuing your education in your junior year?"

"My father was a drunk," she said. "My stepmother clawed. I was already grown up. I already looked twenty-one. I could make all the money I wanted. Arny Pappas gave me a yellow Buick convertible all my own. Honey—" she said, "what did I want with algebra and *Ivanhoe?*"

"Um," said George. "And then Mr. H came along, and he and Mr. G got into a fistfight over you?"

"Knives," she said. "It was knives. Stan Carbo—that was his name. Why call him Mr. H?"

"To protect him—" said George, "to keep this all confidential—to protect anybody you might want to tell me about."

She laughed. She stuck the tip of a finger through the screen, and she wiggled it at George. "You?" she said. "You're going to protect Stan Carbo? I wish you could see him. I wish *he* could see *you.*"

"Well," said George lamely, "maybe someday we'll meet."

"He's dead," she said. She didn't sound sorry. She didn't even sound interested.

"That's too bad," said George.

"You're the first person who ever said so," she said.

"In any event," said George, looking at his notes, "while he was still among the living, Mr. H offered you a job as an exotic dancer in his nightclub in East Chicago—and you accepted."

Gloria laughed again. "Honest to God, honey—" she said, "you should see your face. It's bright red! You know that? Your mouth looks like you've been sucking lemons!" She shook her head. "Rollo—" she said, "tell me again what you think you're doing here."

George had been over the question several times before. He went over it again. "As I told you," he said patiently, "I'm a student of sociology, which is the science of human society." There wasn't any point in telling her that the course was actually criminology. That might be offensive. There didn't seem to be much point in telling her anything, for that matter.

"They made a science out of people?" she said. "What a crazy science that must be."

"It's still very much in its infancy," said George.

"Like you," she said. "How old are you, baby?"

"Twenty-one," said George stiffly.

"Think of that!" she said. "Twenty-one! What is it like to be that old? I won't be twenty-one until next March." She sat back. "You know," she said, "every so often I meet somebody like you, and I realize it's possible for some people to grow up in this country without ever seeing anything, without ever having anything happen to them."

"I was in Korea for a year and a half," said George. "I think I've had a little something happen to me."

"I tell you what," she said, "I'll write a book about your great adventures, and you can write one about mine." And then, to George's dismay, she took a pencil stub and an empty pack of cigarettes from her pocket. She tore the pack apart, flattened it out to make a sheet of paper. "All righty—" she said, "here we go, Rollo. We'll call this *The Thrilling Life Story of Mr. Z*—to protect you. You were born on a farm, were you, Mr. Z?"

"Please—" said George, who really had been born on a farm.

"I answered your questions," she said. "You answer mine." She frowned. "Your present address, Mr. Z?" she said.

George shrugged, told her his address. He was living over the garage of the dean of the Divinity School.

"Occupation?" she said. "*Student*. One word or two?"

"Two," said George.

"*Stew dent*," she said, and she wrote it down. "Now, I'm going to have to investigate your love life, Mr. Z. That's actually kind of the main part of your science, even though it *is* in its infancy. I want you to tell me about all the hearts you've broken during this wild, wild life of yours. Let's start with Miss A."

George closed his notebook. He gave her a bleak smile. "Thanks for your time, Miss St. Pierre," he said. "It was good of you to talk to me." He stood.

She gave him a blinding smile. "Oh, *please* sit down," she said. "I haven't been nice at all—and here you've been so nice to me, no matter what awful things I say. Please—please sit down, and I'll answer any question you ask. Any question. Ask me a real hard one, and I'll do my best. Isn't there one really *big* question?"

George was fool enough to relax some, to sit down again. He did have one big question. He had no more dignity, no more anything to lose, so he asked it—asked it flat out. "You've got a very high I.Q., Miss Pierre. Why is it that somebody as smart as you are should live the way you do?"

"Who says I'm smart?" she said.

"You've been tested," said George. "Your I.Q. is higher than that of the average physician."

"The average physician," she said, "couldn't find his own behind with both hands."

"That's not quite true—" said George.

"Doctors make me sick," she said. And now she turned really nasty, now that she had George relaxed for a full blast of malevolence. "But college kids make me sicker," she said.

"Get out of here," she said. "You're the most boring goon I ever met!" She made a limp, disgusted motion with her hand. "Beat it, Rollo," she said. "Tell teacher I'm the way I am because I *like* the way I am. Maybe they'll make you a professor of people like me."

Out in the anteroom of the jail, a little, dark, vicious young man came up to George. He looked at George as though he wanted to kill him. He had a voice like a grackle. He was Bernard Gratz, the lady's husband.

"You been in there with Gloria St. Pierre?" said Gratz.

"That's right," said George politely.

"Where you from?" he said. "What you want with her?" he said. "Who ast you to come?" he said.

George had a letter of introduction from the professor who was giving the course in criminology. He handed it to Gratz.

Gratz wadded it up and handed it back. "That don't cut no ice with me," he said. "She ain't supposed to talk to nobody but her lawyer or me. She knows that."

"It was purely voluntary on her part," said George. "Nobody made her talk to me."

Gratz took hold of George's notebook. "Come on—lemme see," he said. "What you got in the book?"

George pulled the book away. It not only had his notes on Gloria in it. It contained notes for all of his courses.

Gratz made another grab for the notebook, got it. He tore out all the pages, threw them up in the air.

George did a very un-Christian thing. He knocked the little man cold—laid him right out.

He revived Gratz enough to get Gratz's promise that he

was going to kill George slowly. And then George gathered up his papers and went home.

Two weeks went by without much of anything's happening. George wasn't worried about being killed. He didn't think Gratz had any way of finding him in his room over the garage of the dean of the Divinity School. George had trouble believing that the adventure in the jail had even happened.

There was a picture in the paper one day, showing Gloria St. Pierre leaving the jail with Gratz. George didn't believe either one was real.

And then, one night, he was reading *The Encyclopedia of Criminology*. He was looking for clues that would help him to understand the life Gloria St. Pierre had chosen to lead. The *Encyclopedia,* all-inclusive as it tried to be, said not one word about why such a beautiful, intelligent girl should have thrown her life away on such ugly, greedy, cruel men.

There was a knock on the door.

George opened the door, found two unfamiliar young men standing outside. One of them said George's name politely, read it and his address from a piece of paper torn from a pack of cigarettes. It was the piece of paper on which Gloria St. Pierre had started to write George's biography, *The Thrilling Life Story of Mr. Z.*

George recognized it a split second before the two men started beating the stuffing out of him. They called him "Professor" every time they hit him. They didn't seem mad at all.

But they knew their business. George went to the hospital with four broken ribs, two broken ankles, a split ear, a closed eye, and a headful of orioles.

★ ★ ★

The next morning, George sat in his hospital bed and tried to write his parents a letter. *"Dear Mother and Father:"* he wrote, *"I'm in the hospital, but you mustn't worry."*

He was wondering what to say beyond that, when a platinum blonde with eyelashes like buggy whips came in. She carried a potted plant and a copy of *True Detective*.

She smelled like a gangster funeral.

She was Gloria St. Pierre, but George had no way of recognizing her. Bernard Baruch could have hidden behind a disguise like that. She came bearing gifts all right, but no pity seemed to go with them. George's wounds interested her, but the interest was clinical. She was obviously used to seeing people bashed up, and she gave George low grades as a spectacle.

"You got off easy," she said. She assumed George knew who she was.

"I'm not dead," said George. "That's true."

She nodded. "That's smart," she said. "That's smarter than I thought you'd be. You could have been dead very easily. I'm surprised you're not dead."

"May I ask a question?" said George.

"I'd think you'd be through asking questions," she said. And George finally recognized her voice.

He lay back and closed his one good eye.

"I brought you a plant and a magazine," she said.

"Thanks," he said. He wished she would go away. He had nothing to say to her. She was so wild and unfamiliar that George couldn't even think about her.

"If you want some other plant or some other magazine," she said, "say so."

"Just fine," said George. A whanging headache was coming on.

"I thought of getting you something to eat," she said. "But they said you were on the serious list, so I thought maybe you better not eat."

George opened his eye. This was the first he'd heard of his being on the serious list. "Serious list?" he said.

"They wouldn't have let me in if I hadn't said I was your sister," she said. "I think it's some kind of mistake. You don't look serious to me."

George sighed—or meant to sigh. It came out a groan. And, through the whanging and purple flashes of his headache, he said, "They should have you make up the list."

"I suppose you blame me for all this," she said. "I suppose that's how your mind works."

"It isn't working," said George.

"I'm here just because I feel sorry for you," she said. "I don't owe you any apology at all. You asked for this. I hope you learned something," she said. "Everything there is to learn isn't printed in books."

"I know that now," said George. "Thanks for coming, and thanks for the presents, Miss St. Pierre. I think I'd better take a nap now." George pretended to go to sleep, but Gloria St. Pierre didn't go away. George could feel her and smell her very close by.

"I left him," she said. "You hear me?"

George went on pretending to sleep.

"After I heard what he had done to you, I left him," she said.

George went on pretending to sleep. After a while Gloria St. Pierre went away.

★   ★   ★

And, after a while, George really did go to sleep. Sleeping in an overheated room with his head out of order, George dreamed of Gloria St. Pierre.

When he woke up, the hospital room seemed part of the dream, too. Trying to find out what was real and what was a dream, George examined the objects on his bedside table. Among these things were the plant and the magazine Gloria had brought him.

The cover on the magazine could very well have been a part of the dream George had been having, so he pushed that aside. For utterly sane reading, he chose the tag wired to the stem of the plant. And the tag started out sanely enough. *"Clementine Hitchcock Double-Blooming Geranium,"* it said.

But after that the tag went crazy. *"Warning! This is a fully patented plant!"* it said. *"Asexual reproduction is strictly forbidden by law!"*

George thanked God when the perfect image of reality, a fat policeman, clumped in. He wanted George to tell him about the beating.

George told the lugubrious tale from the beginning, and realized, as he told it, that he didn't intend to press charges. There was a crude fairness in what had happened. He had, after all, started things off by slugging a known gangster much smaller than himself. Moreover, George's brains had taken such a scrambling that he remembered almost nothing about the men who had done the actual beating.

The policeman didn't try to argue George into pressing charges. He was glad to be saved some work. There was one thing about George's tale that interested him, though. "You say you know this Gloria St. Pierre?" he said.

"I've just told you," said George.

"She's only two doors down," said the policeman.

"What?" said George.

"Sure," said the policeman. "She got beat up, too—in the park right across the street from the hospital."

"How badly hurt is she?" said George.

"She's on the serious list," said the policeman. "About the same deal as you—a couple of ankles broken, a couple of ribs, two big shiners. You still got all your teeth?"

"Yes," said George.

"Well," said the policeman, "she lost her upper front ones."

"Who did it?" said George.

"Her husband," said the policeman. "Gratz."

"You've got him?" said George.

"In the morgue," said the policeman. "A detective caught him working her over. Gratz ran. The detective shot him when he wouldn't stop. So the lady's a widow now."

George's ankles were set and put in casts after lunch that day. He was given a wheelchair and crutches.

It took him a while to get nerve enough to go calling on the widow Gratz.

At last, he rolled himself into her room and up to her bedside.

Gloria was reading a copy of the *Ladies' Home Journal.* When George rolled in, she covered the lower part of her face with the magazine. She covered it too late. George had already seen how fat-lipped and snaggletoothed she was.

Both eyes were black and blue. Her hair was immaculately groomed, however. And she wore earrings—big, barbarous hoops.

"I—I'm sorry," said George.

She didn't answer. She stared at him.

"You came to see me—tried to cheer me up," he said. "Maybe I can cheer you up."

She shook her head.

"Can't you talk?" said George.

She shook her head. And then tears ran down her cheeks.

"Oh my—my," said George, full of pity.

"Pleath—go way," she said. "Don't look at me—pleath! I'm tho damn ugly. Go way."

"You don't look so bad," said George earnestly. "Really."

"He thpoiled my lookth!" she said. The tears got worse.

"He thpoiled my lookth, tho no other man would ever want me!"

"Oh now—" said George gently, "as soon as the swelling goes down, you'll be beautiful again."

"I'll have falth teeth," she said. "I'm not even twenty-one, and I'll have falth teeth. I'll look like thomething out of the bottom of a garbath can. I'm going to become a nun."

"A what?" said George.

"A nun," she said. "All men are pigth. My huthband wath a pig. My father wath a pig. You're a pig. All men are pigth. Go way."

George sighed, and he went away.

George snoozed before supper, dreamed about Gloria again. When he woke up, he found Gloria St. Pierre in a wheelchair next to his bed, watching him.

She was solemn. She had left her big earrings in her room. And she was doing nothing to cover her bunged-up face. She exposed it bravely, almost proudly, for all to see.

"Hello," she said.

"Hello," said George.

"Why didn't you tell me you were a minithter?" she said.

"I'm not one," said George.

"You're thtudying to be one," she said.

"How do you know that?" said George.

"It'th in the newthpaper," she said. She had the paper with her. She read the headline out loud: "DIVINITY THTUDENT, GUN MOLL, HOTHPITALITHED BY THUGTH."

"Oh boy," murmured George, thinking of the effect of the headline on his landlord, the dean of the Divinity School, and on his own parents in a white clapboard house in the Wabash Valley, not far away.

"Why didn't you tell me what you were?" said Gloria. "If I'd know what you were, I never would have thaid the thingth I thaid."

"Why not?" said George.

"You're the only kind of man who ithn't a pig," she said. "I thought you were jutht thome college kid who wath a pig like everybody elth, only you jutht didn't have the nerve to act like a pig."

"Um," said George.

"If you're a minithter—or thtudying to be one, anyway—" she said, "how come you don't bawl me out?"

"For what?" said George.

"For all the evil thingth I do," she said. She didn't seem to be fooling. She knew she was bad, and she felt strongly that George's duty was to scare her.

"Well—until I get a pulpit of my own—" said George.

"What do you need a pulpit for?" she said. "Don't you believe what you believe? Tho why you need a pulpit?" She rolled her wheelchair closer. "Tell me I'll go to hell, if I don't change," she said.

George managed a humble smile. "I'm not sure you will," he said.

She backed off from George. "You're jutht like my father," she said contemptuously. "He'd forgive and forgive and forgive me—only it wathn't forgiving at all. He jutht didn't care."

Gloria shook her head. "Boy—" she said, "what a lothy mitherable minithter *you're* going to be! You don't believe anything! I pity you."

And she left.

George had another dream about Gloria St. Pierre that night—Gloria with the lisp this time, Gloria with the teeth missing and the ankles in casts. It was the wildest dream yet. He was able to think of the dream with a certain wry humor. It didn't embarrass him to have a body as well as a mind and a soul. He didn't blame his body for wanting Gloria St. Pierre. It was a perfectly natural thing for a body to do.

When George went calling on her after breakfast, he imagined that his mind and soul weren't involved in the least.

"Good morning," she said to him. Many swellings had gone down. Her looks were improved—and she had a question all ready for him. This was it:

"If I wath to become a houthwife with many children, and the children were good," she said to George, "would you rejoith?"

"Of course," said George.

"That'th what I dreamed latht night," she said. "I wath married to you, and we had bookth and children all over the houth." She didn't seem to admire the dream much—nor had it done anything to improve her opinion of George.

"Well—" said George, "I—I'm very flattered that you should dream of me."

"Don't be," she said. "I have crathy dreamth all the time. Anyway, the dream latht night wath more about falth teeth than it wath about you."

"False teeth?" said George.

"I had great big falth teeth," she said. "Every time I tried to thay anything to you or the children, the falth teeth would fall out."

"I'm sure false teeth can be made to fit better than that," said George.

"Could you love thomebody with falth teeth?" she said.

"Certainly," said George.

"When I athk you if you could love thomebody with falth teeth," she said, "I hope you don't think I'm athking you if you could love me. That itn't what I'm athking."

"Um," said George.

"If we got married," she said, "it wouldn't latht. You wouldn't get mad enough at me if I wath bad."

There was a silence—a long one in which George finally came to understand her somewhat. She treated herself as worthless because no one had ever loved her enough to care if she was good or bad.

Since there was no one else to do it, she punished herself.

George came to understand, too, that he would be worthless as a minister as long as he didn't get angry about what such people did to themselves. Blandness, shyness, forgiveness would not do.

She was begging him to care enough to get mad.

The world was begging him to care enough to get mad.

"Married or not," he said, "if you continue to treat yourself like garbage and God's sweet earth like a city dump, I hope with all my heart that you roast in hell."

Gloria St. Pierre's pleasure was luminous—profound.

George had never given that much pleasure to a woman or to himself before. And, in his innocence, he supposed that the next step had to be marriage.

He asked her to marry him. She accepted. It was a good marriage. It was the end of innocence for them both.

$10,000 A YEAR, EASY

"So you're finally moving, eh?" said Gino Donnini. He was a small, fierce-looking man, who had once been a brilliant operatic tenor. His brilliance was gone now, and, in his sixties, he gave voice lessons in order to pay for his cluttered apartment under mine, a little food and wine, and expensive cigars. "One by one my young friends are going. How will I stay young now?"

"I'd think you'd be glad to get somebody upstairs who wasn't tone-deaf."

"Aaaaaah—you make fine music inside. What's that book there?"

"I was just cleaning out our storage locker, Maestro, and found my old high-school annual." I opened the book to the checkerboard of faces and brief biographies that was the section devoted to the hundred and fifty seniors that year. "See how I've failed? They predicted I'd be a great novelist someday, and here I go to work for the telephone company as a maintenance engineer."

"Aha," said Gino, examining the book, "what great expectations these American children have." He had been an American for forty years, but still regarded himself as a puzzled outsider. "This fat little boy was going to be a millionaire, and this girl the first woman Speaker of the House."

"Now he runs a grocery, and she's his wife."

"Lo! how the mighty are fallen. And here's Nicky! I keep forgetting you two were classmates."

Nicky Marino had come to study voice with Gino, an old friend of his father, after the war, and he'd found an apartment for me in the same building when I'd decided to get an engineering degree under the G.I. Bill. "Well," I said, "the prediction for Nicky has held up beautifully."

"A great tenor," read Gino, "like his father."

"Or like you, Maestro."

Gino shook his head. "He was better. You can't imagine. I could play you records, and as bad as recording was in those days, Nicky's father's voice comes through more thrilling than anything you'll hear today. Generations can go by without knowing a miracle like that voice. And then he had to die at twenty-nine."

"Thank God he left a son."

In the small town in which Nicky and I'd grown up, everyone knew whose son Nicky was—and no one doubted that he'd make our town famous as soon as he was full grown. No civic occasion was complete without his singing whatever was appropriate. His mother, herself an unmusical businesswoman, spent most of her money on voice and language lessons for Nicky, recreating in him the image of her lost husband.

"Yes," said Gino, "thank God he left a son. Will you have a farewell drink with me, or is it too soon after breakfast?"

"This isn't quite farewell. We don't move for two more days. I'll take a rain check on the drink, thanks. Now I've got to return some books to Nicky."

★   ★   ★

Nicky Marino was in the shower, singing with the volume of a steam calliope when I arrived. I sat down in the one-room apartment to wait.

The walls were covered with photographs of his father, and with old posters headed by his father's name. On the table, beside a pot of coffee, a cracked cup in a cigarette-filled saucer, and a metronome, was a scrapbook, its edges festooned with the ragged ends of newspaper clippings about his father.

On the floor were his garish pajamas and the morning mail—a letter with a check and a snapshot clipped to it. It was from his mother, who never wrote without enclosing some memento of his father from a seemingly inexhaustible store of souvenirs. The check was from the earnings of her small gift shop, and, little as the check was, Nicky had to make it last, for he had no other income.

"How did that sound?" said Nicky, stepping from the bathroom, his big dark, slow body glistening wet.

"How should I know? All I can tell is the difference between loud and soft. It was very loud." I'd lied to Gino about returning a book to Nicky. What I was after was ten dollars Nicky'd owed me for three months. "Look, about the ten bucks—"

"You'll get it!" he said expansively. "Everybody who was good to Nicky as an unknown will be rich when Nicky is rich."

He wasn't joking. His mother talked the same way—without a trace of uncertainty about his future. He had been talking and hearing himself talked about in this way all his life. Sometimes, he behaved as though he'd already reached the top.

"That's nice of you, Nicky, but I'll let you off the hook now for ten dollars, and then you won't have to make me rich later. You can keep it all yourself."

"Are you being sarcastic?" said Nicky. He stopped grinning. "Are you trying to tell me that the day won't come when—"

"No, no—hold on. It'll come, I guess. How should I know? All I want is my ten dollars, so I can rent a truck to move my stuff."

"Money!"

"What can you do without it? Ellen and I can't move."

"I've always done without it," said Nicky. "First the war takes four years out of my life, pft! And now money troubles."

"Then ten bucks would take years out of your life?"

"Ten, a hundred, a thousand." He sat down dejectedly. "Gino says it's showing up in my voice—the insecurity. I sing of happiness, he says, and insecurity shows through—poisons it. I sing of unhappiness, and it spoils that, too, because my real unhappiness isn't great or noble but cheap—money unhappiness."

"Gino said that? I thought the worse off an artist was financially, the better he was artistically."

Nicky snorted. "The richer they get, the better they get—especially singers."

"I was kidding, Nicky."

"Pardon me if I don't laugh. People who sell bolts and nuts and locomotives and frozen orange juice make billions, while the people who struggle to bring a little beauty into the world, give life a little meaning, they starve."

"You're not starving, are you?"

"No, not physically," he admitted, patting his belly. "But my spirit is starving for security, a few extras, a little pride."

"Uh huh."

"Ooooooh, what do you know about it? You're set—pension plan, automatic raises, free insurance for everything you can think of."

"I hesitate to mention this, Nicky," I said, "but—"

"I know, I know, I know! You're going to say why don't I get a job."

"I was going to be diplomatic about it. Not give up voice, understand, but pick up a little cash and security while you're studying with Gino, while you're getting ready for the big push. You can't sing all the time."

"I must and do."

"All right, then, get a job out-of-doors."

"And get bronchitis. Besides, you can imagine what working for somebody else would do to my spirit—licking boots, saying yes all the time, grovelling."

"Pretty terrible, all right, working for somebody."

There was a knock on the door, and Gino walked in. "Oh—you still here? Brought the morning paper, Nicky. I've read it."

"Talking about insecurity, Maestro," I said.

"Yes," said Gino thoughtfully, "it's something to talk about, all right. It's broken greater spirits than ours, and robbed the world of God knows how much beauty. I've seen it happen more times than I like to think about."

"It's not going to happen to me!" said Nicky passionately.

"What are you going to do?" said Gino. He shrugged. "Go into business? You're too much of an artist. If you were going to go ahead and try it anyway, I suppose the place to start would be in the want-ad section. But no—I'm against it. It's beneath you. You could get in and maybe make your fortune and get out again, and give your full attention to voice—but no, I don't like it, and I feel responsible for you."

Nicky sighed. "Give me the paper. The average man doesn't even suspect the price an artist pays to bring beauty into his life. Now the son of Angelo Marino is going into business." He turned to me to berate me as a representative of average men everywhere. "You understand what that means?"

"I've adopted a wait-and-see policy," I said.

"Nicky," said Gino gravely, "you've got to promise me one thing: that you won't let business get the better of you, that you'll keep the real end in view—your singing."

Nicky banged his fist on the table. "By God, Gino—here I thought you knew me better than anybody else on earth, next to my mother, and you say a thing like that!"

"Sorry."

"Now what's the stupid paper got to say for itself?"

On the day of our move from the apartment, Nicky insisted on my paying attention to matters far more important than my own piddling affairs—his affairs. He had been tramping the streets for two days, investigating likely ads in the Business Opportunities section.

"Where would I get a thousand dollars?" I grunted, as I lifted a chair onto the rented truck.

He made no effort to help, and stood by with an expression of annoyance, as though I had no business dividing my attention. "Five hundred, then."

"You're crazy. I'm in hock for my car, the new house, and

the baby. If turkey was five cents a pound, I couldn't buy the beak."

"How on earth am I going to buy this doughnut shop?" he asked irritably.

"What the hell am I, the Guggenheim Foundation?"

"The bank'll lend me four, if I'll put in four," said Nicky. "You're passing up a chance of a lifetime. This lousy little shop nets ten thousand a year. The man proved it to me. Ten thousand a year, easy," he said, awe in his voice. "Twenty-seven dollars a day, every day. There it is, just waiting. Machines make the doughnuts; you buy the mix in bags, and sit around making change."

Gino came out of my apartment, carrying two lamps. "Back from the bank, Nicky?"

"They'll only lend me half, Gino. Can you beat it? They want me to put up four thousand, too."

"A nice wad, four thousand," said Gino.

"Peanuts!" said Nicky. "The owner's been making ten G's, even though he doesn't advertise or make a decent cup of coffee or try new flavors or—" He stopped short, and his enthusiasm decayed. "You know," he said flatly, "the stupid things businessmen have to do to make a thing go. Well, the hell with it, anyway."

"Just forget the ten thousand a year," said Gino.

An hour later, as I climbed into the cab of the truck and started the engine, Nicky came running out of his apartment. "Shut off the motor!"

Obediently, I did. "For the last time, Nicky, I can't even afford the ten you already owe me."

"I don't need it," he said.

"Given up? Good. I think you're wise."

"Someone else put up the money as a silent partner. The bank told him about me."

"Who put up the dough?"

"He wants to be known only as a friend of opera," said Nicky triumphantly. "Just like the artists in the old days, I've got a patron."

"First patron of art in history to underwrite a doughnut manufacturer."

"That's not the point!"

"Nicky," called Gino from his basement door. "What are you yelling about?"

Nicky looked at him sadly, ashamed. "I'm in business, Maestro."

"You've got to suffer to be great," said Gino.

Nicky nodded. "I'll use another name. It wouldn't do to use the name of Marino."

"I should say not," said Gino.

"Jeffrey," said Nicky thoughtfully, "George B. Jeffrey."

"Get out there and sell, George," said Gino.

While my new life never came in contact with Nicky's new life, I had only to pick up a paper to see that he was still in business. He had a small ad in almost every issue, and I was amazed by the variety of things he had to say in favor of doughnuts.

"Maybe we should make a point of going over and buying some," said Ellen, my wife, at breakfast one morning. "Maybe he's hurt that we haven't."

"Nothing would hurt him more than if we showed up there," I said. "He's humiliated enough, without his old friends looking in on him. The time to visit him is when this is all behind him, when he's either made a pile or been cleaned out, and is back studying with Gino."

That morning, which was about six months after Nicky'd decided to prostitute himself, I was waiting for a bus by a stoplight, and it seemed to me that someone had his car radio turned up annoyingly loud. I looked up from my paper to be surprised by a doughnut six feet high, with four wheels, a windshield, and bumpers.

Inside sat Nicky, his head back, his white teeth flashing, singing. The mad joy of the song got through to me, even if the melody didn't. "Nick, boy!" I called.

The song stopped, and he became glum, sardonic. He waved, and opened the side of the doughnut. "Come on, I'll give you a lift downtown."

"Don't go out of your way. Your shop's just down three blocks, isn't it?"

"I have business downtown," he said gloomily.

I found that inside the doughnut was a jeep, the back of which was filled with racks of doughnuts, iced in many colors. "Mmmmm. Don't those look good!"

"All right, rub it in."

"They really do look wonderful."

"In six more months I sell out, and if anybody ever offers me a doughnut, I'll break his back."

"You sounded happy enough back there by the light."

"Laugh, clown, laugh."

"Through the tears, eh? Business that bad?"

"Business! Who wants to talk about business?" said Nicky. "How's music?"

"Haaaah, music. Gino says the security is helping."

"Good boy! So you're getting security."

"A little—some, maybe. Gino wants me to take my money and get out."

"But you said you were sticking with it another six months."

"Trapped," he said bitterly. "My partner, the great friend of opera, fixed things so I can't sell without his permission. Lord! What a babe in the woods I was!"

"Gosh, that's too bad. What's his name?"

"Lord knows. The bank represents him."

"Anyway, sounds like you're doing fine."

"It *would* sound that way to you," said Nicky. "You're the kind of guy that ought to be in this business, not me. You're the kind that'd love it—watching the competition, figuring new angles, new lines, new come-ons, all that nonsense." He clapped me on the knee. "Twentieth-century man! Thank your lucky stars you weren't born with talent."

"Nice, all right. Mind my asking what you're going downtown for?"

"Oh—one of the milk companies is kind of thinking about delivering our doughnuts in the morning along with milk. They want to see me."

"Kind of thinking of doing it?"

"They're going to do it," he said absently.

"Nicky! You'll be smothered with cash. You're a ball of fire in business. A natural!"

"How insensitive can you be?"

"Didn't mean to be offensive. Mind if I have a dough-nut?"

"Take a light green one," said Nicky.

"Poisoned?"

"New flavor we're trying out."

I bit into it. "Boy! Mint. Good, huh?"

"Really like it?" he asked eagerly.

"What do you care, artist?"

"If I'm trapped, I might as well make the best of it."

"Well, keep a stiff upper lip. Here's where I get out."

He stopped, but he didn't look at me when I got out. He was staring at something across the street. "That lying son of a gun," he murmured, and pulled away.

Across the street was a restaurant, over which was written in electric lamps, "The Best Cup of Coffee in Town."

On my birthday, just after Easter, a package from Nicky arrived. I hadn't seen him for almost a year, and supposed that his silent partner had let him sell out by now, and that, rich as the devil, he was once more studying full-time with Gino. The doughnuts-delivered-with-milk idea had worked out fine, as nearly as I could tell. I had a standing order with my milkman for a half dozen every three days—with mint icing.

The package, delivered in the evening, confirmed one part of the supposition, at least—that Nicky was rolling in money.

"What is it?" said Ellen.

"Big and heavy enough to be a tricycle," I said. I removed the gaudy wrappings, and was dazzled by a complete sterling tea service, the sort of thing I could imagine ambassadors giving as wedding presents to princesses.

"Good heavens!" said Ellen. "What's that taped to the tray?"

"A ten-dollar bill and a note." I read the note aloud: " 'Bet you thought you'd never get it back. Thanks. Happy birthday. Nicky.' "

"This is embarrassing," said Ellen. "What would I do with it? Where could I put it?"

"We could pay off the mortgage with it." I shook my head. "Well, hell, this is ridiculous. I'm going to get him to take it back." Ellen rewrapped the present, and I drove down to Nicky's apartment with it.

I almost turned away from his door, thinking he'd moved, when I saw the name on the knocker—"George B. Jeffrey." And the noises inside were unfamiliar, too: dance music and women's voices. Nicky hadn't had much to do with women, except for his mother. The assumption, *his* assumption, was that women, hundreds of them and all beautiful and talented, would come his way automatically once his career was going full blast. That had been his father's experience, so it would certainly happen to Nicky, too.

Then I remembered that George B. Jeffrey was Nicky's business name, and I knocked. A uniformed maid, carrying a tray of martinis, opened the door. "Yes?"

Behind her I saw Nicky's one room. It was now spotless, and elegantly furnished in dark Victorian furniture. The scrapbook was still there on the table, but rebound in expensive-looking plush and leather. And the pictures of his father and the posters still covered the walls, but they were now protected by glass in massive gilt frames. The room looked more like a well-run museum than a studio.

The sounds of celebration puzzled me, because I couldn't see anyone in the room behind the maid, and the only rooms opening onto it were the bathroom, the kitchenette, and a closet. "Is Mr. Marino in?" I said.

"Mr. *Jeffrey*?" said the maid.

"Yes—Mr. Jeffrey. I'm a friend of his."

The heavy drapes on one side of the room parted, and Nicky appeared, flushed, happy, and I saw that the wall separating Nicky's old room from the next apartment had been knocked out, and that he now had a suite. The drapes closed behind him, so that I had only a glimpse of what lay beyond— a room hazy with smoke and laughter, garishly modern. It was like looking into a sunset from the mouth of a cave.

"Happy birthday, happy birthday," said Nicky.

"Celebrating the sale of your business?"

"Hmmm? Oh—no, not exactly," he said. As before, my intrusion into his new life seemed to sadden him. "No. Just having some business associates in." His voice dropped to a confidential whisper. "You have to do a little of this to keep things going smoothly."

"Still trapped?"

"Yep. Son of a gun, he's really got me. Maybe in six months—"

"Another deal on?"

"Just one darn thing after another," he said dismally. "An outfit from Milwaukee's trying to open up some shops here, so what can we do but extend our chain? Dog eat dog. But in six months, so help me, George B. Jeffrey's going to disappear, and Nicky Marino's going to be reborn."

"Georgie, boy, sing us a song," called a woman from the other room.

It was plain that Nicky didn't want me to meet his business associates, that he didn't want me to go into the other room. But the woman opened the drapes to call to him again, and I got another look at the door. The walls, I saw, were decorated with framed ads, and over the fireplace was a caricature, a doughnut with Nicky's features, grinning, cocky, happy.

"Look, Nicky, I came about this tea service. It was a wonderful thing to do, but listen, it's too much. Really, we—"

He was restless, seemingly eager to get me out and get back to the party. "No—I want you to have it. You deserve it, or I wouldn't have given it to you. Back in the old days, the ten dollars you gave me was a king's ransom." He started easing me to the door, in friendly fashion, but firmly. "You keep it, and tell Ellen hello from George."

"From who?"

"From Nicky." I was out in the hall again. He winked, and shut the door.

I walked slowly down the stairs with the ridiculous bushel of silver still in my arms, and knocked on Gino's door.

The old man opened the door a crack, smiled broadly, and welcomed me in.

"Greetings, Maestro. I thought maybe you'd moved. Your sign isn't out there anymore."

"Yes—I've taken it down at last, and retired."

"Nicky just threw me out."

"Mr. George B. Jeffrey threw you out. Nicky would never do a thing like that. What would you like to drink?" He had an amiable edge on. "I've got a good bottle of Irish a former student sent me. He's a very successful welder now."

"Lovely."

"Any other time of the year, even Christmas, I enjoy being alone," said Gino, making my drink. "But in the springtime it gets me, and there's nothing to do but quietly tie one on."

"Live!" cried Nicky outside, to the world in general. Gino and I watched the variegated feet of the doughnut king's entourage pass by the cellar window.

"Bears his cross well, don't you think?" said Gino.

"Must break your heart to watch it, doesn't it, Maestro?"

"It must? Why?"

"Seeing a promising artist like Nicky getting deeper and deeper into business, farther and farther from singing."

"Oh—*that*. He's happy, even if he says he isn't. That's the important thing."

"You sound like a traitor to art, if I ever heard one."

Gino poured himself another shot, and, on the way back to his chair, he leaned over and whispered in my ear, "The only way Nicky could ever serve the world of music is as an usher."

"Maestro!" I couldn't believe it. "You said he was the image of his—"

"He said it. His mother said it. I never did. I never contradicted them, that's all. That big lie was his whole life. If I'd told him he was no good, he might have killed himself. And we were getting to the point when I was going to have to tell him something."

"Then this doughnut business was the luckiest thing that ever happened," I said wonderingly. "He can go on believing he's going to be a great singer like his father, and the business keeps him from having to prove it."

"So be careful who you call a traitor to art," said Gino. He lifted his glass in a toast to an imaginary audience. "Last year I gave ten thousand dollars to the Civic Opera Association."

"Ten thousand."

"Peanuts," said Gino.

The din of Nicky's singing filled the apartment courtyard. He was alone now, having said farewell to his guests.

"Exit George B. Jeffrey, enter Nicky Marino," whispered Gino.

Nicky thrust his head through the doorway. "Spring, men! Earth is being reborn!"

"How's business, Nicky?" said Gino.

"Business! Who cares about business? Six more months, Maestro, and the hell with it." He winked and left.

"Ten thousand dollars is peanuts, Gino?" I said.

"Peanuts," said Gino grandly. "Peanuts for the half owner of the world's fastest-growing doughnut chain. Six more months, did he say? In six more months he and doughnuts will probably do as much for opera as his father ever did. Someday, maybe I'll tell him about it." He shook his head. "No, no—that would spoil everything, wouldn't it? No— I guess the whole rest of his life had better be an interlude between the promises his mother made him about himself and the moment when he'll make them all come true."

MONEY TALKS

Cape Cod was in a cocoon of cooling water and autumn mists. It was seven in the evening. The only lights that shone on Harbor Road came from the dancing flashlight of a watchman in the boatyard, from Ben Nickelson's grocery store, and from the headlights of a big, black, Cadillac sedan.

The Cadillac stopped in front of Ben's store. The well-bred thunder of its engine died. A young woman in a cheap cloth coat got out and went into the store. She was blooming with health and youth and the nip in the air, but very shy. Every step seemed to be an apology.

Ben's shaggy head was on his folded arms by the cash register. His ambition had run down. At twenty-seven, Ben was through. He'd lost his store to his creditors.

Ben raised his head and smiled without hope. "Can I help you, ma'am?"

Her reply was a whisper.

"How's that?" said Ben. "I didn't hear."

"Could you kindly tell me how to get to the Kilraine cottage?" she said.

"Cottage?" said Ben.

"That *is* what they call it, isn't it?" she said. "That's what it says on the key tags."

"That's what they call it, all right," said Ben. "I just never got used to it. Maybe that was a cottage to Joel Kilraine. I never saw what else he had to live in."

"Oh dear," she said. "Is it great big?"

"Nineteen rooms, a half mile of private beach, tennis courts, a swimming pool," said Ben. "No stables, though. Maybe that's why they call it a cottage."

She sighed. "I'd hoped it would be a sweet, cozy little thing."

"Sorry to disappoint you," said Ben. "What you do to get there is turn around, and go back the way you came, until you come to a—" He paused. "You don't know the village at all?"

"No."

"Well, it's awful hard to describe," said Ben. "It's kind of hidden away. I'd better lead you there with my truck."

"I don't want to be any trouble," she said.

"I'm closing up in a minute anyway," said Ben. "Haven't anything else to do."

"I'll need some groceries first," she said.

"My creditors will be very happy," said Ben. Loneliness and futility swept over him, and he looked the girl up and down. From her hands he learned she was a nail-biter. From her low-heeled, blocky white shoes, he gathered that she was some kind of servant, usually in uniform. He thought she was pretty, but he didn't like her for being so cowed.

"What are you—her housekeeper or something?" said Ben. "She send you up to find out what she's got here?"

"Who?" she said.

"The nurse—the Cinderella girl—the one who got the whole shebang," said Ben. "The girl with the million-dollar alcohol rubs. What's her name? Rose? Rose something?"

"Oh," she said. She nodded. "That's what I'm doing." She

looked away from Ben to the shelves behind him. "Let's see—I'd like a can of beef-noodle soup, a can of tomato . . . a box of cornflakes . . . a loaf of bread, a pound of oleo—"

Ben gathered her groceries on the counter. He put the oleo down hard, slapping the waxed cardboard against the wood.

The girl jumped.

"Saaaaay—you're nervous as a cat," said Ben. "Rose make you that way? She that kind? Rose wants what she wants when she wants it?"

"Rose is just a plain, dumpy little nurse, who still doesn't know what hit her," she said stiffly. "She's scared to death."

"She'll get over that quick enough," said Ben. "They *all* do. Come next summer, Rose'll be strutting around here like she'd just invented gunpowder."

"I don't think she's that kind," she said. "I certainly hope not."

Ben smiled askance. "Just an angel of mercy," he said. He winked. "By God, for twelve million bucks, *I'd* have nursed him, wouldn't *you?*"

"Rose had no idea he was going to leave her everything," she said.

Ben leaned back against the shelves, pretending to be crucified. "Oh, come now—come, come," he said.

"A lonely old man on his deathbed in a big apartment on Park Avenue—hanging on to life, begging for life, begging for somebody to care." He saw the scene vividly. "Kilraine calls out in the night, and who comes?" Ben smiled demurely. "*Rose*—the angel of mercy. She fluffs his pillow, rubs his back, tells him everything's going to be fine, and gives him his sleeping pills. She's the whole world to him."

Ben waggled his finger at the girl. "And you mean to tell me it didn't pop into Rose's little head that maybe he might leave her just a little something to remember him by?"

She dropped her gaze to the floor. "It might have crossed her mind," she murmured.

"Might?" said Ben triumphantly. "It *did*—and I don't mean once; I mean *hundreds* of times." He added up her bill. "I've never laid eyes on her," he said, "but, if there's one thing I learned about in this business, it's how the human mind works." He looked up. "Two ninety-five."

He was amazed to see tears on the rims of her eyes.

"Oh, hey—say, now," said Ben remorsefully. He touched her. "Gosh—hey, listen—don't mind me."

"I don't think it's very *nice* for you to talk that way about people you don't even know," she said tautly.

Ben nodded. "You're right, you're right. Don't mind me. You picked a lousy time to come in. I was looking around for something to hit. Why, hell—Rose is probably the salt of the earth."

"I didn't say that," she said. "I never claimed that."

"Well, whatever it was you *did* claim," said Ben. "Don't pay any attention to me." He shook his head, and he wondered at the two dead years in the grocery store. Anxiety and a million nagging details had held him prisoner all that time, numbed him, dried him out. There'd been no time for love or play—no time, even, for thoughts of them.

He worked his fingers, unsure that love and playfulness would ever come back into them.

"I shouldn't be ragging a nice girl like you," he said. "I should give you a smile and a gardenia."

"Gardenia?" she said.

"Sure," said Ben. "When I opened up two years ago, I gave every lady customer a smile and a gardenia." Since you're my last customer, seems like you ought to get a little something, too." He gave her the opening-day smile.

The smile and the offer of a gardenia pleased and confused the poor, pretty mouse of a girl, and made her blush.

Ben was fascinated. "Gee," he said, "now you make me *really* sorry the florist shop is closed."

Her pleasure went on and on, and so did Ben's. Ben could almost smell the gardenia, could almost see her pinning it on, her hands all thumbs.

"You're selling your store?" she said.

There was radiance between them now. There were overtones and undertones to everything they said. The talk itself was formal, lifeless.

"The business failed," said Ben. It didn't matter much anymore.

"What are you going to do now?" she said.

"Dig clams," said Ben, "unless you've got a better idea." He cocked his head, and, with the control of an actor, he showed in his face how keenly hungry for a girl he was.

Her fingers tightened on her purse, but she didn't look away. "Is that hard work?" she said.

"Cold work," said Ben. "Lonely work, out there with a fork."

"Is there a living in it?" she said.

"The way *I* live," said Ben. "No wife, no kids—no bad habits. Won't make as much as old man Kilraine spent on cigars."

"Toward the end, all he had was his cigars," she said.

"And his nurse," said Ben.

"He's dead, and you're young and alive," she said.

"Eeeeeeeeeeeyup," said Ben. "Guess I'm the big winner after all."

He picked up her small bag of groceries, went outside, and saw the big car she'd come in.

"Rose let you take *this* big boat?" he said. "What does that leave her?"

"It's embarrassing," she said. "It's too big. It makes me want to hide under the dashboard when I go through towns."

Ben opened the front door for her, and she slid into the leather chauffeur's seat. She seemed no bigger than a ten-year-old, dwarfed by the great steering wheel and instrument panel.

Ben set the groceries on the floor beside her, and he sniffed. "If ghosts had smells," he said, "that's what the ghost of Joel Kilraine would smell like—*cigars*." He wasn't about to say goodbye to her. He sat down beside her, as though resting and gathering his thoughts. "You ever hear how he made his money? Clear back in 1922, he figured out that—" His words trailed off as he saw that the spell was broken, that she was about to cry again.

"Miss," said Ben helplessly, "you sure cry *easy*."

"I cry all the time," she said pipingly. "Everything makes me cry. I can't help it."

"About what?" said Ben. "What's there to cry about?"

"About *everything*," she said wretchedly. "I'm Rose," she said, "and everything makes me want to cry."

Ben's world yawed, shimmered, and righted itself. "You?" he said softly. "Rose? Twelve million dollars? Cloth coat? Cornflakes? Oleo margarine? Look at your purse! The patent leather's all chipping off."

"That's how I've always lived," she said.

"You haven't lived very long," said Ben.

"I feel like Alice in Wonderland," said Rose, "where she shrank and shrank and shrank until *everything* was too big for her."

Ben chuckled emptily. "You'll grow back," he said.

She rubbed her eyes. "I think Mr. Kilraine must have done it as some kind of joke on the world—making somebody like me so rich." She was trembling, white.

Ben took her arm firmly, to calm her.

She went limp gratefully. Her eyes glazed over. "Nobody to turn to, nobody to trust, nobody who understands," she said in a singsong. "I've never been so lonely and tired and scared in all my life. Everybody yammering, yammering, yammering." She closed her eyes and lay back like a rag doll.

"Would a drink help?" said Ben.

"I—I don't know," she said dully.

"*Do* you drink?" said Ben.

"Once," she said.

"Do you want to try again, Rose?" said Ben.

"Maybe—maybe that would help," she said. "Maybe. I dunno. I'm so sick of thinking, I'll just do anything anybody tells me to do."

Ben licked his lips. "I'll go get my truck and a bottle my creditors don't know about," he said. "Then you follow me."

Ben put away Rose's groceries in the vast kitchen of the Kilraine cottage. The tidbits were lost in canyons of porcelain and steel.

He mixed two drinks from his bottle, and carried them into the entrance hall. Rose, her coat still on, lay on the spiral staircase, looking at her wedding-cake ceiling far above.

"I got the oil burner going," said Ben. "It'll be a while before we feel it."

"I don't think I'll ever feel anything again," said Rose. "Nothing means anything anymore. There's too much of everything."

"Keep breathing," said Ben. "That's the big thing for now."

Rose inhaled and exhaled rattlingly.

Some of what she felt began to creep into Ben's bones, too. He had a spooky sense of a third person in the house— not the shade of Joel Kilraine, but the phantasm of twelve million dollars. Neither Rose nor Ben could speak without a polite, nervous nod to the Kilraine fortune. And the twelve million, a thousand dollars a day at three percent, took full advantage of their awe. It let nothing go by without comment— without giving the conversation a hard, rude wrench.

"Well, here we are," said Ben, giving Rose her drink.

"And here *I* am," said the twelve million dollars.

"Two sleepy people—" said Ben.

"I never sleep," said the Kilraine fortune.

"Fate's a funny thing," said Ben, "bring us together like this tonight."

"Heh heh heh," said the twelve million. The *heh*s were spaced far apart, and the sarcasm in them squawked like rusty hinges.

"What's this house and everything got to do with me?" said Rose. "I'm just a plain, ordinary person."

"With a plain, ordinary twelve million simoleons," said the Kilraine fortune.

"Sure you are," said Ben. "Just like the girls I used to go around with in high school."

"Only with twelve million iron men," said the Kilraine fortune.

"I was happy with what I had," said Rose. "I'd graduated from nursing school—was making my own way. I had nice friends, and a green '49 Chevy that was almost paid for."

The twelve million let out a long, wet raspberry.

"And I was *helping* people," said Rose.

"Like you *helped* Kilraine for twelve million spondulics," said the twelve million.

Ben drank thirstily. So did Rose.

"I think it speaks very well for you that you feel the way you do," said Ben.

"And somebody's going to bamboozle her out of the whole works, if she doesn't brighten up," said the twelve million.

Ben rolled his eyes. "Gee—it's funny about troubles," he said. "You got troubles, I got troubles—everybody's got troubles, whether they've got a lot of money or a little money or no money. When you get right down to it, I guess love and friendship and doing good really *are* the big things."

"Still, it might be kind of interesting to shuffle the money around," said the twelve million, "just to see if somebody might not get happier."

Ben and Rose covered their ears at the same time.

"Let's get some music in this mausoleum," said Ben. He went into the living room, loaded the big phonograph with records, and turned the volume up loud. For a moment, he thought he'd driven the Kilraine fortune away. For a moment, he was free to appreciate Rose for what she was—pink, sweet, and affectionate.

And then the twelve million dollars started singing along with the music. "Bewa, scratch, and lucre," it sang, "Mopus, oof, and chink; Jack and bucks and rhino; Bawbees, specie, clink."

"Dance?" said Ben wildly. "Rose—you wanna dance?"

They didn't dance. They huddled together to music in a corner of the living room. Ben's arms ached, he was so grateful to have Rose in them. She was what he needed. With his store and his credit gone, only a woman's touch could make him whole.

And he knew he was what Rose needed, too. He pitted muscle against muscle, to make himself hard and bulging. Rose fawned against the rock he was.

Bundled up in each other, their heads down, they could almost ignore the hullabaloo from the Kilraine fortune. But the twelve million dollars still seemed to prance around them, singing, cracking wise—hell-bent on being the life of the party.

Ben and Rose talked in whispers, hoping to keep a little something private.

"It's a funny thing about time," said Ben. "I think maybe that's the next big thing science is going to turn up."

"How you mean?" said Rose.

"Well, *you* know—" said Ben. "Sometimes two years seems like ten minutes. Sometimes ten minutes seems like two years."

"Like when?" said Rose.

"Like now, for instance," said Ben.

"How like now?" said Rose, letting him know with her tone that she was way ahead of him. "How you mean?"

"I mean," said Ben, "it seems like we've been dancing for hours. Seems like I've known you all my life."

"That's funny," said Rose.

"How you mean?" said Ben.

"I feel the same way," murmured Rose.

Ben caromed back through time to his high school senior prom—when childhood had ended, when the scrabbling curse of maturity had begun. The prom had been an orgy of unreality. Now that feeling was back. Ben was somebody. His girl was the prettiest thing on earth. Everything was going to be just fine.

"Rose," said Ben, "I—I feel kind of like I was coming home. You know what I mean?"

"Yes," said Rose.

She tilted her head back, her eyes closed.

Ben leaned down to kiss her.

"Make it good," said the Kilraine fortune. "That's a twelve-million-dollar kiss."

Ben and Rose froze.

"Four lips into twelve million dollars gives three million dollars a lip," said the Kilraine fortune.

"Rose, listen—I—" said Ben. No thoughts came.

"He's trying to say he'd love you," said the twelve million, "even if you *didn't* have a thousand dollars a day, without even touching the principal. He'd love you even if the principal *wasn't* going right through the roof in the bull market; even if he *had* two dimes of his own to rub together; even if he *wasn't* dead sick of working. He'd love you even if he *didn't* want money so bad he could taste it; even if he *hadn't* dreamed all his life of going bluefishing in his own Crosby Striper, with a Jacobson rod, a Strozier reel, a Matthews line, and a case of cold Schlitz."

The Kilraine fortune seemed to pause for breath.

Ben and Rose let each other go. Their hands fell away from each other lifelessly.

"He'd love you," said the twelve million dollars, "even if he *hadn't* said a hundred times that the only way to make big money, by God, was to marry it." The Kilraine fortune closed in for the final kill. There was no need of it. The perfect moment of love was already dead, stiff and bug-eyed.

"I guess I'd better say good night," said Rose to Ben. "Thanks a lot for starting the oil burner and everything."

"Glad to be of help," said Ben desolately.

The twelve million dollars administered the *coup de grâce.* "He loves you, Rose," it said, "even though you *aren't* what anybody'd call a raving beauty or a personality girl—even though nobody but a sick old man *ever* fell in love with you before."

"Good night," said Ben. "Sleep tight."

"Good night," said Rose. "Sweet dreams."

All night long, Ben, in his rumpled, narrow bed, took inventory of Rose's virtues—virtues any one of which was more tempting than twelve million dollars. In his agitation, he peeled wallpaper from the wall by his bed.

When dawn came, he knew that a kiss was all that could drown out the twelve million dollars. If he and Rose could kiss, ignoring all the nasty things the Kilraine fortune could say about it, they could prove to each other that they had love above all. And they'd live happily ever after.

Ben decided to take Rose by storm, to overwhelm her with his manliness. They were, after all, when all was said and done, a *man* and a *woman*.

At nine that morning, Ben lifted the massive knocker on the front door of the Kilraine cottage. He let it fall. The *boom* echoed and died in nineteen rooms.

Ben was in clamming clothes, as big as Paul Bunyan, in hip boots, two layers of trousers, four layers of sweaters, and a villainous black cap. He carried his clam rake like a battle-ax. Beside him was a bucket stuffed with a burlap bag.

The heiress to the Kilraine fortune, wearing an old bathrobe patterned with daisies a foot across, answered the door. "Yes?" said Rose. She took a step backward. "Oh—it's you," she said. "I'm not used to you in boots."

Ben, supported by his clothing, maintained an air of ponderous indifference. "I'd like to go clamming off your beach, if that's all right with you," he said.

Rose was shyly interested. "You mean there are clams right out there?"

"Yes, ma'am," said Ben. "Cherrystones."

"Well, I never," said Rose. "Like in a restaurant?"

"That's who'll buy 'em," said Ben.

"Now, isn't God good to Cape Codders," said Rose, "putting all that food out there for anybody who needs it?"

"Yes," said Ben. He touched his cap. "Well, thanks for everything." He timed his turn carefully, so she would be sure he was walking out of her life. And then he turned back to her suddenly, passionately, and grabbed her.

"Rose, Rose, Rose," said Ben.

"Ben, Ben, Ben," said Rose.

The Kilraine fortune seemed to yell at them from some-where deep in the cottage. Before they could kiss, it was with them again. "This I've got to see—this twelve-million-dollar kiss," it said.

Rose ducked her head. "No, no, no, Ben, no," she said.

"Forget everything else," said Ben. "We're what matters."

"Forget twelve million dollars like you'd forget an old hat," said the Kilraine fortune lightly. "Forget all the lies most men would tell for twelve million dollars."

"I'll never know what matters again," said Rose. "I'll never be able to believe anything or anybody again." She wept quietly, and closed the door in Ben's face.

"Goodbye, Romeo," said the twelve million to Ben. "Don't look so blue. The world is full of girls just as good as Rose, and prettier. And they're all waiting to marry a man like you for love, love, love."

Ben walked away slowly, heartbroken.

"And love, as we all know," the Kilraine fortune called after him, "makes the world go 'round."

Ben laid the burlap bag on the beach before the Kilraine cottage, and waded into the sea with his bucket and rake. He buried the tines of the rake in the bay floor, and worried them through the sand.

A telltale click ran through the handle of the rake to Ben's gloved fingers. Ben tipped the handle back, and lifted the rake from the water. Resting on the tines were three fat clams.

Ben was glad to stop thinking about love and money. Swaddled in the good feel of thick wool, listening only to the voices of the sea, he lost himself in the hunt for treasure under the sand.

He lost himself for an hour, and in that time he gathered almost half a bushel of clams.

He waded back to the beach, emptied his bucket into the bag, and rested and smoked. His bones ached sweetly with manly satisfaction.

For the first time in two years, he saw what a fine day it was, saw what a beautiful part of the world he lived in.

And then his mind began to play with numbers: six dollars a bushel...three hours a bushel...six hours a day...six days a week...room rent, eight dollars a week...meals, a dollar and a half a day...cigarettes, forty cents a day...interest on bank loan, fifteen dollars a month...

Money began talking to Ben again—not big money this time, but little money. It niggled and nagged and carped and whined at him, as full of fears and bitterness as a spinster witch.

Ben's soul knotted and twisted like an old apple tree. He was hearing again the voice that had held him prisoner in the grocery store for two years, that had soured every smile since the milk and honey of high school.

Ben turned to look at the Kilraine cottage. Rose's haunted face peered out from an upstairs window.

Seeing the captive maiden, remembering his own captivity, Ben understood at last that money was one big dragon, with a billion dollars for a head, and a penny on the tip of its tail. It had as many voices as there were men and women, and it captured all who were fools enough to listen to it all the time.

Ben threw the bag of clams over his shoulder, and went to the door of the Kilraine cottage once more.

Again, Rose opened the door for him. "Please—please go away," she said weakly.

"Rose," said Ben, "I thought you might want some clams. They're very good, steamed, dipped in melted butter or oleo."

"No, thank you," said Rose.

"I want to give you *something*, Rose," said Ben. "Clams is all I've got. Nothing like twelve million clams, but clams, anyway."

Rose was startled.

"Of course," said Ben, strolling past her and into the living room, "if we fell in love and got married, then I'd be as rich as you are. That'd be a nutty break for me, just like the nutty break old man Kilraine gave you."

Rose was shocked. "Am I supposed to laugh?" she said. "Is this supposed to be funny, talking this way?"

"It's the truth," said Ben. "All depends on what you make of it. God's honest truth." He took an old cigar from a humidor. The outer leaves crumbled in his fingers and fell to the carpet.

"I asked you to leave nicely," said Rose angrily. "Now I'm going to tell you in no uncertain terms to please get out. I can see now how right I was—how little I knew about you." She quivered. "Rude, insulting—"

Ben put down his clams, and lit what was left of the cigar. He put one foot on a windowsill, and cocked his behind to one side, in a pose of superb male arrogance. "Rose," he said, "do you know where that damn fool bonanza of yours is?"

"It's invested all over the country," said Rose.

Ben pointed into a corner with his cigar. "It's sulking over there in the corner, where it belongs," he said, "because *I* said everything *it* was gonna say."

Rose looked into the corner, puzzled.

"The thing about money is," said Ben, "you can't be polite to it. Leave something suspicious to say, and it'll say it." He took his foot down from the windowsill. "Leave something greedy to say, and it'll say it." He put his cigar in an ashtray. "Leave something scary to say, and it'll say it.

"Give it an inch," said Ben, "and it'll take a mile." He took off his gloves, and laid them on the windowsill. "As near as I can tell, I love you, Rose," he said. "I'd do my best to make you happy. If you love me, kiss me, and make me rich beyond my wildest dreams. Then, after that, we'll steam these clams."

Rose thought a moment, still looking into the corner. And then she did what Ben had asked her to do.

The Kilraine fortune seemed to speak once more. "At your service," it said.

NUDE
BEACH

THE HUMBUGS

Life had been good to Durling Stedman. He drove a new Cadillac the color of lobster bisque. And on the back bumper of the Cadillac was a big trailer-hitch that hauled Stedman's silver home on wheels to Cape Cod in the springtime and to Florida in the fall. Stedman was an artist—a picture painter. But he didn't look like one. Part of his stock-in-trade was looking like a four-square businessman, like a no-nonsense free-enterpriser who knew what it was to meet a payroll, like a man's man who thought most artists were dreamers, who thought most art was bunk. He was sixty years old, and he looked a good deal like George Washington.

The sign over his studio in the art colony of Seminole Highlands, Florida, said it all: "Durling Stedman—Art Without Bunk." He set up shop right in the middle of struggling abstract painters. That was slick of him, because a majority of the tourists were confused and angered by the abstractionists. And then, in the middle of all the gibberish, the disgruntled tourists came upon Stedman and his work. Stedman's paintings were as pretty as postcards. And Stedman himself looked like a friend from home.

"I am an oasis," he liked to say.

Every night he did a demonstration painting on an easel in front of his studio. He did a painting in an hour flat with a crowd watching. He signified that he was done by putting a golden frame around the painting. The crowd knew then that it was all right to talk and applaud. A sudden noise couldn't spoil the masterpiece now, because the masterpiece was done.

The price of the masterpiece was on a card tacked to the frame: "65.00, frame included. Ask about our lay-away plan." The "our" on the card referred to Stedman and his wife Cornelia. Cornelia didn't know much about art, but she thought her husband was another Leonardo da Vinci.

And Cornelia wasn't the only one who thought so.

"I swear," said a thunderstruck woman in the demonstration crowd one night, "when you was doing them birch trees, it looked like you was using some kind of birch-bark paint—like all a body had to do was gob it on and it'd come out birch bark. And the same with them clouds—like you was using cloud paint, and all a body had to do was scrootch it on up top without hardly thinking."

Stedman offered her his palette and brush playfully. "Help yourself, Madam," he said. He smiled serenely, but it was an empty smile—a case of the show's going on. All was not well. When he had come out to do his demonstration on schedule, he had left his wife in tears.

Cornelia, he supposed, was still weeping in the trailer behind the studio—was still weeping over the evening paper. In the paper, an art critic had called Stedman an iridescent humbug.

"Land-a-mercy, no!" said the woman to whom Stedman had offered his palette and brush. "I couldn't make nothing look like nothing." She drew back, put her hands behind her.

And then Cornelia appeared, white and trembling—came

out of the studio and stood beside her husband. "I want to say something to all these people," she said.

All those people had never seen her before. But she made them understand instantly an awful lot about her. She was scared and humble and shy—had never spoken to a crowd before. Plainly, only a cataclysm of the first magnitude could have loosened her tongue. Cornelia Stedman was suddenly universal—representing all sweet, quiet, affectionate, bewildered housewives full of years.

Stedman was speechless. He had expected nothing like this.

"Ten days from now," said Cornelia unevenly, "my husband's gonna be sixty. And I just wonder how much longer we're gonna have to wait before the world finally wakes up and admits he's one of the greatest painters who ever lived." She bit her lip and fought back tears.

"Some high art muckety-muck from the paper says in the paper tonight that my husband's some kind of a humbug." Now the tears came. "There's a nice birthday present for a man who's given his whole life to art," she said.

The thought broke her up so much that she could hardly begin her next sentence. "My husband," she said at last, "entered ten beautiful pictures in the Annual Exhibition of the so-called Seminole Highlands Art Association, and every one of 'em got rejected." She pointed to a painting in the window of a studio across the street. Her lips moved. She was trying to say something about the painting, a huge, shocking abstract, but no coherent sounds came from her throat.

Cornelia's speech was over. Stedman led her tenderly into the studio, closed the door.

Stedman kissed his wife and made her a drink. He was in a peculiar position, since he knew perfectly well that he was a humbug. He knew his paintings were awful, knew what a good picture was, knew what a good painter was. But he had somehow never passed the information on to his wife. Cornelia's high opinion of his talent, while showing dreadful taste, was the most precious thing that Stedman had.

When Cornelia had finished her drink, she finished her speech, too. "All your beautiful pictures got rejected," she said. She pointed to the painting across the street with a hand that was now steady and deadly. "And that mess across the street won first prize," she said.

"Well, honey bunch," said Stedman, "like we've always said, we've got to take the bad with the good, and the good's been mighty good." The painting across the street was superbly imaginative, powerful, sincere—and Stedman knew it, felt it in his bones.

"There's all kinds of painting styles, honey bunch," he said, "and some kinds of people like one kind and some kinds of people like another kind, and that's the way the ball bounces."

Cornelia continued to stare across the street. "I wouldn't give that awful thing houseroom," she said darkly. "There's a big conspiracy going on against you," she said, "and it's high time somebody blew the whistle."

Cornelia stood up, slowly, dangerously, still staring across the street. "Now what's she think she's pasting in the window?" she said.

Across the street, Sylvia Lazarro was taping a newspaper article to the front window of her husband's studio. It was the article that called Stedman a humbug.

Sylvia was putting it up for all to see, not because of the humbug crack but because of what it said about her husband, John Lazarro. It said Lazarro was the most exciting young abstractionist in Florida. It said Lazarro was capable of expressing complex emotions with extraordinarily simple elements. It said Lazarro painted with the rarest of all pigments—Lazarro painted with soul.

It said also that Lazarro had begun his art career as a boy wonder, discovered in the Chicago slums. He was now only twenty-three. He had never been to art school. He was self-taught.

In the window with the clipping was the painting that had won all the praise and a two-hundred-dollar first prize besides.

In the painting, Lazarro had tried to trap on canvas the pregnant stillness, massive ache and cold sweat in the moment before the break of a thunderstorm. The clouds didn't look like real clouds. They looked like big gray boulders—as solid as granite, but somehow spongy and sopping, too. And the ground didn't look like real ground. It looked like hot, tarnished copper.

There was no shelter in sight. Anyone caught in that godforsaken moment in that godforsaken place would have to cower on that hot copper under those big wet boulders—would have to take whatever Nature was going to hurl down next.

It was an upsetting painting, a painting that only a museum or a dedicated collector would give houseroom to. Lazarro's sales were few.

Lazarro himself was upsetting—seemingly crude and angry. He liked to seem dangerous, to seem the hoodlum he'd almost been. He wasn't dangerous. He was afraid. He was afraid that he was the biggest humbug of all.

He lay fully dressed on his bed in the dark. The only light in his studio came from the overflow of Stedman's profligate lighting scheme across the way. He was thinking morosely about the presents he had hoped to buy with his two-hundred-dollar first prize. The presents would have gone to his wife, but creditors had snatched the prize money away.

Sylvia left the window, sat down on the edge of his bed. She had been a pert, uncomplicated waitress when Lazarro had wooed her. Three years with a complicated, brilliant husband had put circles under her eyes. And bill collectors had reduced her pertness to gamely gay despair. But Sylvia wasn't about to give up. She thought her husband was another Raphael.

"Why wouldn't you read what the man said about you in the paper?" she said.

"Art critics never make any sense to me," said Lazarro.

"You make a lot of sense to them," said Sylvia.

"Hooray," said Lazarro emptily. The more praise he got from critics, the more he secretly cowered on hot copper under a boulder sky. His hands and eyes were so poorly disciplined that he could not draw the simplest likeness. His paintings were brutal, not because he wished to express brutality, but because he could paint no other way. On the surface, Lazarro had only contempt for Stedman. Down deep, he was in awe of Stedman's hands and eyes—hands and eyes that could do anything Stedman asked them to do.

"Lord Stedman has a birthday in ten days," said Sylvia. She had nicknamed the Stedmans "Lord and Lady Stedman" because they were so rich—and because the Lazarros were so poor. "Lady Stedman just came out of the trailer and made a big speech about it."

"Speech?" said Lazarro. "I didn't know Lady Stedman had a voice."

"She had one tonight," said Sylvia. "She was clear off her rocker because the paper called her husband a humbug."

Lazarro took her hand tenderly. "Will you protect me, baby, if anybody ever says that about me?"

"I'd kill anybody who said that about you," said Sylvia.

"You haven't got a cigarette, have you?" said Lazarro.

"Out," said Sylvia. They had been out since noon.

"I thought maybe you'd found a pack hidden around," said Lazarro.

Sylvia was on her feet. "I'll borrow some next door," she said.

Lazarro clung to her hand. "No, no—no," he said. "Don't borrow anything more next door."

"If you want a cigarette so badly—" said Sylvia.

"Never mind. Forget it," said Lazarro, a little wildly. "I'm giving 'em up. The first few days are the hardest. Save a lot of money—feel a lot better."

Sylvia squeezed his hand, let go of it—went to the beaverboard wall and drummed with her fists. "It's so unfair," she said bitterly. "I hate them."

"Hate who?" said Lazarro, sitting up.

"Lord and Lady Stedman!" said Sylvia through clenched teeth. "Showing off all their money over there. Lord Stedman with his big, fat twenty-five-cent cigar stuck in his face—selling those silly pictures of his hand over fist—and here's you, trying to bring something new and wonderful and original into the world, and you can't even have a cigarette when you want one!"

There was a firm knock on the door. There were the sounds of a small crowd out there, too, as though Stedman's demonstration crowd had crossed the street.

And then Stedman himself spoke up outside the door, said plaintively, "Now, honey bunch—"

Sylvia went to the door, opened it.

Outside stood Lady Stedman, very proud, Lord Stedman, very wretched, and a crowd, very interested.

"Take that rotten thing out of your window this very instant," Cornelia Stedman said to Sylvia Lazarro.

"Take what out of my window?" said Sylvia.

"Take that clipping out of your window," said Cornelia.

"What about the clipping?" said Sylvia.

"You know what about the clipping," said Cornelia.

Lazarro heard the women's voices rising. The voices sounded harmless enough at first—merely business-like. But each sentence ended on a slightly higher note.

Lazarro reached the door of the studio just in time to witness the moment before the break of a fight between two nice women—between two nice women pushed too far. The clouds that seemed to hang over Cornelia and Sylvia weren't wet and massive. They were a luminous, poisonous green.

"You mean," said Sylvia crisply, "the part of the clipping that says your husband is a humbug or the part that says my husband is great?"

The storm broke.

The women didn't touch each other. They stood apart

and whaled away with awful truths. And no matter what they yelled, they didn't hurt each other at all. The mad joy of a battle finally joined improved them both.

It was the husbands who were being dilapidated. Every time Cornelia hurled a taunt, it hit Lazarro hard. She knew him for the clumsy fraud he was.

Lazarro glanced at Stedman, saw that Stedman winced and sucked in air every time Sylvia let a good gibe fly.

When the fight entered its declining phase, the women's words were clearer, more deliberate.

"Do you honestly think my husband couldn't paint a silly old picture of an Indian in a birch-bark canoe or a cabin in a valley?" said Sylvia Lazarro. "He could do it without even thinking! He paints the way he paints because he's too honest to copy old calendars."

"You really think my husband couldn't paint big hunks of glunk just any which way, and think up some fancy name for it?" said Cornelia Stedman. "You think he couldn't ook and gook paint around so's one of your high muckety-muck critic friends would come around and look at the mess and say, 'Now there's what I call real soul'? You really think that?"

"You bet I think that," said Sylvia.

"You want to have a little contest?" said Cornelia.

"Anything you say," said Sylvia.

"All righty," said Cornelia. "Tonight your husband'll do a picture of something that really looks like something, and tonight my husband'll paint with what you call soul." She tossed her gray head. "And we'll just see who eats crow tomorrow."

"You're on," said Sylvia happily. "You're on."

★　★　★

"Just squook the old paint on," said Cornelia Stedman. She felt marvelous, looked twenty years younger. She was looking over her husband's shoulder.

Stedman was seated bleakly before a blank canvas.

Cornelia picked up a tube of paint, squeezed it hard, laid a vermilion worm on the canvas. "All righty," she said, "now you take it from there." Stedman picked up a brush listlessly, did nothing with it. He knew he was going to fail.

He had been living cheerfully with artistic failure for years. He had managed to coat it with the sugar of ready cash. But now he was sure that his failure was going to be presented to him so nakedly, so dramatically, that he could only take it for the ghastly thing it was.

He did not doubt that Lazarro was now creating across the street a painting so well drawn, so vibrant, that even Cornelia and the demonstration crowds would be struck dumb. And Stedman would be so shamed that he would never touch a brush again.

He looked everywhere but at the canvas, studied the paintings and signs on the studio walls as though he had never seen them before. "A ten percent deposit holds anything Stedman does," said a sign. "At no extra charge," said a sign, "Stedman will work the colors of a customer's drapes, carpet, and upholstery into a sunset." "Stedman," said a sign, "will make a genuine oil painting from any photograph." Stedman found himself wondering who this bustling Stedman was.

Stedman now considered Stedman's work. One theme occurred in every painting—a cunning little cottage with smoke coming from its fieldstone chimney. It was a sturdy little cottage that no wolf could ever huff and puff down. And the cottage seemed to say, no matter where Stedman set it down, "Come in, weary stranger, whoever you are—come in and rest your bones."

Stedman wished he could drag himself inside the cottage, close the doors and shutters, and huddle before the fire. He comprehended vaguely that that was where he had been, in fact, for the last thirty-five years.

Now he was being dragged out.

"Sweetheart—" said Cornelia.

"Hm?" said Stedman.

"Aren't you glad?" she said.

"Glad?" said Stedman.

"About how we're having out about who's the real artist?" said Cornelia.

"Glad as can be," said Stedman. He managed a smile.

"Then why don't you go ahead and paint?" said Cornelia.

"Why not?" said Stedman. He raised his brush, made flicking thrusts at the vermilion worm. In seconds he had created a vermilion clump of birch. A dozen more thoughtless thrusts, and he had erected a small vermilion cottage next to the clump of trees.

"An Indian—do an Indian," said Sylvia Lazarro, and she laughed because Stedman was always doing Indians. Sylvia put a fresh canvas on Lazarro's easel, sketched on it with her fingertip. "Make him bright red," she said, "and give him a big eagle beak. And put a sunset over a mountain in the background, with a little cottage on the side of the mountain."

Lazarro's eyes were glazed. "All in one picture?" he said glumly.

"Sure," said Sylvia. She was a frisky bride again. "Put all

kinds of stuff in, so people will shut up once and for all about how their kids can draw better than you can."

Lazarro hunched over, rubbed his eyes. It was absolutely true that he drew like a child. He drew like an astonishing, wildly imaginative child—but like a child all the same. Some of the things he did now, in fact, were almost indistinguishable from things he had done in childhood.

Lazarro found himself wondering if perhaps his greatest work hadn't been his very first. His first work of any importance had been in stolen colored chalk on a sidewalk in the shadows of a Chicago El. He had been twelve.

He had begun his first big work as a piece of slum-craftiness, part racket, part practical joke. Bigger and bigger the bright chalk picture had grown—and crazier and crazier. Green sheets of rain, laced with black lightning, fell on jumbled pyramids. It was daytime here and nighttime there, with a pale gray moon making daytime, with a hot red sun making night.

And the bigger and crazier the picture had become, the more a growing crowd had loved it. Change had showered on the sidewalk. Strangers had brought the artist more chalk. Police had come. Reporters had come. Photographers had come. The mayor himself had come.

When young Lazarro had arisen at last from his hands and knees, he had made himself, for one summer day at least, the most famous and beloved artist in the Middle West. Now he wasn't a boy anymore. He was a man who made his living painting like a boy, and his wife was asking him to paint an Indian that really looked like an Indian.

"It will be so easy for you," said Sylvia. "You won't have to put soul in it or anything." She scowled and shaded her eyes, pretended to scan the horizon like a Stedman Indian. "Just do um heap big Injun," she said.

By one in the morning, Durling Stedman had driven himself almost out of his wits. Pounds of paint had been laid on the canvas before him. Pounds had been scraped away. No matter how abstract Stedman made his beginnings, the hackneyed themes of a lifetime came through. He could not restrain a cube from turning into a cottage, a cone from turning into a snow-capped mountain, a sphere from becoming a harvest moon. And Indians popped up everywhere, numerous enough at times for a panorama of Custer's Last Stand.

"You just can't keep your talent from busting right through, can you?" his wife Cornelia said.

Stedman blew up, ordered her to bed.

"It would be a hell of a help if you wouldn't watch," John Lazarro said to his wife peevishly.

"I just want to keep you from working too hard at it," said Sylvia. She yawned. "If I leave you alone with it, I'm afraid you'll start putting soul in it and get it all complicated. Just paint an Indian."

"I *am* painting an Indian," said Lazarro, his nerves twanging.

"You—you mind if I ask a question?" said Sylvia.

Lazarro closed his eyes. "Not at all," he said.

"Where's the Indian?" she said.

Lazarro gritted his teeth, pointed to the middle of the canvas. "There's your lousy Indian," he said.

"A green Indian?" said Sylvia.

"That's the underpainting," said Lazarro.

Sylvia put her arms around him, babied him. "Honey," she said, "please don't underpaint. Just start right off with an Indian." She picked up a tube of paint. "Here—this is a good color for an Indian. Just draw the Indian, then color him with this—like in a Mickey Mouse coloring book."

Lazarro threw his brush across the room. "I couldn't even color a picture of Mickey Mouse with somebody looking over my shoulder!" he yelled.

Sylvia backed away. "Sorry. I'm just trying to tell you how easy it should be," she said.

"Go to bed!" said Lazarro. "You'll get your stinking Indian! Just go to bed."

Stedman heard Lazarro's yell, mistook it for a yell of joy. Stedman thought that the yell could mean one of two things—that Lazarro had finished his painting, or that the painting had jelled and would very soon be done.

He imagined Lazarro's painting—saw it now as a shimmering Tintoretto, now as a shadowy Caravaggio, now as a swirling Rubens.

Doggedly, not caring if he lived or died, Stedman began killing Indians with his palette knife again. His self-contempt was now at its peak.

He stopped working completely when he realized how profound his contempt for himself was. It was so profound that he could decide without shame to go across the street and buy a painting with soul from Lazarro. He would pay a great deal for a Lazarro painting, for the right to sign his own name to it, for Lazarro's keeping quiet about the whole shabby deal.

Having come to this decision, Stedman began to paint

again. He painted now in an orgy of being his good old, vulgar, soulless self.

He created a mountain range with a dozen saber strokes. He dragged his brush above the mountains, and his brush trailed clouds behind. He shook his brush at the mountainsides, and Indians tumbled out.

The Indians formed at once for an attack on some poor thing in the valley. Stedman knew what the poor thing was. They were going to attack his precious cottage. He stood to paint the cottage angrily. He painted the front door ajar. He painted himself inside. "There's the essence of Stedman!" he sneered. He chuckled bitterly. "There the old fool is."

Stedman went back to the trailer, made sure Cornelia was sound asleep. He counted the money in his billfold, then stole back through his studio and across the street.

Lazarro was exhausted. He didn't feel that he had been painting for the past five hours. He felt that he had been trying to rescue a cigar-store Indian from quicksand. The quicksand was the paint on Lazarro's canvas.

Lazarro had given up on pulling the Indian to the surface. He had let the Indian slip away at last to the Happy Hunting Ground.

The surface of the painting closed over the Indian, closed over Lazarro's self-respect, too. Life had called Lazarro's bluff, as he'd always known it would.

He smiled like a racketeer, hoped to feel that he had gotten away with a very funny swindle for a good number of years. But he couldn't feel that way. He cared terribly about painting, wanted terribly to go on painting. If he was a racketeer, he was the racket's most pathetic victim, too.

As Lazarro dropped his clumsy hands into his lap, he thought of what the deft hands of Stedman must now be doing. If Stedman told those magical hands to be worldly, like Picasso's, they would be worldly. If he told those hands to be rigidly rectilinear, like Mondrian's, they would be rigidly rectilinear. If he told those hands to be wickedly childish, like Klee's, they would be wickedly childish. If he told those hands to be fumblingly angry, like Lazarro's, those magical hands of Stedman's could be that way, too.

Lazarro had sunk so low that it actually flashed into his mind to steal a painting of Stedman's, to sign his own name to it, to threaten the poor old man with violence if he dared to say a word.

Lazarro could sink no lower. He began to paint now about how low he felt—about how crooked, how crude, how dirty Lazarro was. The painting was mostly black. It was the last painting Lazarro was ever going to do, and its title was *No Damn Good*.

There was a sound at the studio's front door, as though a sick animal were outside. Lazarro went on painting feverishly.

The sound came again.

Lazarro went to the door, opened it.

Outside stood Lord Stedman. "If I look like a man who's just about to be hanged," said Stedman, "that's exactly how I feel."

"Come in," said Lazarro. "Come in."

Durling Stedman slept until eleven in the morning. He tried to make himself sleep longer, but he could not. He did not want to get up.

In analyzing his reasons for not wanting to get up, Stedman found that he wasn't afraid of the day. He had, after all, solved his problem of the night before neatly—by trading paintings with Lazarro. He no longer feared humiliation. He had signed his name to a painting with soul. Glory was probably awaiting him in the strange stillness outside.

What made Stedman not want to get up was a feeling that he had lost something priceless in the lunatic night.

As he shaved and examined himself in the mirror, he knew that the priceless thing he had lost wasn't integrity. He was still the same old genial humbug. Nor had he lost cash. He and Lazarro had traded even-Steven.

There was no one in his studio as he passed through it from his trailer to the front. It was too early for tourists to be coming through. They wouldn't appear until noon. Nor did Cornelia seem to be around.

The feeling that he had lost something important was now so strong that Stedman gave in to a compulsion to rummage through drawers and cabinets in the studio for only-God-knew-what. He wanted his wife to help him.

"Honey bunch—?" he called.

"There he is!" Cornelia cried outside. She came in, hustled him merrily out to the easel where he did his demonstrations. On the easel was Lazarro's black painting. It was signed by Stedman.

In daylight it had an altogether new quality. The blacks glistened, were alive. And the colors other than black no longer seemed merely muddy variations on black. They gave the painting the soft, holy, timeless translucence of a stained glass window. The painting, moreover, was not obviously a Lazarro. It was far better than a Lazarro, because it wasn't a picture of fear. It was a picture of beauty, pride, and vibrant affirmation.

Cornelia was radiant. "You won, honey—you *won*," she said.

In a grave semicircle before the painting stood a small audience altogether different from that to which Stedman was accustomed. The serious artists had come quietly to see what Stedman had done. They were confused, rueful, and respectful—for the shallow, foolish Stedman had proved that he was the master of them all. They saluted the new master with bittersweet smiles.

"And look at that mess over there!" crowed Cornelia. She pointed across the street. In the window of Lazarro's studio was the painting Stedman had done the night before. It was signed by Lazarro.

Stedman was amazed. The painting looked nothing like a Stedman. It looked something like a postcard, all right, but like a postcard mailed from a private hell.

The Indians and the cottage and the old man huddled in the cottage and the mountains and the clouds didn't conspire this time for bombastic romance and prettiness. With the storytelling quality of a Brueghel, with the sweep of a Turner, with the color of a Giorgione, the painting spoke of an old man's troubled soul.

The painting was the priceless thing that Stedman had lost in the night. It was the only fine thing he had ever done.

Lazarro was crossing the street now, coming toward Stedman, looking wild.

Sylvia Lazarro was with him, protesting as they came.

"I've never seen you like this," she said. "What's the matter with you?"

"I want that picture," said Lazarro, loudly, indignantly. "How much you take for it?" he snarled at Stedman. "I haven't got any money now, but I'll pay you when I get some—anything you want. Name your price."

"Have you gone crazy?" said Sylvia. "That's a lousy painting. I wouldn't give it houseroom."

"Shut up!" said Lazarro.

Sylvia shut up.

"Would—would you by any chance consider an even trade?" said Stedman.

Cornelia Stedman laughed. "Trade this beautiful thing here for that slop pile over there?" she said.

"Silence!" said Stedman. For once he was really as grand as he seemed. He shook Lazarro's hand warmly. "Done," he said.

ILLUSTRATIONS

ABOUT THE AUTHOR

KURT VONNEGUT was a master of contemporary American literature. His black humor, satiric voice, and incomparable imagination first captured America's attention in *The Sirens of Titan* in 1959 and established him, in the words of *The New York Times,* as "a true artist" with the publication of *Cat's Cradle* in 1963. He was, as Graham Greene declared, "one of the best living American writers." Mr. Vonnegut passed away in April 2007.